MURDER
in a
FRENCH
VILLAGE

BOOKS BY MERRYN ALLINGHAM

MURDER
in a
FRENCH VILLAGE

Merryn Allingham

bookouture

Published by Bookouture in 2023

An imprint of Storyfire Ltd.
Carmelite House
50 Victoria Embankment
London EC4Y 0DZ

www.bookouture.com

ISBN: 978-1-83790-753-3
eBook ISBN: 978-1-83790-752-6

To Vaison-la-Romaine and the much-loved house I once owned.

PROLOGUE
PARIS, SEPTEMBER 1957

Headlights blazing and engines revving, a queue of cars waited behind the traffic lights – an impatient platoon of soldiers, hungry for the signal to advance. Except for one who wasn't waiting. His foot on the accelerator, the driver hurtled forward in a direct line for the two women crossing the Rue de Rivoli. Sybil Carrington, caught in the vehicle's lights, froze. For an instant she appeared mesmerised by the machine rushing towards them but then, grabbing her friend's hand, ran for the pavement and safety. Not swiftly enough. The car was on them, a hulking mound of hot metal. Sounds. Sounds everywhere. The sickening thump as a woman's soft body crumpled beneath the impact, the roar of an engine as the vehicle sped into the distance, the screech of brakes as other cars joined the scene. And, finally, the sirens.

1

ABBEYMEAD, SUSSEX, THE SAME NIGHT

The telephone rang just before three o'clock in the morning. Jack Carrington stretched a hand towards the bedside light and, grabbing tortoiseshell spectacles, peered groggily at the alarm clock. He'd been writing until midnight, absorbed in making notes for a new crime novel, and was half inclined to let it ring itself out. No one called at three in the morning. But a vague premonition of disaster had him scramble out of bed and grope his way down the stairs to the hall, while the telephone continued its shrill demands.

'Hello,' he croaked into the receiver, shivering in his pyjama bottoms while he stood barefoot on the black and white tiles. Summer was over, and nights had turned chilly this last week, though Overlay House was never warm. In his reclusive days, he'd chosen the house for its out-of-the-way location rather than its comfort.

'Jack?'

'Yes,' he said mystified, thinking he should recognise the voice, but didn't.

'It's your mother.'

Of course it was. He should have known, except that he

hadn't spoken to her for six, maybe seven years, not since the fearful kick-up over who should pay for a wedding that had never happened. His wedding – Helen Milsom, his one-time fiancée, deciding at the last moment that, after all, she preferred Jack's best friend. His parents had immediately abandoned their fragile truce and fought tooth and nail over the costs they'd been landed with.

'I'm in trouble,' Sybil said, not waiting for a response. 'I need you here.'

Jack pushed a recalcitrant flop of hair back from his forehead and tried to focus. 'What trouble? Where are you?'

'I'm in Paris and I need you,' she repeated.

That fitted with what he'd learned from his father. *Your mother has found a new boyfriend*, Ralph had said. *An Italian count, no less, with a flashy apartment in central Paris as well as God knows how much land in Italy. She'll love that title. Love the money, too.*

'Ruby is dead,' Sybil blurted suddenly, but her voice faltered.

The conversation was becoming more surreal by the minute. 'Ruby? Who is Ruby?' he asked.

'Ruby King, my friend. She was run down on the boulevard.'

'I'm sorry to hear that.' He was sorry, anyone would be, but why was his mother calling him at three o'clock in the morning about someone he didn't know? Why was she calling him at all?

'The car drove straight at us,' his mother went on. 'Ruby was hit. Tossed to one side like a doll. They took her to hospital – I'm at Hôpital St Louis now. But they couldn't save her, Jack. They couldn't save her... and she's dead.' Her voice broke completely.

'It sounds a terrible accident, Mum, but I don't know what you think I can do.'

There was a pause until she said in barely a whisper, 'It

wasn't an accident. A car jumped the red light and drove straight at us.'

'You must be mistaken. Who would do that? It has to have been an accident – Parisian drivers take no prisoners, do they, and accidents happen all the time.' He fidgeted from one foot to the other, trying to warm frozen toes.

'It *wasn't* an accident,' she repeated, her voice stronger now. 'It was quite deliberate. It was murder!'

'But who would want to murder your friend?' The questions kept coming. It seemed a bizarre proposition.

'That's it,' his mother countered, almost triumphantly. 'It wasn't Ruby they wanted to kill. It was me!'

For a moment, Jack said nothing, too stunned to speak, and she filled the silence between them. 'They're trying to get rid of me. Things have been happening while I've been in Provence. They've been happening for weeks. Things to make me leave France. But now someone is actually trying to kill me.'

'But who are "they"?' he asked, grappling with the improbability of the claim.

Sybil did not answer directly. 'I need you to find out who did this.'

'Me? Why me? If you think it was deliberate, the police are the ones to speak to.'

'The French police! Have you any idea how they'll deal with it? They'll laugh me out of the station.'

Jack was inclined to agree with the French police, but at this time in the morning his job was to soothe a distressed parent rather than argue. Before he could begin the soothing, though, his mother went on, 'You're my son and you're a crime writer, aren't you? Stop worrying about pretend murders and solve a real one. You need to be here – with me, in Paris.'

'But—' he began to say.

'You're the only person I can ask, Jack. Your father is miles away and, in any case, he'd not be willing to help. Even if he were, he'd be useless,' she added with asperity. 'But you can help.' Her tone changed to one of pleading. 'Please... please come.'

It was a laughable prospect that he could trot over to France at a minute's notice to spend time tracking down a supposed murderer. For one thing, he couldn't think her friend's death had been anything but an accident and, for another, his mother and he had virtually no relationship to speak of. He'd been ten when his parents had separated and, though he'd lived with his mother when not imprisoned in boarding school, it had been a wretched experience, Sybil's violent mood swings, her complete indifference to his happiness, resulting in a move to live with his father. Ralph had been no less indifferent but spared Jack the histrionics.

Why she had turned to him in what was clearly a personal crisis was a mystery. But she was in trouble – he had never heard Sybil Carrington so close to hysterics – and, if he were to be true to himself, he couldn't decently desert her. If he could calm her, make her see that she was overreacting to what had been a dreadful experience, he supposed he had a duty to do so.

'OK,' he said reluctantly. 'I'll come.'

'When?' Her voice was still not secure, but the old exasperation was there, underlying the tears.

'Today,' he said, making an instant decision. 'I'll take the afternoon ferry from Newhaven and, as long as I can buy a ticket at such short notice, I'll be with you this evening.'

Four hours later, he walked along Greenway Lane to Flora Steele's cottage. She answered his knock, toothbrush in hand, and blinking against the early morning sun.

'I know I'm a fascinating companion, Jack, but this early?'

'Sorry. I wanted to get to you before you left for the bookshop.' Her chestnut hair was freshly brushed, he saw, and she was wearing her work uniform of short-sleeved blouse and neat skirt.

Flora studied his face and stopped brushing her teeth. She knew that look from old. From any number of adventures they'd shared these past two years, the latest only months ago at Abbeymead Farm.

'You're in trouble,' she decided. Grabbing his hand, she pulled him over the threshold into the narrow hall. 'What is it?'

'It's not me that's in trouble. It's my mother.'

'Your mother!' Flora gaped. 'But you never—'

'Speak to her. I know. She's been the one speaking to me, ringing at some godawful hour this morning. She's in Paris and a friend of hers has been knocked down and killed. My mother wants me there.'

'Really? That sounds a bit extreme.' She led the way into the kitchen, while he followed. 'Can I get you a hot drink? You're looking a tad dishevelled.'

'Anything. And toast, if you're doing it. The thing is... the thing is... I don't really know what the thing is,' he finished hopelessly.

'Sit down and tell me slowly. I'll put the kettle on.'

While Flora made tea and toast, he tried to recount the strangest telephone call he'd ever taken.

'It still sounds extreme to me. But you're definitely going to Paris?' Her eyebrows formed question marks. 'That is sudden.'

'It's all sudden,' he complained. 'It's lucky I'm between books and only just beginning to sketch out a new idea. Lucky, too, that I've enough cash for the journey. But I haven't a clue what I'm supposed to do when I get there.'

'Find Ruby King's murderer,' she said blithely, then gave him a loving hug. 'If anyone can, you can.'

'But there isn't a murderer, is there? It's my mother having an uncharacteristic fit of the vapours.'

'You'll go anyway?'

'I have to. She sounded distraught – I've never heard her so close to collapse. And Dad's out of range, somewhere in the Far East doing whatever he does.'

'Gambling?'

'Probably. It's pointless trying to get hold of him and, in any case, it would only make things worse. They can't stand the sight of each other.' He gave a sigh that came from the depths. 'You know, Flora, since she phoned what's struck me is the fact that I'm the only person she feels she can turn to. A son she hasn't seen, hasn't spoken to, since an almighty row years ago. Poor, dead Ruby appears to have been her sole friend.'

'That is sad,' she agreed, 'but good that you're going. You can hold your mother's hand for a few days and, when she's calmed down, come home. When will you leave?'

'I'm planning on this afternoon.' Flora's eyebrows arched further. 'I have this feeling that if I don't go immediately, she might do something stupid. On the phone, she sounded nothing like the woman I know.'

'There's an afternoon ferry to Dieppe, I think, if they're not completely booked.'

'That's the one. Then a train to Paris.' Jack paused, wondering whether to dare the suggestion he'd been turning in his mind on his way to the cottage. Anything that increased Flora's fear of too close a commitment made her twitchy.

He decided to brave it. 'I don't suppose... you'd like to come with me?' he asked.

She stared at him but said nothing.

'It might give you the chance to look for your parents' graves,' he gabbled on.

Her parents' last days were shrouded in mystery, buried, according to Flora's ex-boyfriend, in the south of France rather than the cemetery in Highgate where she'd always believed them to be. It was a mystery he knew Flora was desperate to lay to rest, yet at the same time frightened of what she might discover.

'And you always wanted to visit Paris,' he reminded her.

'I still do,' she said sharply. 'But how? I'd have to shut the shop. I don't have Sally to look after the All's Well this time.' Sally Jenner, now proud owner of the Priory Hotel, had managed the bookshop for Flora when, last year, she and Jack had spent weeks together in Cornwall. I don't know if it's possible.'

'I'll be leaving the village before midday.' He took his empty cup and plate to the sink, then turned and hugged her tightly, kissing her on both cheeks. 'Ring me before I go. You've a few hours to decide.'

Flora had been sent into a flurry of anxiety. Should she go? How could she go? The lure of visiting Paris had remained strong over the years but, more important was the unease she felt regarding her parents' deaths. It had become a constant, always humming in the background. And, recently, humming more loudly than ever. This might be her opportunity to find out. She could travel with Jack and, once in the city, contact Richard Frant, her one-time sweetheart. It was Richard who was convinced he'd seen their graves in a French village church-yard, a thousand miles from where they should be.

Aunt Violet, her father's sister, had told a small Flora that Highgate was the place from where her mother and father would go to heaven, and her dear aunt had never once deviated from that conviction. Yet Jack, wandering through the cemetery a year or so ago, had been unable to locate their graves. It was a mystery Flora needed to solve, but a mystery that scared her. The sense that their deaths in a car crash might have been the result of an unhappy marriage, that her father's temper – even Violet had let slip that on occasions her brother's rages could be frightening – had been to blame. Did she really want to know what had happened?

Then there was Richard Frant. She would have to meet him again, a man who had let her down at the worst time of her life. When her beloved Violet had fallen gravely ill and she had needed his support, he'd left her to deal with her aunt's decline and death completely alone. How could she face him with equanimity?

Perhaps, though, with Jack beside her, it would be bearable. Partners in crime for several years, since the moment an inconvenient body had appeared in Flora's bookshop, they'd become friends, too. Very good friends. Before, that is, they'd crossed the line into what Abbeymead's older generation called sweethearts. It was something Flora hadn't expected, hadn't even wanted until she found that, in fact, she did.

After past romantic disasters, both she and Jack had been reluctant to commit themselves, but since their dinner at the Priory – a thank you from Sally Jenner for helping to solve a murder and get her hotel back on its feet – their relationship had changed. In truth, it had changed long before, but neither had been willing to acknowledge it. That evening at the Priory, though, the barriers had finally tumbled. It would be Jack, she knew, who would give her the strength to stay indifferent to Richard, to face her past and not care.

And she had to confess, she was curious about Jack's mother. Flora had met Ralph Carrington the previous year and liked him despite Jack's discomfiture with his father. Ralph was a gambler, a womaniser, a man who'd been happy to break up his family for his own pleasure and, since then, had shown only a lazy interest in the son he'd left behind. But Sybil Carrington was another matter. For a mother to have no contact with her child whatsoever for some seven years spoke of a relationship that was deeply troubled. Knowing more of Jack's previous life, Flora thought, might help her understand him that little bit better. She'd grown to care for him deeply, but there were times when she could feel they were still strangers.

It was the bookshop, however, that was causing her the most disquiet. The shop had remained open through every one of the war years. It had not even closed on the day Aunt Violet was buried. It was what her aunt had wanted and, as her successor and new owner of the All's Well, Flora had abided by Violet's dictum. Surely, though, she could close for a short while. Financially, she could afford it – just – this year having finally found herself on an even keel. She could put a notice in the bookshop's latticed window, explaining her sudden disappearance and promising to reopen very soon. The villagers would understand. They would nod and be glad she was travelling with Jack. Expecting a wedding that wasn't coming, she thought wryly. Particularly Alice, Sally's aunt and head chef at the hotel. Alice Jenner, though single herself and likely to remain so, was a great advocate of weddings.

And the deliveries? Flora's mind was ticking over. Maybe she could transfer the parcels she'd recently packed – they were currently in the bookshop's cellar – to the Teagues' house in Swallow Lane. Betty, her faithful bike, could go along, too, meaning that Charlie Teague, her enterprising young helper, could make his usual Friday delivery round. Yes, she decided, she could do it.

Picking up the telephone, she dialled Jack's number.

2

Halfway through the four-hour journey to Dieppe, Flora decided she had made a mistake. The wind had been noticeable on the Newhaven quayside while she'd waited for Jack to buy tickets for the ferry but, once out of the harbour, its strength had increased markedly. Now mid-Channel, the water chopped and boiled, a discomforting grey swell riven by droves of white-topped waves. The horizon, too, was tilting at the oddest angles. Flora felt wretchedly ill.

Jack, on the other hand, was striding the deck, as though born to live on water. Flora watched him from the chair he'd found her in a sheltered spot, saying it was far better she stay on deck than go below into the stuffiness of the lounge or the sickly grease of the cafeteria. It was unfair. How could he revel in this ghastly journey while her stomach was turning itself inside and out and back again?

'Have you finished being Horatio Nelson?' she asked, a touch acidly, when he dragged across a second deckchair to sit beside her.

'Still feeling sick?' He sounded sympathetic.

'Very. How much longer of this hell do I have to endure?'

Jack consulted his watch. 'An hour or so, I'm afraid.'

'Or so?' She groaned. 'Right now, I should be back in Abbeymead, on dry land and selling books. Checking that Charlie has organised the deliveries and Betty is safe.'

'Charlie knows what he's doing, and no one is going to harm Betty.'

'People have tried,' she retorted. They'd been rammed into a ditch along Fern Hill, and more recently narrowly escaped the wheels of a double decker bus when Betty's tyres had been deliberately slashed. 'And then there's the Friday supper with Alice and Kate. I should have been hosting it this week.'

Alice and Kate were her best friends in the village and together they formed a tight circle that for years had taken it in turns to host a meal every week. Friday evening was their time to eat together, to exchange news and enjoy whatever gossip was meandering its way along the village grapevine.

'Will Kate still want to do Friday suppers?' he asked and, when Jack saw her puzzled expression added, 'Now that she's married.'

'What difference does that make?' In her indignation, Flora forgot how ill she felt. 'Why should being married mean you no longer meet your female friends?'

'I just wondered,' he said mildly. 'The happy couple are only just back from their honeymoon. Maybe they're still catching their breath.'

'Kate will have had more than enough time with Tony. I should think she'll be desperate for a break by now.'

'So harsh, Flora! At least you did her proud at her wedding. You were a stunning maid of honour, everyone agreed.'

'It was a lovely day,' she conceded. 'And a lovely dress, though I don't suppose I'll ever wear it again. Still, I can always fish it out of the wardrobe every so often and drool.'

'You can, and it was good the wedding went without a hitch.'

It was good that she'd gone along with it, was what Jack was really saying. Kate's wedding had been a bone of contention for Flora from the day her friend had told her she was marrying again, her first union having ended in the blessed relief of widowhood. Bernie Mitchell had been an errant and wholly unsatisfactory husband in Flora's view and, since his death, Kate had grown ten times happier, throwing herself into village life and taking a real interest in how she looked. And she looked beautiful. Flora had never understood why her friend would willingly relinquish her new-found freedom to take on another husband, even a pleasant chap like Tony Farraday.

Jack got to his feet again at the same time as the ship went into an even more pronounced roll, causing Flora to clutch at her stomach. 'How much longer now?'

It seemed a never-ending dip and wallow before the outline of Dieppe came into view but, once Flora saw the town appear on the horizon, she gathered what energy she had to stagger to the deck railings and watch as the waves gradually calmed and the ferry drew close to the harbour walls. By the time they were ready to disembark, she needed only a gentle hand beneath her elbow to steady her. Head high, she walked down the gangway and on to dry land, Jack following.

He rammed a straw trilby on his head – the fedora had been abandoned for summer – and straightened his crumpled jacket. 'I thought we'd grab a quick snack at the bar while we're here. The train for Paris doesn't leave for a couple of hours.'

He must have seen the stricken look on her face. 'You have to eat, Flora. Something solid,' he urged, 'and perhaps a cup of tea although maybe' – he was thinking of the last cup of French tea he'd had – 'a coffee would be better.'

'I couldn't eat a thing,' she declared.

But once they'd found seats in the bar and Jack had brought

her a roll and butter and a large chunk of cheese with what
looked like a dark chutney but probably wasn't, she managed a
few mouthfuls.

'What do we do when we get to Paris?' she asked, chewing
her way slowly through a resistant roll.

'I've booked a couple of rooms at the Hôtel Regina. It's in
the Place des Pyramides, fairly close to the Rue Royale which is
where Count Falconi has his apartment.'

'I'll take your word for it. These are just names to me. Is
your mother staying at the apartment then?'

'According to my father, she's been living with the count for
some months – mainly in Provence – and when he came to
Paris, she travelled with him. But why they're in the city, I've no
idea. The phone call told me little. Her mind was so fixed on
getting my agreement to come to France that nothing else
seemed to matter. If we meet her for supper this evening – you
should have your appetite back by then – we can ask her.'

'Ask her, too, why she's so convinced the driver of that car
was targeting her and not her friend. Or targeting anyone.'

'She seems to believe she's been victimised for some time.
Things have been happening to her in Provence, she said.'

'What things?'

'Exactly. What things? She wasn't specific. Only that
someone was trying to make her leave Provence, possibly leave
France and, because she hadn't taken the hint, was now willing
to kill her.'

'That's quite an accusation. Did she mention who she
thought it might be?'

'The conversation was too brief and she was in no proper
state to answer questions. All she wanted from me was that I
promised to make this journey. She *was* badly rattled –
completely out of character. I felt as though I was talking to a
woman I'd never met. Something must have been going on to
throw her into such a state, whether it's real or imagined.'

'Let's hope she can tell us more this evening.' Flora abandoned most of her roll and took a cautious sip of the dark brown liquid Jack had assured her was coffee.

'Talking of this evening, we should be going. The station is a ten-minute walk away, and we have a platform to find. We're on the train to Rouen and from there we need to change for Paris St Lazare. That's if you've eaten all you can.'

Flora nodded and, getting to her feet, bent down to pick up the small suitcase she'd brought.

'That's mine,' he said, taking it out of her hands. 'After your bravery at sea, you need looking after!'

'And you're the one to do it?'

'Who else?'

He gave her a quick kiss on the lips, then a suitcase in either hand, led the way out of the café and set off towards the station.

3

Jack had hurried them through the Paris St Lazare station, past a bewildering number of lines and platforms, and out into a wide-open space where Flora came to a halt. While he walked on, she stood and simply looked. Her first sight of a city that for years she'd yearned to visit! Elegant mansard-roofed buildings filled the surrounding streets, their soft gold colour half shadowed in the setting sun and beyond, stretching into the distance, a tree-lined boulevard. Rooted to the spot, she had been thrilled by this new and fascinating world. Jack, though, suitcases in hand, had already reached the taxi rank.

Now, ensconced in her bedroom at the Hôtel Regina, Flora was thrilled all over again. The view from her window was magnificent.

'That's the Eiffel Tower,' she said, almost squeaking in excitement, her face pressed against the window. 'Jack, I can see the Eiffel Tower!'

His eyes smiled through the tiredness. 'I'll leave you to enjoy it. I'd better phone my mother and arrange to meet for supper. Eight o'clock has long gone, but are you up to eating?'

Flora beamed. 'Absolutely. I feel a new woman.'

Her first dinner in Paris, she thought, after Jack had left her to telephone. A dinner together. A warm, intimate restaurant with ruched curtains, candles on the table and plush Empire-style chairs covered in velvet. She could see it all and, for a moment, indulged herself with the picture she'd conjured. But only for a moment. However warm and intimate, however many candles, they would not be eating alone. Sybil Carrington would be sharing their evening.

Sybil had named a nearby Italian restaurant as the place to meet and was already there when they arrived. Flora knew her at once. Jack might have his height from his father, but it was Sybil's face she saw reflected in his. Except his mother's was less kind and a great deal more groomed than his would ever be, her hair streaked a subtle blonde, her make-up perfect, and the dress she had chosen expensive and well-fitted to a mature but still shapely figure.

'This is Flora Steele, a good friend,' Jack introduced her. 'Flora, my mother.'

She felt Sybil's glance slowly travel the length of her body, then linger for a moment on her face. Weighing me up and finding me lacking, Flora decided. Jack must have warned his mother that he was here in Paris with a companion, but she was evidently not what Sybil had expected.

'I'm pleased to meet you, Miss Steele,' his mother said mechanically, while her face suggested otherwise.

'Flora, please. I hope you don't mind my gate-crashing. I was planning a trip to France and when Jack said he was travelling here...' He wouldn't want his mother to know their true relationship, Flora knew instinctively. She had needed an excuse.

Sybil's brown eyes were hard. 'Really? Well, no matter.

Perhaps two heads will be better than one.' It was a cliché she obviously didn't believe.

They had dispensed with the *aperitivo*, worked their way through the *antipasti* and were waiting for the *primi* to arrive before Sybil approached the matter that had brought Jack to France.

'I'm being threatened,' she said abruptly.

Jack fidgeted with a knife, tapping it against the linen table-cloth. 'You said as much on the telephone.'

'And not just in Paris, mind. Threatened at the chateau, too.'

'The chateau is the vineyard in Provence?' he asked.

'Chateau Constantin,' she said impatiently. 'Massimo – the count – has decided to live in Provence full time, at least for a year or so. He's found an exceptionally good manager for the Veneto winery and prefers the south of France, particularly in the winter.'

'Winters in northern Italy can be cold and damp,' he agreed. 'But the threats – you never spelled them out.' He was sounding cautious.

Sybil smoothed back a particularly blonde lock of hair and huffed slightly. 'I had no time on the phone. The most important thing was to get you here.'

'And now?'

She settled herself further into her chair. 'It was money first,' she began. 'I had a huge sum stolen. Five hundred pounds! It was all I had left from the miserable settlement your father agreed. I withdrew it before I left England.'

Ralph Carrington had been a great deal more generous than Jack had been aware, it seemed. 'In cash?'

'Yes,' she said snappishly. 'In cash. I don't trust French banks. The theft left me virtually penniless.'

'I can see that would be uncomfortable... The count, though?' Jack asked delicately. 'Couldn't he have helped?'

'Massimo won't see me starve, if that's what you mean,' she said acidly. 'But I prefer independence. I've had enough of playing second fiddle to a man – years of being forced to suffer a dilettante's whims. Your father's,' she said, as if he needed an explanation.

Flora saw Jack's shoulders stiffen. He hadn't come all the way from Abbeymead to listen to a litany of complaints he could probably recite backwards.

'Did you or the count try to discover who might have taken the money?' he asked, his voice carefully neutral.

'Of course we tried, but all it did was upset the servants. Massimo stopped the interrogation when two of the maids put in their resignation.'

Two of the maids, Flora observed to herself. Massimo evidently kept a large establishment and must be a very wealthy man. Sybil seemed to have fallen on her feet despite losing what appeared to be her life savings.

'In any case,' his mother went on, 'it wasn't just the money disappearing. It was the fact that it left me stranded – that's what they must have planned for when they took it.'

'They?' Jack interrupted.

'The count's wife. His ex-wife,' she corrected herself. 'I'm pretty sure she was behind it. And his daughters – well, maybe not Clio. They hate me and will do anything to be rid.' She leaned forward. 'It wasn't just the money, you know,' she said in a low voice. 'It was the attempt to poison me.'

Flora's eyebrows shot up along with Jack's but, before he could ask the obvious question, the waiter arrived bearing the seafood risotto all three had ordered. There was a fuss of clearing plates and delivering new ones, before Jack got round to his question.

'What makes you think you were poisoned?'

'I didn't say I was.' She waved a fork at him in remonstration. 'I said there was *an attempt* to poison me. Someone changed my pills. Substituted the ones I take for high blood pressure with... I don't know what.'

'How did you know they'd been swapped?'

'Because contrary to your usual assumption, Jack, I am not stupid. The pills were the same colour and the same shape, but slightly different in size, and I noticed.'

'Not a particularly clever deception then.'

'It might have been,' she snapped. 'If I hadn't been wearing my glasses when I took the pills.'

Flora had so far said nothing, allowing mother and son the space to talk while quietly enjoying the food. It was simply delicious. La Cantina was apparently one of Massimo's favourite restaurants. The man had taste as well as money, she thought. Alice, if she were here, would be so jealous and probably already in the kitchen trying to snaffle recipes. It was a shame that tension around the table was making the meal less than comfortable. Mother and son might be talking, but the atmosphere was far from harmonious and Flora's sympathy for Jack's predicament – after all, he'd willingly come to his mother's aid after years of silence; well, fairly willingly – encouraged her to break into the conversation.

'The other night,' she began, 'what happened with your friend? That's if you feel you can talk about it.'

Sybil looked a little kindlier on her. 'It is painful,' she acknowledged. 'And terrifying, too. We were coming away from Galerie Lambert. It's the new gallery that Count Falconi has helped to fund and there'd been a big reception that evening to launch the project. I'd taken Ruby with me. She seemed to be enjoying herself, but then began to feel unwell. A little faint.'

Sybil paused, staring blankly ahead, as though straining to remember the details of that evening.

'The gallery was very hot and very noisy,' she said. 'Too many people talking and drinking and jostling each other and, when she suggested we walk back to my apartment and have a nightcap there, I thought it a good idea. The apartment isn't far and I felt it would give Ruby a chance to recover if she fancied going back to the party.'

'It was just the two of you who left together?' Jack asked.

His mother nodded. 'The traffic lights were red,' she said slowly. 'We'd begun to cross the road... we were halfway across when...' She stopped, visibly upset. 'The lights hadn't changed, the other cars were still waiting but this one, a big black beast of a thing, ignored the red light and came at us at top speed. I grabbed Ruby's hand and ran but the car was travelling too fast and...'

'OK, Mum, we get the picture. No need to say more.' Jack's voice held concern. 'The police didn't get a number plate from anyone, I suppose?'

'The police!' she exclaimed sourly. 'They couldn't have been more useless. Apart from alerting local garages for any car brought in for repair, they've done nothing. There are thousands of large black saloons in Paris, they told me, and, unless we had amazing luck, it was a hopeless task. All they really wanted to do, of course, was close the case.' Sybil's mouth pursed. 'Massimo wasn't much help either. He kept agreeing with them that it must have been an accident. That the driver mistook the lights, then didn't see us. Didn't see us! The road was floodlit!'

She paused and took a deep breath. 'It was deliberate,' she said sternly, 'and it's clear to me that I was the target.'

'Have you known Ruby long? Was she an old friend?' It had occurred to Flora that if this had been a deliberate hit-and-run, it might well have been *Ruby* who'd been the target. She wondered how much Sybil knew of her friend's history.

'No, not old,' Sybil said thinking about it, 'but she'd become a good friend.'

Flora nodded sympathetically, encouraging Sybil to say more.

'I met her a few weeks ago. I was having tea at Galeries Lafayette waiting for Massimo to arrive and she came over to say how much she liked my dress. It was Dior,' she said in an awed voice. 'A birthday present from the count.'

'Goodness!' Flora hoped that was the right response.

It was. Sybil seemed happy to continue. 'We got talking over tea. Ruby knows— knew Paris well, and was happy to take me around. I know hardly anybody here, just a few acquaintances from when I first arrived in France, and when Massimo is busy it can be lonely. And he's been exceptionally busy with the gallery. It's why we travelled up from Provence. He's putting a good deal of money into the venture and wanted to make sure the launch went without a hitch.'

'And Ruby is a retired lady?' Flora asked, being careful to use the present tense.

'She didn't work, I know. We didn't really talk about jobs, but I assumed she was a widow. Wealthy, too. She was never short of money.'

'Where did she live?' Jack asked suddenly, interrupting the female conversation. 'You were on your way to your apartment, but did you ever visit her?'

'Why should that matter? As it happens, I didn't, and I don't know precisely where she lived. Not far from Rue Royale, I suppose. She'd telephone and we'd meet in a café or a shop or in the park.'

In other words, Flora thought, Sybil knew very little about this very good friend.

'Do you have her telephone number?'

'What on earth do you want that for, Jack? Ruby won't be on the other end of the line, will she?'

'No, but it might help us make a start on finding the driver of that vehicle,' he said calmly.

'Well, if you must.' She scribbled a number down on the menu almost angrily and thrust it at her son. 'Here. Take it.'

The conversation dwindled as they ate their way through baked branzino, crushed potatoes and a variety of vegetables. By the time Flora laid aside her knife and fork, she was full to bursting. The puddings had looked wonderful – she'd seen the dessert trolley go by – but there was no chance she could manage one. Another day, she thought, luxuriating in the knowledge that this evening would be the first of several.

'So, Miss Steele' – evidently she was not to be Flora – 'why are *you* in France?'

The question had been sudden and startled Flora out of her dreamy mood. She had no idea how much Jack had confided to his mother and stuck to the bare bones of why she was here.

'I'm looking for my parents,' she said. 'Or rather, looking for their graves. Where they were buried has been a mystery, but an old friend has given me a clue that it's somewhere in the south of France.'

'Goodness! That's a huge area. You'll have quite a quest on your hands. Tell me, doesn't your husband mind you travelling on your own like this? Well, hardly on your own.' She looked at Flora's bare hand, then accusingly at Jack.

'I'm not married.'

'You should be. At your age.'

Nettled, but unwilling to upset Jack, Flora kept her voice steady. 'I have a business to run. I own a bookshop and work long hours. Marriage wouldn't be easy.'

Sybil gave a dismissive snort. 'That's all very well, but don't leave it too late. Books won't keep you warm at night.'

'I'll get the bill,' Jack said brusquely, and signalled to the waiter.

Before they left the restaurant, he arranged to meet his mother at the Hôtel Regina the following evening.

'I'll be in the bar,' he said. 'Around eight o'clock? I need some time to think over what you've told me and by then I should have a better idea of what to do.'

'Let's hope so,' was Sybil's only comment, as she climbed into a taxi on her way back to the Rue Royale.

Once the cab had disappeared from sight, he turned to Flora, putting his arms around her and kissing her first on one ear and then on the other. 'Thank you, thank you.'

She broke free, amused. 'Whatever for?'

'For not stuffing a napkin down her throat!'

'You didn't either.'

'She's my mother, unfortunately, and I have to put up with her. But you endured her rudeness magnificently. I know you did it for me.'

'I did,' she said, tucking her hand through his arm as they walked back to their hotel, having decided the night was too beautiful to waste by taking a cab. 'And because I'm intrigued as well. Ruby whatshername...'

'Ruby King.'

'Ruby King,' Flora continued, 'is what Inspector Ridley would call a person of interest.'

Alan Ridley of the Brighton police was an old combatant of Flora's, but a friend of Jack's and a valuable source of information for a crime writer.

'Isn't she, though? Just happening to be in the Galeries Lafayette tearoom when my mother was waiting for the count.'

'Just happening to know it was a Dior dress that Sybil was wearing.'

'And sussing immediately that her victim was someone who would very easily succumb to flattery.'

'The fact that Ruby never disclosed her address – was that an oversight or was it deliberate?' Flora asked. 'That she didn't want your mother to know where she lived?'

'The latter, I'm sure. I'm thinking that maybe she painted a picture of herself as a wealthy widow, a woman about town, who was happy to befriend my mother when, in fact, she was anything but. This phone number' – he pulled the menu from his pocket – 'could be crucial. Where Ruby laid her head at night might expose her lies and more.'

'Of course,' Flora said judiciously, 'she *could* have died by accident.'

'It's what we need to find out. The police obviously want to think so – they can forget the case – but I agree with them that looking for a large, black car in this city is pretty hopeless. The best thing we can do is try to discover more about Ruby. I'll call the number first thing tomorrow.'

4

Jack said good night to Flora at the door of her bedroom, not wanting to cause unnecessary chatter among the hotel staff and aware of how very tired she must be. He sympathised. Having to deal with his mother – he'd forgotten how wearing she was – had exhausted him as well. Along with the worry that at any moment Flora might stray into one of her fits of devastating honesty. His fingers had been crossed for the entire meal.

Now, lying on his bed, studying the ornate ceiling above, his mind travelled over what had been said during that awkward meal. It might be that Ruby King's death was an accident. The count seemed to accept the explanation and certainly the police were unwilling to investigate further. But then that made their life easier, and the count's, too, in all probability. Preoccupied with his new project, Galerie Lambert, he'd have little time for what might seem to him a fantasy of Sybil's, brought on by the appalling death of her friend.

But if it had been an accident, why hadn't the car stopped? That wasn't too difficult to fathom, was it? If the driver had stopped, he would be charged with a criminal offence. At best, with dangerous driving and at worst, after Ruby's death, with manslaughter. Driving away, he stood a very good chance of escaping altogether.

Go back a step, Jack thought, concentrating on the tracery of plaster flowers and leaves above his head. Why had the driver jumped the lights in the first place? An errand so urgent it was worth the risk? Sheer impatience, perhaps? Even bad eyesight? Accident or not, there were questions to answer.

As for Provence – the missing money and the switching of his mother's pills – Jack wasn't sure what to make of them. Was she imagining threats when there weren't any? He knew from family history that Sybil had a habit of dramatising when she felt overlooked. Was that the case here? Had the count been remiss in not paying her sufficient attention? His mother had evidently been living at the chateau for some months and was now installed in Falconi's Paris apartment. It suggested a serious relationship, so surely the count would have understood his lover sufficiently to know that she needed attention and plenty of it?

The questions went round and round in Jack's mind, until finally in the early hours of the morning, he closed his eyes and slept.

After a good night's rest, he felt more sanguine, if not hopeful, of cracking the mystery of Ruby King's death. At least more willing to try. Before he met Flora for breakfast, he rang the telephone number his mother had reluctantly handed him. It was a wild card but right now the only lead he had. He was slipping on his shoes, phone in hand, when his call was answered. A man's voice! Had Ruby been married after all?

'*Bonjour, Monsieur.*'

He would have to try his schoolboy French since he'd never lived in the country as a journalist and the language had largely eluded him. There hadn't been much cause for French after D-

Day, he thought wryly, too busy fighting his way across France to need much in the way of language. In a few words, he managed as sensitively as he could to ask about Ruby.

The voice at the other end answered in heavily accented English. 'Who is this Ruby?'

'Ruby King.' Jack was relieved. Schoolboy French could be put away for another day. 'She lived in your apartment, I believe.'

'*Non*,' came the response, curt and uncompromising. 'Never. I do not know this woman.'

That was something Jack hadn't expected. For a moment, he grappled with the situation, then said the only thing he could. 'I wonder, would you have time to speak to me if I called on you. It is important.'

There was a short silence. 'I am a busy man, but Café Mistral,' the man said sharply. 'Place de la Madeleine in thirty minutes.'

'Thank you. I'll be there.'

Flinging a jacket over his shoulders, Jack grabbed his wallet and hat and, within seconds, the lift had delivered him to the reception desk where he checked with the clerk for directions to Place de la Madeleine and left a message for Flora.

The café turned out to be within walking distance or, in Jack's case, running distance. He was fearful of being late, sensing that his unknown informant would not be willing to wait a second longer than the time he'd stipulated. On the telephone, the man had been formal, verging on brusque.

When Jack pushed open the Mistral's glass door, his quarry was already at a table drinking his morning coffee and acknowledged his visitor's presence by a slight rise from his seat. A smartly tailored suit, crisp shirt and modest silk tie, spoke the businessman loud and clear.

'Laurent Michon,' he said, holding out his hand.

'Jack Carrington. Thank you for meeting me.'

'I cannot be long. I have a train to Lyons in less than an hour. This woman, Ruby?'

'She is dead. An accident on the Rue de Rivoli.'

'Ah!' The man didn't sound surprised. Accidents on that road were evidently not unusual. 'But why are you here?'

'She gave my mother your telephone number.' When Monsieur Michon gave an indifferent shrug, Jack continued, 'She telephoned my mother from that number, which means she must have had access to your apartment. My mother believed that was where Ruby lived.'

'*Mais non*, it is not possible. This woman is an imposter.'

It was what Jack had been thinking ever since their meal last night. 'You've been living at your apartment all this time?'

'I am back from a trip – to Martinique. My company has offices there.'

Was this a clue to what had happened? 'Tell me please, how long were you away?'

'Around three months.'

'And you got back?'

'Last night.'

It was definitely a clue. 'But you saw no sign that anyone had been living in your apartment while you were away?'

Laurent spread his hands in a gesture of contempt for such a ridiculous notion. '*Naturellement*. Such a crazy idea.'

'Crazy,' Jack repeated, his mind in a fury, puzzling how Ruby King could have used this man's telephone while he was away working in the Caribbean.

'Can I ask who else holds a key to your apartment?'

'No one. I have no family. My work is my family.'

That didn't surprise Jack. The man was austere, impatient to be starting his day. There would be no time for family, or for that matter, friends.

'But if you lost your key...'

'Oh,' Laurent said offhandedly. '*La conciergerie*, of course. She has one.'

A concierge who could be bribed? Jack wondered.

'Just one more thing. Would you give me your address? I promise not to bother you any further.'

Another shrug. 'It is an English thing, this needing an address?'

And therefore inexplicable, Jack thought. 'An English thing,' he agreed, pocketing the slip of paper Laurent handed him. 'And thank you.'

The man sprang to his feet, dropping several coins on the table before disappearing through the door into the Place de la Madeleine.

Jack watched him out of sight, then walked to the counter to ask the server where he might find the address he'd been given. Boulevard Malesherbes was a mere step away, she told him. He made a swift decision. He would take that step before returning to the hotel. Flora would probably be furious at being sidelined in what was supposedly a joint investigation, but he was on the trail of something, he knew, and he needed to continue.

The boulevard, as Jack expected, turned out to be a very grand avenue, tree-lined and home to block after block of elegant stone mansions. They must once have been grand family homes, he imagined, but turned now into stylish apartments. Standing outside number eighty-one, he glanced up at the façade of smooth stone punctuated by a trellis of ironwork balconies. On each floor, louvred shutters guarded French windows, the top cornice slanting inwards to allow light to filter down to the lower floors. The design was perfect, the overall effect immaculate. The building exuded a subtle but considerable wealth.

Wondering how best to tackle the concierge if he could find her, he noticed an archway to one side of the mansion block, half covered in winter jasmine, there to brighten the colder

months ahead. Beyond the arch, he discovered a small interior
courtyard built, it seemed, to hide the unsightly necessities: the
pipes, the lift machinery, the ventilation shafts. At the lower
end of the courtyard a one-storey dwelling slumbered in the
morning sun. Jack made for it. It had to be where the concierge
lived.

He was lifting his hand to knock when the front door was
pushed open and a woman pulling a shopping trolley
backed out.

'*Bonjour, madame,*' he said, smiling as the woman turned to
face him. '*Une belle journée.*'

She scowled at him. It seemed it was not such a beautiful
day.

'I met Monsieur Michon this morning. Monsieur Laurent
Michon.'

The woman stared at him.

'He has just returned from a long trip.' His basic French
wasn't doing too badly, he reckoned.

There was an impatient huff of the shoulders. So far, the
concierge had said not a word.

'I wonder, do you have a key for him?'

'*Mais bien sûr,*' she snapped.

'And did anyone take the key while he was away?'

Jack hadn't known the word for 'borrow' and maybe had
sounded more accusatory than he'd meant, because the
woman's face turned red, bunching itself into a furious expression. Pushing forward, she made sure to run his toes over with
the trolley.

He put out a detaining hand. 'Please. I'd like to know. I'm a
friend of Ruby King's.'

The name made the concierge halt her destruction of his
feet.

'I think you know Miss King,' he said, smiling benignly.

For a moment, Jack thought she was going to agree, but then

she thrust past him and stomped out of the courtyard, making for the boulevard beyond.

Was that proof of her guilt? The name had meant something to the woman, that was certain, and why would a concierge in the Boulevard Malesherbes know Ruby King unless she'd had dealings with her? Had there been some business arrangement between them? But that was mere speculation and, without a police investigation, would stay so. However strongly he sensed a connection, he'd nothing to prove it.

It hadn't been a wasted journey, though. He could be fairly sure that his guess was right, that Ruby had bribed the concierge to give her access to Laurent's apartment on certain days at certain times. Where she had actually lived would probably remain a mystery. One more question to answer before he could be certain he was thinking along the right lines, but that would have to wait until this evening and the meeting with his mother.

5

Flora slept late. Grabbing her wristwatch from the bedside table, she peered hazily at the dial. Past nine o'clock already! She threw back the covers, anxious that Jack could be waiting for his breakfast. She hadn't realised how very tired she'd been last night, but the long journey, the excitement of seeing Paris at last, and the meeting with Sybil Carrington – dinner had probably tipped the scales – had wrung her dry.

Rather than throwing on her daily uniform of blouse and skirt, she chose carefully from the few clothes she'd brought. Unlikely to match the fashions she'd glimpsed from the taxi, she could at least try. The weather was still warm and a navy-and-white polka dot cotton should be smart enough for whatever Jack had in mind for the day.

He was walking through the swing doors of the hotel and making his way to the reception desk as she emerged from the lift.

Flora cut across his path, 'Where have you been?' she asked suspiciously. 'I thought you'd be waiting for me.'

There was a shade of guilt in those grey eyes, she could swear.

'I left you a note.'

'Jack! You've been freelancing again!'

'I had to,' he defended himself, and gave her a hug. 'There honestly wasn't time to involve you. Come and have some breakfast and I'll tell you about it.' He turned to the reception clerk. 'The note I left for Miss Steele, can you destroy it, please?'

'Your story had better be good.'

But when Jack had finished his recital to the accompaniment of warm croissants and coffee from a tall silver pot, she was forced to agree that it *had* been good and worth pursuing while she slept.

'So, Ruby King bribed the concierge to let her into this man's, this Laurent's apartment, and called your mother from there?'

'It's beginning to look that way. It suggests what we thought, that she didn't want my mother to know where she actually lived.'

'Because it might give the lie to her being a wealthy widow.' Flora broke apart her second croissant.

'Something like that. It's clear that Ruby set up the meeting with my mother at Galeries Lafayette and then played along with a pretend friendship. But why? What did she have to gain?'

'If she wasn't the wealthy widow she pretended, she might have been hopeful of getting money. Perhaps she thought that if she wheedled her way into your mother's life, Sybil would be willing to fund her. Or maybe...' Flora could feel a tingle of excitement. 'Maybe she was being paid to do it. Someone else was pulling her strings, someone hoping for the opportunity to do your mother harm.'

'I'm not so sure.' Jack signalled for the waiter to bring a second pot of coffee. 'You heard my mother last night – she has this bee in her bonnet that she's been victimised for months.

The hit-and-run certainly fits your suggestion, but if that story is true, it means the threat to her has moved from Provence to Paris. What connection, if any, does Ruby King have to the vineyard in Provence? And it might not be true. Whatever my mother claims, Ruby's death could still be an accident. Equally, Ruby could have been the actual target and the killer spot on. It's perfectly possible she insinuated herself into Sybil's life for her own purposes. Maybe for money, maybe not. She appears to have been living a lie so who knows what secrets she was hiding?'

'I can't believe it was an accident and whichever one of the women was supposed to die, someone could have paid the driver to jump the lights and drive at them. Someone who followed Sybil from Provence intent on murder? The daughter she spoke about, the ex-wife?'

'They would have the money to pay a hitman, I guess, but it sounds pretty far-fetched. I'm more inclined to believe it was something from Ruby's past life coming back to bite her. My mother's here tonight – just a drink, I promise – and she might be able to tell us more. Until then... how would you like to spend your first full day in Paris?'

Flora knew how she *should* spend the day, or at least part of it. Trying to contact Richard Frant, and arranging a journey to the village where her parents were supposedly buried. Guiltily, she pushed the demand to the back of her mind. It was the single reason she had come to France but, now she was here, she shied away from making the phone call.

'I'd like to go to Notre Dame and Montmartre and the Eiffel Tower,' she said in one breath.

'Hold on – one expedition at a time. Which comes first?'

'Notre Dame,' she said, without a shadow of doubt.

. . .

It was a wonderful day. The sun continued to shine more or less unbrokenly and, when they'd climbed the four hundred odd steps of the cathedral towers, Flora was rewarded with a panoramic view, not just of the Île de la Cité, but of a huge part of Paris as well. On the way up, they had stopped at the Salle Haute and admired its Gothic architecture, the Galerie des Chimères for a close view of the famous gargoyles, and finally the belfry.

'The famous bell – Emmanuel,' Flora said excitedly.

'All thirteen tons of it.'

'Did you ever read *The Hunchback of Notre Dame*?'

Jack shook his head. 'I don't think so. Should I have?'

'Definitely. It's good that, for once, I know something you don't.'

'Ah!' He gave her hair a gentle flick. 'But did you know that when Paris was liberated in the summer of 1944, the Magnificat was sung here in celebration?'

'Were you in the congregation?'

'Sadly, no. I was moving east and shooting people.'

They had lunch by the river, an onion galette and salad, followed by crème brûlée, Jack persuading her after some effort to drink a glass of wine. The terrace where they sat was hot and drowsy and Flora felt her eyelids drooping, ready to sleep again. How shameful!

'Back to the hotel for you, I think.' Jack was laughing at her.

'What on earth's the matter with me?'

'Too much excitement crammed into too short a time. Let's go back to the Regina and you can have *un petit repos*.'

'And you?'

'Oh, me too. I've another dose of Sybil to gird myself against.'

.   .   .

It had been a good day, Jack reflected, towelling himself dry from a reviving shower. He'd visited the cathedral several times in the past but today had been special – seeing Flora's eyes alight with pleasure, her smile wide; seeing the joy she'd taken in the glorious building and the view of Paris below. The way that having made short work of her lunch, she'd dozed blissfully on the café terrace. If every day was like this, it would be the best trip ever.

Except there wouldn't be an every day – she wouldn't be with him much longer. She hadn't spoken of Richard and the quest to find her parents' graves and he hadn't wanted to mention it. It would have spoiled their time together. But soon she would have to decide whether to make the journey south or stay here with him in Paris. He was half hoping she'd stay, but that wouldn't be fair. Flora suffered a very real sense of unease about the way her parents had died and anything that could put it to rest should be welcomed.

Perhaps – a thought came to him – he could travel with her. Whether he liked it or not, he owed a duty to his mother to discover what was behind that night on the Rue de Rivoli but, if he hit a dead end in the city, which looked more than likely, he could drive Flora to whatever village or town this Frant character named.

Right now, he had an evening with his mother to endure. Hopefully, not an entire evening which was why he'd suggested a drink in the Regina's bar. He glanced at the travel clock that always came with him and saw he'd only minutes to finish dressing. A pair of casual slacks, a short-sleeved shirt plus a sombre looking blazer would do the trick. His mother would like the blazer – it had a pinch of snob value. For her part, he hoped she had abandoned Dior for the evening.

Flora was waiting for him by the lifts, and his first thought was how beautiful she looked. Her red-brown waves fell loose to her shoulders, and she had caught the sun today, her skin very slightly tanned. She was wearing the elegant cream crêpe she'd worn the night they'd decided that maybe they were more than just friends. He could have scooped her up and kissed her soundly, then happily abandoned this evening's meeting. Instead, he pressed the lift button and sent them on their way to the bar.

Sybil Carrington was late arriving and they were halfway through their drinks when Jack saw her hovering in the doorway.

He stood up to arrange a seat for her. Taking the leather-bound chair, she made no apology for being late. 'It's been a fearful rush. Can you imagine – having to pack up in a few hours? And I hate being rushed.'

'What can I get you to drink?' he asked.

'A large gin,' she said decidedly. 'But I can't stay long.'

'You're packing up?' Flora was interested. There'd been no mention yesterday of leaving Paris.

'Annoying, isn't it, but Massimo insists. He says I've had a terrible shock, which is true enough, and that I need to take things easy. I need to be in the countryside, away from this madhouse.'

'You're leaving Paris?' Jack had caught the last few words as he finally managed to get the waiter's attention. The dimly lit bar was busy tonight, most of its small tables occupied, the hum of conversation competing with corks popping and the crackling of ice.

'Yes, and I'm not entirely sorry. The chateau is wonderfully quiet which is more than I can say for the Rue Royale. Massimo has done what he wanted, seen the gallery launched – very successfully, I might say – and he has business back in Provence. It makes sense for us to leave as soon as we can.'

Probably, Jack thought, but it smacked a little too much of unnecessary haste. He was about to start on the questions he hoped to get an answer for when his mother demanded, 'Have you found out who did this terrible thing to Ruby?'

He stared at her. 'I've been in Paris a single day.'

'Well, how long do you need? I shall be gone tomorrow.'

'That won't prevent me investigating. The incident happened here.'

'Other things happened at the chateau,' she reminded him.

'But they weren't fatal, were they? Tell me, when you and Ruby decided to meet each other, who did the arranging?'

'What do you mean?' she said crossly, taking a large sip of the gin that had just arrived.

'Did you telephone Ruby or did she phone you, or maybe a little of both?'

'I can't see what relevance that has, but Ruby telephoned, I think. Yes, I'm almost certain.'

'She gave you her number, but you never used it?'

'She was cut off once when she was phoning and gave me the number to ring back if we were disconnected again.'

'But otherwise you never rang it? Why not?'

Sybil's forehead fell into a deep crease. It was evident she thought his questions pointless.

'Ruby wasn't home much. She had a very busy social life and thought it easier if she was the one to get in touch with me. *My* life, you see, is not exactly a social whirl.' She said this with a tight smile.

'She had other interests, though,' Jack pursued. 'An interest in art that you shared? Did you visit many galleries together?'

'No, I can't say we did. As I say, she enjoyed the social aspect. The parties, that kind of thing. That's why I invited her to the Galerie Lambert launch.'

'You invited her, or she invited herself?'

Sybil glared at him. 'I don't know. I don't remember. Really, does it matter?'

'It might. And when you decided to leave the launch and go

for a nightcap, whose idea was that?' Jack offered round the dish of mixed olives the waiter had left and took one himself.

'I told you. Ruby felt faint. The atmosphere was crushing.'

'And she suggested you walk back to your apartment?'

'It was the sensible thing to do.'

'Did you know your way to Rue Royale from the gallery?'

'What kind of question is that?'

'You could have used a taxi,' he pointed out. 'Did you know how to find your way walking? Why did you walk?'

'We walked because Ruby needed fresh air. And she knew the way – she'd lived in Paris for years.'

Flora had said nothing, but Jack had sensed her weighing up his mother's answers and coming to the same conclusion as he. The walk back to Rue Royale had been part of a plan and Ruby King was at its centre.

His mother had drained her glass in a few gulps as though she needed to recover from his interrogation, and he was about to offer her a second drink when a small, plump woman with brightly coloured hair rushed into the bar and made straight for their table.

'You are here!' she said in fractured English. 'With another man. I knew it!'

'This is my son, Isabella,' his mother said frigidly. 'And my son's friend.'

The woman was unabashed. 'Then go home with your son. Go back to England. You have no right to be here, no right to be in my apartment, to go to my husband's gallery.'

'He is not your husband.' Sybil had risen from her seat and Jack saw her fists clenched. He sprang up and stood between them.

'I don't have the pleasure—' he began.

'Pleasure!' his mother snapped, pushing him away.

The intruder jabbed her finger at Sybil. 'You.' The woman's eyes, unusually light against such deep olive skin, burnt with anger. 'You... you are a bad woman.' And then the English broke down and a stream of furious Italian poured forth.

'I think perhaps...' Jack began again, when a waiter intervened. 'Madame, signora,' he said placatingly, holding out his arm to shepherd the unwanted guest to the door. 'Please, come.'

With a final burst of Italian, an insult from what Jack could make out from his somewhat sketchy knowledge, Isabella went. His mother collapsed back in her chair.

Flora leaned towards her, her face concerned. 'I'm so sorry that that should have happened.'

His mother rallied. 'Don't be, my dear. I am quite inured to it by now. I've had months of harassment. The woman is deluded, convinced she is still married to Massimo despite a civil divorce. She's not stopped harrying him, accusing him of abandoning her, of breaking his vows, of being a bad Catholic. And since I've been in Massimo's life, she's gone into overdrive. I'm an intruder, a debauched woman and a heathen at that. I don't speak Italian, but it doesn't take too much to understand the gist. She hangs around the chateau and when Massimo took me to Venice for what was supposed to be a romantic weekend, she followed us! Stopping us in the street, haranguing us on the vaporetto, causing a scene at our hotel.'

'And now she's followed you to Paris,' Jack said thoughtfully.

'Allegra will have told her we're in Paris. Told her of the Galerie Lambert event. Allegra is Massimo's eldest daughter. She hates me, too.'

'What does Isabella – that was her name? – hope to achieve?' Flora asked.

'She wants to wear us out. Wear Massimo down until he agrees that he has made a terrible mistake, that they are still married after all and that he'll send the divorce papers back.'

'Would he do that? Could he do that?'

'I really don't know.' For the first time Jack thought his

mother looked genuinely vulnerable. 'Thirty something years is a long time to be married and lose it all.'

'When you go back to Provence,' Flora put in, 'is she likely to follow you?'

'Why not?' Sybil asked wearily. 'She has a house nearby, so every reason to be there.'

'Should you be returning to the chateau then?' Jack asked. 'If you believe you're being threatened there?'

'What else can I do?' The snap was back in Sybil's voice.

'Stay in the Paris apartment. Isabella will follow her ex-husband rather than camping on your doorstep, I'd guess.'

'I can't stay,' his mother said dully. 'It's Massimo's apartment. I'm his guest. If he goes, I must go.'

'You could move to a hotel,' he suggested.

'What chance of that?' His mother's fight had reappeared. 'Ralph left me with next to nothing.' Jack stared at her. This was the woman who had lost a whole five hundred pounds. 'And what little money I had was stolen.'

She sprang to her feet, narrowly avoiding sending their empty glasses spinning. 'I have to go. There's still packing to do and we leave after lunch tomorrow. Let me know what you discover – if you do ever find anything.'

He was dismissed. No thanks for coming to Paris, no grateful encouragement to keep probing the mystery, and not a word of affection. His mother hadn't changed.

6

The following morning, Jack returned to the neighbourhood of Laurent Michon's apartment. Saying good night to Flora, he'd warned her that he intended to miss breakfast the next day hoping, if he was at the flat early enough, to talk to as many local people as possible.

Initially, he had little luck. A small stream of people passed him by, making for the nearest Metro station, but all of them too preoccupied with getting to work and with little time to speak. Most, in any case, would not have known Monsieur Michon or his apartment.

Jack had more luck when the first rush of travellers abated. An elderly man with a canvas shopping bag came through the wide glass door of the mansion block, an overweight pug snuffling by his side. He seemed happy to stop and talk, but he hardly knew Laurent Michon. He was a businessman, he thought, this Michon, and rarely at home. A newcomer, one of those money men who could afford the sky-high price these days for an apartment on the boulevard. Not like him, the old man said comfortably – he'd been here for years, had been able to buy when he'd returned from the First War.

Jack's second interviewee was no more helpful but, noticing a woman at one of the ground-floor windows, her stare fixed on him, he decided boldness might win the day. Her apartment was the perfect spot from which to view people coming in and out of the building, and the way she had taken up position at her window suggested she spent a good deal of time doing just that.

The vestibule was as comfortable as he'd expected, the floor thickly carpeted and with expensive-looking artwork decorating the walls. Knocking on what he thought must be the door in question, he waited to see if he was right.

'*Oui?*' the woman asked imperiously. He'd guessed correctly. This was the woman he'd seen at the window. He caught a glimpse of a spacious hall beyond, crammed full of antique furniture. There was money here – and a life needing to be filled, he imagined.

'*Bonjour, madame,*' he began, then struggling with his words, 'I wonder if you know Monsieur Michon who lives on the third floor?'

'You are English?' Her voice was educated and her accent barely noticeable. He'd struck lucky.

'Yes,' he admitted. 'An acquaintance of Monsieur Michon.' He hoped that wasn't stretching the truth too far.

'I don't know the man. I've seen him from time to time but I don't know him.'

Jack's spirits fell. 'No one seems to know him,' he said. 'He's been abroad for a while and is only just back, but there was a woman—'

'Oh, that one.'

'You saw her?' Jack asked eagerly.

'A few times. She is a friend of Monsieur Michon?'

'Possibly,' he extemporised.

She nodded. 'I thought so. She was here one day, then another.'

'How often would you say?'

The woman put her head on one side. 'Two, three times a week. I thought maybe she was living here, but she came and then she went.'

'She was always alone?'

'Of course. She was a single lady,' she said repressively. 'I saw no ring. There was a man, the one time, but I don't think he was... special, you know. He came in a car.'

'You saw the car?' At last he seemed to be getting somewhere. 'What make was it, do you know?'

She shrugged her shoulders, slumping slightly against the doorpost. His interrogation was beginning to tire her, Jack could see. 'Cars – I have no interest. It was big. Black.'

'There are a great many cars like that in the city,' he said ruefully.

'*Non*, this one was not from Paris. Why do you want to know?'

He'd been expecting that question sooner or later and had been dredging his mind for an excuse. 'I'm trying to trace the lady,' he said. 'I have some property of hers that I'd like to return. Can I ask, what made you think the car wasn't from here?'

'The number plate. Cars are... *bof!*' She gave an indifferent shrug. 'But I know a Paris number plate when I see one.'

'Maybe he was a relative of hers or a friend who was visiting,' Jack tried.

'I do not think so. They were arguing. They did not look friends.'

'It would be difficult to hear their conversation, I imagine.' Another try.

'I went outside,' she said naively, 'to water the petunias. They stopped talking when they saw me. In any case, I did not understand what he was saying. Such a thick accent.'

'He wasn't French?'

'*Mais, oui*, he was French but from the Midi. He spoke French, not Provençal, but even so I could not understand a word.'

'He came from Provence?'

'*Certainement*. There is no doubt. My husband had a friend for many years. He was from Nîmes and I never understood him either.' She frowned. 'I am not sure you will find the lady.'

'I've made a start,' he said gratefully, 'and you've been a great help.'

The woman smiled complacently. '*Pas de tout*. We are here to help each other.'

And to spy on each other whenever possible, but he kept that thought to himself.

Walking back to the Hôtel Regina, he had a clear idea of what he should do. Ruby King had had dealings with a man who came from Provence, driving a car that he strongly suspected was registered in that region. It was this man, this car, he reckoned, that had killed her, whether by design or accident. It was enough. He would go to Provence. It was where his mother believed she'd first been threatened, and it was where Flora should herself be heading. He wondered if she'd found the courage to pick up the telephone and ring Richard Frant.

Flora had. After a solitary breakfast, she'd returned to her room and dialled Richard's number. He'd sounded pleased to hear her voice, very pleased, which was a little concerning, but when he'd suggested they meet at the Madeleine, a short walk from the hotel, Flora had agreed.

She chose the same frock as she'd worn yesterday – the only other day dresses hanging in the wardrobe were a rather dowdy floral and a beautiful rainbow print. He didn't deserve the rainbow but she wanted to look smart. Not because she had any wish to reignite Richard's interest, but from a strong desire to prove that over the years she'd not languished from his rejection. Brushing her hair till it shone, she tied it into a secure knot, flicked a powder puff at her freckles and attached a fresh pair of earrings. She was ready to go.

The Madeleine was easily found, its neo-classical façade more like a Greek temple than a church and, at any other time Flora would have been itching to explore. But Richard was waiting by the steps – she knew him immediately, even though the intervening years had given him a more stolid figure and a sprinkling of grey hair beneath the cotton cap he wore. He was only a year or so older than Flora and she was surprised to see that he wasn't wearing particularly well. She felt an instant of guilty pleasure.

He came towards her, his arms outstretched, which with some niftiness she managed to avoid, offering her hand instead. Richard took it, looking a little disappointed, but then pointed out the café on one side of the square and suggested they head for its striped sunshade.

'It's so good to see you,' Richard enthused, once he'd drunk his first cup of coffee. 'And looking so good!'

She smiled slightly. 'It's... interesting... to meet again. But you have news for me?'

He seemed taken aback by her directness. Evidently, he saw this as a social occasion while, for her, the goal was nothing more than information.

'You want to know about your parents?'

'It's why I am here,' she said crisply.

'I have to say your call was a surprise, but I'm very glad you've made it to Paris. You know, if you'd rung me from Sussex, I would have been happy to have found you accommodation.'

'I'd no wish to bother you. And it was easy enough to book a hotel. Now, tell me exactly what you saw, please, and where you saw it?'

'Before I do, I want to say sorry. I *am* very sorry, Flora.'

'For?' Her eyebrows rose in a sceptical arch.

'For leaving you as I did.'

'You should be sorry.'

'I can't excuse my behaviour. The more I think of it, the more deeply ashamed I am but, at the time, I felt I had to go. Escape. Miss Steele was unwell – you were convinced she would get better, but I looked at your aunt and knew she wouldn't. I was terrified the trip we'd planned would never happen, that I'd be stuck waiting while your aunt declined. And it wouldn't have ended then. You'd inherit that damn bookshop and say you couldn't go after all.' He tugged nervously at the sleeve of his linen jacket.

'How perceptive of you, Richard. My aunt did die after a long and painful illness, and I did inherit that damn bookshop of which I'm extremely proud.'

'Yes, I'm sure,' he stammered, 'but you can see the dilemma I faced.'

'A dilemma I faced, too,' she reminded him. 'One we should have faced together, but you chose otherwise. However, I'm not here to rake over old miseries. Tell me please what you know.'

Seeming to accept he would get no further, Richard told his tale. 'I was staying with a friend in Avignon,' he began. 'An old university buddy. I don't think you knew him. He was actually a friend of Lowell's – you'll remember Lowell?'

Flora nodded. Lowell Gracey had been Richard's roommate at college and the three of them had spent most winter evenings together in or around the student bar.

'I haven't seen Lowell for an age, haven't heard a dicky bird, but one of his mates in the chemistry group is teaching English, would you believe? At a language school in Avignon. He got in touch, quite out of the blue, and invited me down. Wanted to show me around the department. Vaucluse, it's called. The countryside in that part of Provence is stunning and has a fascinating history. Anyway, I drove down, and we used my car to visit a number of the villages round and about. One of the places we went to was a small town called Vaison-la-Romaine. It was once a Roman settlement. You'd never guess that, eh?'

It was an attempt at a joke, Flora imagined, but unsmilingly she brushed it aside, intent on getting to the nub of the business, the reason she was here meeting a man she didn't want to be with.

'Vaison isn't large but it has a pretty big church,' he said stiffly, seeming to relinquish any idea of winning her round. 'And after we'd done the Roman remains, we spent some time there. Most of the graves in the cemetery were old, really old, but – well, I couldn't believe my eyes – there were two grave-stones that looked fairly new. Matching gravestones, side by side, one dedicated to Christopher Steele and the other to Sarah Steele. They'd died on the same day as each other and the dates fitted with what you'd told me of your parents' accident. Unless there was another English couple who'd suffered the same fate on the same day, it had to be them.'

'Christopher and Sarah aren't unusual names,' she said stoutly. 'Neither is Steele. And how do you know they're English? They could be American, Canadian, Australian.'

'They were English. The dedication made that clear.'

'What did it say?' Her voice held a tremble she couldn't control.

'I remembered it exactly. It was such an extraordinary find. It said: "Erected by the commune of Vaison-la-Romaine in remembrance of our English visitors who tragically lost their lives far from home."'

'I see.' Flora swallowed hard, still unwilling to believe. 'If it is them, what I don't understand is why they were in France. Aunt Violet never mentioned France.'

'Did she ever say where the accident happened?'

Flora shook her head. 'She was vague, and I never knew precisely. I think she didn't want me to know – it was too sad.'

'Then what I'm saying is likely to be true, but why don't you check for yourself?' he said practically. 'I'd be very happy to drive you down any time you say.'

'I've no wish to trouble you, Richard. I can get a train, I'm sure.'

'You can,' he agreed. 'One to Avignon, but then it's a bus that trundles around a dozen or so villages before it gets to Vaison. Or you could take a taxi which will be super expensive. It's up to you.' He looked hopefully at her over his coffee cup.

Flora held a furious inner debate. She couldn't afford a taxi, that was certain, but was she going to take the easier option? Superficially easier, at least.

'Thank you for the offer,' she said at last. 'If it really is no bother, I'd like you to drive me.'

'Wonderful!' With one quick movement, he was on his feet and leaning across the table, seemingly expecting to embrace her, but Flora escaped, pushing back her seat and picking up her handbag.

'Shall we say tomorrow then?' he asked uncertainly.

'Won't you have to work?'

'I'm freelance,' he said. 'I work when I want to. I'm a journalist now.'

Flora lowered her gaze. The coincidence was ironic. From one journalist to another, she thought.

Aloud, she said, 'I'm at the Hôtel Regina. It's very close.'

'I know it. I'll be in reception around ten tomorrow.'

'Thank you,' she said again, not at all sure she had done the right thing.

Jack was eating a baguette in the snack bar that nestled alongside the hotel when she walked past. Seeing him at a window table, she went in and sat down opposite. She had news to tell and it seemed that he, too, had news for her.

'I'm going to Provence,' was the first thing he said. 'Can I get you a drink, by the way?'

'I'm full to here with drink.' She indicated her throat. 'Two coffees and a juice already. But Provence. How come? Aren't you supposed to be investigating in Paris?'

'I was but the trail leads south, my fellow sleuth. When I get back to the hotel, I'll telephone my mother. Find out the nearest town or village to Chateau Constantin and book myself a room. Amazingly, I've managed to find a hire car at short notice. The chap behind the counter here gave me a tip.'

'Have you ever driven abroad?'

'Seriously?' He smiled indulgently, making her feel foolish. Jack had worked as a journalist in half a dozen foreign countries.

He paused and Flora felt herself being scrutinised. 'If you did decide to travel south,' he said carefully, 'I could drop you off wherever you want.'

'I did decide. I'm going.' She fiddled with the cutlery on the table.

'That's good.' Jack laid aside the rest of his baguette. 'I wondered whether you'd get round to phoning the chap or not. Presumably you've met up?'

She nodded.

'And?'

'He's driving me down tomorrow, to a place called Vaison-la-Romaine.' There was another long pause. 'I'm not happy, Jack,' she burst out suddenly. 'I don't want to be with Richard. He seems so... so proprietorial.'

'He wants to get you back,' he said smugly, sitting back in his chair. 'It's what I always thought. Those letters – it was clear he was using them as a way of currying favour.'

'If he was, it hasn't worked. I've agreed to travel with him, but it stops there. And don't look like that. I can be as good as my word.'

'You can, but he seems a persistent gentleman.'

'A gentleman he is not,' she declared. 'I wish, I wish—'

'You hadn't agreed? Don't agree then. He's told you where he thinks your parents are buried. He's done his job. Ring him up and tell him you're coming with me.'

She hadn't been thinking straight – Jack's news had changed everything. Why hadn't she realised?

Flora's smile lit her whole face. 'Of course! That's exactly what I'll do!'

7

The journey to Provence could have been tedious – the car Jack had hired was an ancient Citroën with no intention of going any faster than it wanted – but the countryside on either side of the N6, the main road south from Paris, held Flora's interest. Travelling through lush farmland, past vineyards and in and out of the pretty villages of Burgundy, helped speed the hours.

'We should decide where we stay tonight,' Jack said, well into the afternoon. 'Beaune is a possibility. I can't drive much longer and we'll be there in an hour or so.'

It was a rare admission. Most usually, he refused to acknowledge the wound he still carried from fighting across Europe during the last war. He must be in real pain, Flora thought.

'Beaune it is,' she said, stretching her legs to relieve the cramp. The Citroën wasn't exactly roomy, and she couldn't imagine how bad it must be for Jack. 'We can't keep driving anyway, or we'd be arriving at the chateau in the middle of dinner. Not the best impression to make!'

When Jack had telephoned his mother the previous afternoon to tell her they were driving south, Sybil had been adamant he should stay at Chateau Constantin. Flora, too. The count wouldn't hear of them booking a hotel, she said. They were to be his guests. To Flora's ear, Jack had sounded less than enthusiastic but, when a further question established the chateau was only a few miles from Vaison-la-Romaine, he'd agreed.

The matter settled, Flora had straight away dialled Richard's number, delighted to be spared the strain of an uncomfortable journey. She would be travelling to Provence with a friend, she'd told him, and wouldn't need to trouble him after all, but thanked him several times for his offer of a lift. Richard didn't sound too happy at not being troubled. She felt his suppressed anger humming down the line but, when she replaced the receiver, her heart was a great deal lighter.

Now, sharing the drive with Jack, the sun shining, the sky azure, and the countryside on either side gleaming, she felt content. And even greater content when they drove into the small town of Beaune. Its narrow streets, timbered houses and stone fortress seemed barely to have changed since the Middle Ages and their hostelry in the heart of the town, Hôtel Le Cep, chimed with the period.

Flora's bedroom that night, all wood, antiques, trompe l'oeil and even a Renaissance sculpture, was so perfect she'd no wish to leave. No wish to leave Beaune itself, it was so very beautiful. But they had promises to keep, Jack to his mother and Flora to herself, and the following day saw them throw suitcases onto the back seat of the Citroën and, after a hasty breakfast, resume the long journey.

The landscape was changing. Flora, gazing through the car window, watched fascinated as vineyards rather than pasture-land began to line each side of the road, stretching so far into the distance that the whole world seemed to be one huge winery. By late afternoon they were travelling by the side of the

Rhône, the great river on its way to the Mediterranean Sea, and so into Provence.

'I hope this works out,' Jack murmured, once they'd left Avignon and taken the signposted road to Carpentras. 'I'd have preferred a hotel, but my mother was so insistent it would be seen as bad manners, I had to agree.'

'Staying at the chateau might have its advantages,' she said thoughtfully. 'If Sybil is being hounded as she says, it could help that we're on the spot. Deter any further attack perhaps.'

'I suppose it might. She's certainly been careful in what she's said, made sure that Massimo believes ours is a family visit. I'm in France to support her after what happened in Paris, that's her story. It should provide good cover – whichever Falconis live at the chateau won't be expecting us to poke around where we shouldn't.'

Flora nodded in silent agreement, her attention diverted by the appearance to their right of a jagged range of hills, massive against the setting sun.

'Just look at those! The scenery *is* stunning, just as Richard claimed.'

Jack glanced towards the limestone cliffs. 'The Dentelles de Montmirail,' he announced.

'You *would* know, of course!'

'I'll confess. I looked at the map last night. "*Dentelle*" means "lace" – and I guess its peaks could be seen as lace-like. Just. Great countryside for climbers, though.'

'But not us,' she said quickly.

'No, not us! We've other fish to fry. Talking of which, we're just about to hit Chateau Constantin.' He pointed to the painted sign they were passing, hanging motionless in the still air.

A short drive uphill along a narrow lane, then through a sturdy pair of gates, and they were in the spacious courtyard of the house that would be their home for the next few days. It was a bastide or large farmhouse, Flora realised. Miss Bancroft, a teacher at the Abbeymead school, had shown her pictures of one in a travel magazine she'd brought into the bookshop. Basking in the late afternoon sun, the two-storeyed rectangular building was decorated a Provençal pink, its façade partly covered by jasmine. Blue-painted shutters framed full-length windows on both upper and lower floors and a continuous iron-work balcony ran along the entire first storey. A sloping terra-cotta-tiled roof completed the picture.

'Mum seems to have done well,' was Jack's wry comment, as he manoeuvred the Citroën between a row of potted cordyline.

They had barely come to a halt when a man's substantial figure emerged from the main door and strode across the court-yard. Flora judged him to be in his sixties, still a handsome man with silver hair and dark brown eyes, and tall enough to carry his weight without looking portly. He was followed out of the door by Sybil, eschewing Dior today, Flora guessed, but dressed in what must still be designer wear. Her boxy jacket looked very much like a magazine picture Flora had seen recently, the magic name of Chanel appearing beneath.

Massimo came steaming towards them, a broad smile on his face and, as Jack clambered out of the car, he had his hands seized in a warm clasp.

'Signor Carrington!'

'Jack,' his mother put in.

'Jack!' he repeated. It sounded almost romantic, Flora thought, spoken by an Italian voice.

'And signorina.' It was Flora's hands that got the treatment this time. 'Come, please! We are waiting for you.'

The 'we' turned out to be several servants busily arranging refreshments on the shaded terrace at the rear of the house. Small dishes of olives, cheese balls, and tiny squares of tapenade toast awaited, with a long cold drink poured for them both.

Sitting upright in a wicker chair, Massimo made polite

enquiries of their journey from England, their stay in Paris, their drive today. It felt to Flora as though the initial boisterous greeting had metamorphosed into something a good deal more formal, and she was unsure why.

What conversation there had been had dwindled to nothing when the count rose to his feet. 'We must not keep you,' he said expansively, another wide smile on his face. 'You will wish to settle into your rooms before dinner. Corinne will escort you.' He pointed to a young woman who had been standing unnoticed to one side of the terrace. 'Corinne will be your maid, Signorina Flora. And for you, Jack, you will share my very own Pierre.'

Massimo had a smooth manner, Flora thought, the perfect host – superficially friendly, socially at ease – but her sense of an underlying entitlement, an assumed ability to control events, was something she couldn't like. The idea, too, of having a servant wait on her made her uncomfortable – she wondered how Jack would fare with Pierre.

When she was shown to her room, she discovered her small suitcase had already been unpacked, the two other dresses and two skirts she'd brought hung in the wardrobe and her blouses and underwear put away in drawers. Again, the same discomfort, the sense that her life had somehow been taken over by a power she couldn't see.

The room itself was charming, looking out over acres of vines and furnished in French country fashion. A pretty painted chest sat in one corner and a basketweave chair with cushions of blue silk in the other. Thick, floral rugs were spread across the polished wood floor and both wardrobe and bed boasted the flowing curves of a rococo style. The coverlet, a beautiful patchwork quilt, looked temptingly soft and, on impulse, Flora swung her legs on to a bed that proved as plump and soft as she'd imagined. She would rest a while, she decided. Just half an hour or so – it had been a long journey.

It was two hours later that she woke with a start and, grabbing her watch from the bedside table, saw that she was in danger of being late to dinner. A hasty wash in the adjoining bathroom and a change into a clean skirt and blouse – now she was staying in France longer than she'd intended, she would have to find a new dress or two, perhaps in a local market – and Flora was ready for whatever the evening had to throw at her.

8

When she opened the bedroom door, Corinne was waiting. For a moment, Flora was startled – how long had the maid been there?

'*Suivez-moi, mamselle*,' she said and, without allowing Flora to speak, led the way down the stairs and along a wide, tiled hall to a room at the far end. Gesturing with her hand to go in, she melted away before Flora could offer her thanks.

In the centre of the dark-timbered room, Massimo's impressive figure stood at the head of a long table spread with what appeared to be a satin tablecloth. Silver cutlery and gold-rimmed plates glinted beneath the glare of an ornate candelabra, speaking loudly of wealth but deepening the surrounding gloom. Every pair of eyes was fixed on Flora as she walked through the door, and she hurried to take the one empty place. With a hardly discernible wave of his hand, Massimo signalled they should sit.

Two young women flanked the count, his daughters Flora presumed, one unsmiling – a tall, heavy-boned woman who had inherited her father's aquiline profile – and a younger, prettier sister. She must be Clio, the one Sybil preferred, despite the girl

being an almost precise copy of Isabella, her mother. Sybil
herself, wearing yet another expensive creation, sat at the foot of
the table while Jack had been placed opposite the unsmiling girl
with Flora beside him. A third chair had been set to Flora's right
and a stocky man, his strawberry-blond hair and blue eyes
seeming more Germanic than French, was introduced as Pascal
Dufour, the manager of the vineyard.

This evening's meal bore all the signs of being an uncomfortable experience, and so it proved. Although beautifully
cooked and beautifully presented, Flora hardly tasted the food.
Massimo's mood had changed again, it seemed, and the
resulting tension had Flora lose much of her appetite. When
one of the maids tripped on a rug and almost dropped a tureen
of onion soup, Massimo barked at her to be more careful. When
Clio, speaking English, began to recount her success that day of
finding a prestigious Paris law firm who would offer her the
chance to shadow their work, her father brought her to a halt by
saying that it was a triviality and no one around the table was
interested.

There was a sour feeling to the gathering. What had
happened to the genial host and his earlier welcome? Whether
it was the eldest daughter's sullen attitude or Massimo's barely
suppressed annoyance or Sybil's occasional nervous titters,
Flora didn't know. What she did know was that the final course
couldn't appear soon enough and her penance and Jack's – he'd
barely spoken – would soon be over.

Not soon enough, it seemed. The daughter Massimo had
introduced as Allegra waited until everyone had been served
from the dish of patisserie before she spoke. Flora had watched
her intermittently during the meal, wondering how long it
might be before her face cracked into any kind of expression,
and noticed that the only person in whom the woman had any
interest was Flora's neighbour, Pascal, the manager. A
disturbing interest. Allegra's gaze had been trained on him

throughout, her black eyes almost feverish, in what seemed to Flora a curious mixture of longing and greed. Dufour himself had addressed not one word to the woman and barely glanced in her direction.

Flora suddenly became conscious that Allegra was staring across the table at Jack. When she spoke, it was in French, relying on her father to translate, while her carefully made-up face remained unsmiling.

'You are a crime writer, Mrs Carrington tells us.' The formality jarred. Sybil might be her father's *chère amie* but to his daughter she clearly remained an outsider.

'I am,' Jack confirmed. 'Do you read crime?'

'I have no time for such books.' She waved her hand in dismissal. 'No time for books that are not serious. Novels – *bof*, they mean nothing.'

How rude, Flora thought. Jack was a guest and why go out of your way to be insulting?

Jack himself appeared unperturbed. 'All of us have different interests,' he said peaceably, while Massimo continued his struggle to translate.

Allegra's stare intensified, her hand clasping the crucifix she wore around her neck. 'And what interests do you have when you are not writing, Monsieur Carrington? Perhaps crime that comes not from a book?'

Jack's face was a picture of bland incomprehension. 'I'm not sure what you mean. Perhaps you could explain.' How well he does that, Flora thought. And why would this unpleasant woman ask such a question unless she suspected the reason Jack had travelled south and was here at the chateau?

'I love crime novels,' Clio chimed in, tossing her long plait of hair to one side while ignoring her father's frown. 'You must be very clever, Jack, to write these books,' she said in English. 'And very hard-working. But you will not be away from your desk for long, I imagine?'

Flora gave Jack's leg a gentle pinch – he would be thinking the same. They had only just arrived and already their departure was expected. If Allegra had suspicions, they seemed to be shared by the whole family.

'Not long, I hope,' he said in answer to Clio's question. 'I'm here to spend time with my mother. She's been through a difficult experience, as you know. But now she's home' – he emphasised the word 'home' – 'I'm sure she'll feel a great deal better very soon.'

'Were you in Paris when that poor lady was killed?' Clio asked. 'We were so sad to hear of the accident.'

'I wasn't there at the time, no. My mother phoned me with the news and asked me to join her. She'd had a very nasty shock.'

'And Miss Steele, too?'

'Flora was already intending to come to France,' he lied. 'For her own reasons. It made sense to travel together, so here we are.' He smiled benignly around the table.

'And what *was* your reason, if I may ask?' Allegra intervened, her stare swivelling towards Flora.

'It's a family matter,' she answered abruptly. 'A private matter.' If necessary, she could be as rude.

Allegra was undeterred. '*Your* family matter? Then you and Monsieur Carrington are not related?'

'No, we're not.' Flora glared at her across the table. 'We are very good friends.'

'But not married?'

She was stunned. This woman's discourtesy knew no bounds. 'Husbands aren't always necessary,' she retorted. 'As I'm sure you'll agree.' She stared pointedly at the woman's bare hand.

Massimo had continued to translate, though Flora could see how awkward he felt in doing so. But she wouldn't feel sorry for him: his daughter was in need of a lesson in manners.

'Thank you for a wonderful meal,' Jack said swiftly, speaking directly to his host. 'I hope you'll excuse Flora and myself.' He pushed back his chair. 'It's been a long day.'

'But of course,' Massimo said a trifle testily. 'We will not be far behind you.'

Outside the dining room, Jack caught her by the arm. 'The garden,' he said in a low voice and together they walked past the stairs, past the kitchen, and out of the rear door.

They hadn't seen the garden in daylight but at night it was magical: amid the chattering of cicadas, an avenue of cypress, sprinkled silver by the moon, vanished into the night while, on either side of the main pathway, the dark outlines of what seemed a hundred different shrubs. And holding court on the surrounding lawns any number of statues, the white purity of their marble gleaming beneath a sky crowded with stars.

'What a place! And what a night!' Flora breathed in the warm, still air, her gaze on the bats that arrowed back and forth.

'It would be, anywhere but here,' Jack muttered glumly.

'So, what do you think?'

She had no real need to ask. It was evident he thought as she did – that the Falconi family was riven with unspoken dislike. Of each other? Of their visitors?

He reached up to smooth back the flop of hair that never lay flat. 'I can't say I love my mother dearly, but I sincerely hope she doesn't throw her lot in with that family. I don't like them – any of them.'

'Massimo seemed welcoming,' she tried. 'At least, at first.'

They began to saunter beneath the avenue of trees, the fresh clean aroma of the cypress filling the air. 'On the surface maybe. But would you trust him?'

She shook her head.

'Exactly. And neither should my mother. I did wonder if

she was exaggerating when she said that someone, maybe more
than one, was trying to force her into leaving. Now, I'm not so
sure. Sitting through that meal felt like being thrown into a pit
of snakes.'

It was unusual for Jack to be so damning, but Flora had
been conscious of the same feeling. Silent snakes waiting their
chance to strike, except for Allegra. She had been far from
silent.

But maybe she was being unfair to dislike the whole family.
'Clio said she was sorry about your mother's friend – and Sybil
likes the girl.'

Jack stopped and faced her. 'She's the best of the bunch, I
agree, but what a bunch. The eldest daughter is a horror. And
why was the manager there eating with the family? He didn't
say a word.'

'Perhaps he's learnt not to. Did you notice the way Allegra
hardly took her eyes off him?'

'You gave her as good as you got.' There was a laugh in his
voice. 'She did *not* like being reminded that she's still unmar-
ried. How old do you think she is?'

Flora pursed her lips. 'Early thirties, maybe. For an Italian
woman that must be old to be still single.'

'Hence the yearning looks at the silent Dufour. It must be
galling to have a far better-looking sister.'

'I wondered when I first saw Clio why Sybil preferred her –
she's a copy of her mother, did you notice? – but now I don't.
She's a great deal more pleasant than the rest.'

'So where do we start looking? Or perhaps we shouldn't.
They're already suspicious of us.' Hand in hand, they turned to
retrace their steps. 'Perhaps we should prioritise *your* search.'

'No,' she said quickly, releasing her hand. 'There's trouble
in this house, it's clear, and that comes first. Before I start
looking around churchyards.'

'We're back to the question of where to start. When we left

Paris, I had in mind that I'd search for the car that hit Ruby. It was almost certainly the same one the woman in Michon's building told me about. She reckoned the man was from Provence, but how many large black saloons must there be locally? Now that we're here, trying to find it seems pointless.'

'Why don't I be the one to make a start? I could question my maid – gosh, doesn't that sound weird? Corinne must have access to all the rooms, including Sybil's.'

'You're thinking of the money and the pills?'

'It's where the campaign against your mother began – if there is a campaign.'

He nodded. 'That makes sense. It has to be someone close to her which narrows the field considerably. She was only saved from taking the wrong tablets because she'd put on glasses to read a letter. Otherwise, she would have swallowed them without thinking – they were virtually the same size, shape and colour as her normal blood pressure medicine. So... it has to be someone who knows what her pills look like.'

'And knows that Sybil wears glasses to see clearly.'

'The switched pills might not have harmed her, we can't know for sure – Mum stupidly threw them away – but why change them in the first place unless you wanted to create trouble?'

'The maid,' Flora said definitely. 'She's my first witness. But that's for tomorrow. Let's get to bed now. Suddenly, I'm exhausted all over again.'

Putting his arms around her, Jack kissed her thoroughly. 'I'll say good night here, away from Allegra's prying eyes.'

'There couldn't be a better place,' she said, returning his kisses.

'Flora? Thinking romance? Really?' He was laughing at her, but she'd already turned back to the house.

In single file they walked quietly through the rear door and along the bluestone-tiled hall to the staircase. She was only vaguely aware of Corinne brushing past them on her way to the kitchen. The maid had finished her night-time duties, it seemed.

Jack had been given the room at the head of the stairs and he paused before opening the door. 'No Allegra!' He grinned and grabbed hold of her again.

'Be careful,' she warned. 'Remember we're the best of friends, nothing more.'

He kissed her again, long and tenderly. 'Who says?' he said in her ear.

Giving him a gentle push, she disentangled herself and walked along the landing to her own room. Her hand was on the doorknob when she heard Jack's shout.

'What is it?' She walked quickly back to him.

'That!' He pointed to something on the floor of his bedroom that looked to Flora like a small, pink lobster.

'What is it?' she repeated.

'It's a scorpion.'

She took a breath in and held it. 'Is it dangerous?'

'They're rarely life threatening, but their sting can be painful. I certainly don't fancy sharing my room with him tonight. He needs another home. Maybe a job for the valet Massimo has kindly awarded me? You best go to bed while I find Pierre.'

Flora didn't move. 'It's a warning,' she announced.

He gave a half smile. 'Don't let's get paranoid. Scorpions aren't uncommon in a hot climate.'

'Uncommon or not, it's a warning,' she said decidedly.

9

————

Flora was awake at dawn, before most of the household, she suspected, but, lying in bed watching the plaster cherubs playing across her ceiling, she heard the tell-tale knocking of a broom in the corridor beyond. Corinne must already be at work. It was a perfect time to question the girl when no one else was around and the maid was at the beginning of her day. She could go the bathroom, pretend she was surprised to see Corinne so early, and stop to talk to her. Frame her questions as casually as she could.

Toilet bag in hand, Flora greeted the maid with a cheerful *Bonjour*. Corinne smiled faintly and continued to dust the banister.

'Corinne, I wanted to ask you. Should I lock my bedroom door during the day?'

It took some miming and a few repetitions before the maid-servant understood. 'It is not necessary,' she said, in halting English.

'No one locks their doors?'

The maid shook her head, but then seemed to have second thoughts. 'Mamselle Allegra.'

'Just Allegra. Madame Carrington's bedroom is open?' she pursued. This time the girl gave a nod. 'Can anyone go there?'

She shrugged. '*Peut-être.* Maybe.'

Corinne was not designed to be helpful, it seemed.

'Have you seen anyone going into Madame Carrington's room?' she asked, giving up the idea of casual questioning. 'When Madame was not there?'

The maid thought it over, whether she didn't understand or was searching her memory or deciding she wasn't going to say, Flora was unsure.

'Mamselle Clio,' she said at last.

'Do you know why?'

'*Pour une écharpe.* A scarf.' The maid paused, her eyes taking on a dreaminess. '*Très belle,*' she said last. 'Hermès. It was beautiful.'

'It would be.' Did Sybil buy anything from Marks and Spencer?

Corinne turned away and, picking up a feather duster, began to whisk it around the row of family portraits that lined walls of coloured stone. The maid had said all she was going to.

As luck would have it, Flora met Jack's mother at the dining room entrance some half an hour later. Though another early riser, Sybil was already groomed to perfection, make-up and hair in place and today wearing a cream silk shirt and matching slacks.

'Did you sleep well?' she asked Flora, in a voice devoid of any real concern.

'Thank you, yes. I was very tired from the journey.'

Sybil's interest switched to the buffet table set up against the far wall and their conversation seemed at an end. Flora, however, decided she would take a chance and ask the woman directly.

'Did you ever lend a scarf to Clio Falconi?'

Sybil swivelled around, dangling a croissant from the pair of tongs she held. 'Yes, I did. Why do you ask?'

'I just wondered,' Flora said lamely. She hadn't had time to concoct an explanation for what, on the surface, must appear an odd question. 'It was a kind thing to do,' she offered, trying to dig herself out of the hole.

'The girl had an interview in Avignon,' Sybil said indifferently, filling her plate with small, sweet cakes alongside the croissant. 'She had a desperate need of something to smarten up that awful suit she wears to such things. I told her to pile the hideous plait on top of her head and wear my scarf.' Wincing, she cast a critical eye over Flora's skirt and blouse. 'I thought the Hermès might do the trick.'

'I'm sure it did.'

'I'm not. She didn't get anywhere, but then it's such a man's world here. Clio graduates from law school this year – all she's asking is for a chance to learn from a professional. Actually doing the job rather than reading God knows how many books to pass exams.'

'Last night she spoke of an offer in Paris.'

'Hmm. Not a job, though. They're not offering a sou. I can't see that being any more successful.'

'Her father didn't seem to think so either.' Flora had been dismayed at the way Falconi had brushed aside his daughter's news.

'Massimo has been very good to her.' Sybil glowered. 'Paid for years of education, and he's still paying. At her age, she shouldn't expect to be funded.'

'Was your scarf returned?'

'What do you mean? You're suggesting that she stole it?'

Jack hadn't exaggerated. Sybil Carrington was a difficult woman, a mean-spirited woman, Flora decided.

'Not at all. I simply wondered if you'd allowed her to keep it for other interviews.'

'Oh, right,' she said, sounding bored and once more returning her interest to the pastries.

When Flora met Jack later that morning – he'd decided to sleep rather than eat and had missed breakfast – she told him the result of her questioning.

'It doesn't get us very far,' she said sadly, as they strolled together across the courtyard towards the cluster of vineyard buildings a short walk away. 'Your mother's room is always unlocked and the only other person the maid remembers being there is Clio, who had a perfectly valid reason.'

'You're right. It doesn't get us far. And how many people work on this estate? Falconi seems to employ a huge staff and the doors to the main house appear constantly open. Anyone could have gained access to my mother's room and not been seen.'

Slowly, they wandered through the warehouse, past a cellar that housed the bottling lines and another containing huge steel tanks, then back into the garden and down to the lake which lay beyond the avenue of cypress. At every spot, they saw people. Overalled staff moving cases in the warehouse, a delivery lorry outside one of the cellars, gardeners weeding and mowing the lawns. Even the lake where they now stood sported a lone fisherman, a vineyard worker on his day off perhaps.

'The scarf is a non-starter,' Jack said at last, his tone gloomy. 'And...' He frowned, his expression hardening. 'I've been thinking about this so-called campaign. It could be my mother is mistaken. She could have mislaid the money.'

'Five hundred pounds, Jack!'

'She may have spent a lot more of it than she realised. And she could have easily muddled her pills.'

Flora looked sceptical. 'She'd have to have made a huge miscalculation to believe she'd been left with no money, and so muddled in her head that false pills could be taken for the true ones.'

'It's possible there were no false pills. Have you thought of that? Mum seems extraordinarily jumpy these days. I've sensed it ever since I met her again. She's a difficult woman, but she's always been quite sure of herself, yet now every so often I've noticed the façade slips and the certainty vanishes. I'm beginning to wonder if she panicked and imagined she'd had money stolen and her pills switched.'

'Why would she panic?' The suggestion was too vague for Flora's liking.

'Wouldn't you, living with this family?'

'The family, yes, but your mother loves Massimo, doesn't she? And he's welcomed her into his home. A stunning home at that.'

Flora spread her arms wide to encompass the immaculate grounds, the faded stone of the winery, and the hazy mauve of mountains in the distance. 'And think of all that drink on tap!'

'Rosé, primarily, and not my favourite.'

'Don't be such a grump. It's a most beautiful estate and I can't see why your mother would be so anxious that she'd make such stupid mistakes. Unless – there's something seriously awry. In which case, her panic is justified.'

'All I'm saying is that she could have worked herself into a state where she imagines things are happening that simply aren't. In her present mood, she could have tucked the money away for safekeeping and forgotten she'd done so, then muddled the pills herself. Add in the fact that Ruby King's death might still be an accident, and you have a series of coincidences that amount to nothing more than that.'

'And last night's scorpion, waiting for you in your room? How do you explain him?'

'I told you. Hot climate, natural habitat. Pierre did a good job with a brush and pan and panic over. Come on, let's shift the dust from our feet and go exploring. I want to see the local town or village or whatever it is. It was given a great commendation in the travel mag I read.'

Vaison-la-Romaine, the large village that Richard Frant had visited months ago, proved charming. It was more like a small town, Flora thought, divided into two distinct halves by a slow-flowing river, the Ouvèze. Topped by a ruined castle, the *haute-ville* or high town had been built on top of a rocky spur and, from what Flora could see, had changed little from the Middle Ages, while the modern town of houses and shops spread across the opposite bank, with signposts to the site of an ancient Roman settlement. An interesting mix!

Jack made for the modern town and parked their hire car beneath the plane trees of the central square. Businesses selling everything from paintings to hardware, tablecloths to face cream, lined all three sides, while the fourth boasted a row of cafés, restaurants and bars. It was at Le Festival Café that they were sitting now, drinking *citron pressé* and enjoying the afternoon sun.

'I think I'll telephone while we're here,' Flora said. 'I didn't want to ask permission to use the chateau phone and I saw a kiosk on the corner as we drove into the square.'

'You're ringing Richard?'

'No, I'm not! Why would I?' It appeared Richard Frant was still an angry wasp buzzing in Jack's head. 'I want to ring Alice.'

'Alice! Abbeymead will still be there when we get back,' he teased.

'I know, but I need to check on the All's Well. Alice should be home around now. Thursday is her day off and she'll have finished her shopping.' Putting down her empty glass, she got up to go. 'I won't be long, I promise.'

It took Flora a while to work out the mechanics of making

the call to an operator, but her patience was rewarded when her friend eventually answered, delighted to hear Flora's voice.

'I've been wonderin' how you were gettin' on,' she said. 'The journey and all.'

'The journey was fine, well, maybe a little long. Maybe a bit tiring,' she admitted. 'But Paris was wonderful, what I saw of it. I so wanted to stay.'

'You're not there now, then? Where are you? Is Jack with you?' Alice's voice had risen an octave.

'It's OK, honestly.' Flora laughed. 'Jack is with me and we've not been kidnapped. We're in Provence, Alice.'

'Ah! Isn't that where—'

'Yes. But it's also where Jack's mother is living – she was only in Paris a short while – and it seemed sensible to travel together. We're staying in the same house as Mrs Carrington. A chateau, believe it or not! Anyway, I have to ask. How is the All's Well? Has the village forgiven me for shutting up shop?'

'There's been a few murmurs,' her friend admitted, 'but everyone is pleased that you're with Jack.' There was a hopeful silence at the other end of the line, but when Flora said nothing, Alice gave a barely audible sigh and went on, 'Charlie's been a good lad, delivered all the parcels you left him. And he's lookin' after Betty, too. He's efficient, I'll give him that. When he leaves school, I'm thinkin' I might train him at the Priory.'

'What!' Flora was amused.

'He's a practical lad and he loves food. And I need someone who's reliable.' There was an acerbic note to her friend's voice.

'What's happened?' Flora braced herself for bad news.

'It's that Tony.' Tony Farraday was apparently back to being 'that Tony' rather than 'Tony, love'. 'He's off to help Kate run the Nook now they're married.'

'Really?' Flora took a while to adjust her thinking. On balance, it seemed a sensible move, husband and wife working in the café together. It meant Kate would no longer be run off

her feet or scrabbling to find part-time staff. But it also meant
that Alice would be losing her sous-chef.

'You'll find someone else,' she said soothingly. 'Or Sally will.
She found Tony, didn't she?'

'And look how that's turned out.' Alice sniffed.

'You must be happy for Kate, though?'

'Course I am... I'll get used to it, I s'pose, but it's a bitter pill,
Flora. I'd just got the lad doin' things as I liked. Anyways, when
are you comin' back? If you've got a date, I can tell folks when
the shop'll be open again.'

'I can't be completely sure, but very soon. Jack is starting to
wonder if his mother is just overly nervous, imagining things
that didn't really happen. Once he feels Sybil is more settled,
we'll be on our way.'

'There was a woman who died, wasn't there? That's not
imagination.'

'No,' she conceded. 'But in all probability it was an accident.' The lie tripped off Flora's tongue. She didn't believe it
herself but she'd no wish to alarm Alice all those miles away. 'I'll
telephone again when we're on our way home,' she promised.

'Mind you do. It's that strange here without you. I know you
went off to Cornwall t'other year and that's a heathen enough
place. But at least it's still England.'

'I'll phone again,' she said once more.

'How's Alice? How's Abbeymead?' Jack asked, as she
slipped back into her seat.

'Both surviving, though Alice is not a happy woman.' With
a grimace, she recounted her friend's woes.

'Tony and Kate working together makes sense, but can you
see Charlie in the Priory kitchen?'

'I can see him in the kitchen, but he'd be eating not working!' Flora smiled at the image in her mind.

'Although perhaps not with Alice behind him.' Jack waved
his empty glass. 'Fancy another one?' When she shook her head,

he said a little too brightly, 'Then should we look for the church-yard you've come to see?'

They had passed a large church as they'd driven in, and Flora had found herself deliberately looking away. 'Another day, perhaps,' she murmured.

She sensed Jack's eyes on her, trying no doubt to gauge her true feelings, but she refused to meet his gaze. Instead, she adjusted her sunhat and looked across to the far side of the square, seemingly fascinated by the picture-perfect scene. Beneath the plane trees, a woman's figure stood motionless, staring in their direction. She wore a headscarf and outsize sunglasses, yet she seemed familiar.

'Isn't that Allegra Falconi?'

Jack followed her gaze. 'You're right. I wonder what she's doing here?'

'Watching us,' Flora said shortly. 'That's what she's doing. Do you think she followed us from the chateau?'

10

_____

'She may have followed someone else,' Jack said quietly. 'Look who's also in the square.'

Flora looked again. Allegra had left the plane trees behind and was walking in the footsteps of Pascal Dufour as he crossed the open space to its southern corner.

'Do you think he realises that she's following him?' Flora asked.

'He soon will if he doesn't now. Her pursuit looks pretty dogged.'

'There's something going on between those two.' Flora jumped up from her chair, grabbing his arm as she did. 'Let's follow them.'

'Why?' Jack was bewildered.

'Because I want to know just what their relationship is. Can Dufour rustle up a large black saloon if required?'

'While Allegra steals money and mixes pills,' he finished for her, understanding exactly how Flora's mind worked.

'A partnership made in heaven,' she suggested lightly. 'Hurry up, or we'll lose sight of them.'

Jack was reluctant. He thought it unlikely they would learn

very much. On the contrary, they might confirm suspicions, already aroused at the chateau, that their visit to Provence was not the simple holiday they claimed. But knowing Flora's determination, he allowed himself to be hauled to his feet and set off after the swiftly disappearing couple.

When they reached the narrow street that led from the southern tip of the square, he saw nothing remarkable: a large number of people strolling the cobbles, others stopping to gaze at window displays, and yet others making an occasional foray into one of the shops that lined each side of the road. It was a bustling thoroughfare and the time of day when people emerged from an early afternoon rest to finish their marketing.

Then, in the distance, he caught sight of Dufour's close-cropped head walking into what looked like a bookshop and, just behind him, Allegra idling on the pavement outside.

'We'd best wait,' he cautioned. 'They're only a little ahead and from here I can just about see what's happening.'

It wasn't easy. Figures weaving a path in and out of the crowd temporarily hid the bookshop from sight but, at length, he saw Dufour walk through its door and pull up sharply when he saw the woman waiting for him.

Their talk was brief.

'What's happening?' Flora demanded.

'They're talking.'

'And we're too far away to hear anything! We should be closer.'

'Too risky,' he muttered. 'The crowd has cleared a little and you should be able to see now. Let's just watch.'

Together they watched. There appeared to be a disagreement of some kind, a refusal maybe on Dufour's part to say or do whatever Allegra was asking. After only a few minutes' conversation, the man turned and walked away, his irritation made plain by ramrod shoulders and an angry stride.

Allegra stood looking after him for what seemed a long time

and Jack could feel Flora's restlessness. 'Let's wait a bit longer,' he urged. 'See what she does next.'

But what Allegra did next surprised them both. Following at a discreet distance, they trailed her to the end of the road and, just before they reached the Roman bridge which spanned the river and led to the *haute-ville*, she walked up the steps of a large building. It was a church.

Without speaking, they followed her through the door, lingering in the porch rather than taking a seat. Jack peered in at the candlelit interior. It was dark, yet welcoming. Several of the pews were occupied, women in the main, kneeling with heads bowed while a church official, not the priest, he thought, trimmed candles and tidied hymnals and hassocks.

'That's her,' Flora whispered. 'One of the rear pews, in a row to the left.'

Jack caught sight of an angular figure bent in prayer, the woman's long black hair visible beneath a hastily tied headscarf and streaming almost to her waist. As they watched, she pulled a Bible from her handbag and began reading.

There was little point in their staying and he gestured to Flora that they should go.

'Was she praying for Dufour, do you think?' Flora couldn't prevent a grin as they retraced their steps back to the square and the Citroën.

'Things didn't seem to be going too well between them, so maybe.'

'But we still don't know what *is* between them, do we?' She sounded dejected and, once in the car, he put his arms around her and gave her a long hug.

'Don't be downhearted. Whatever's going on with Dufour might have nothing to do with what's happened to my mother.'

'It's possible, but it doesn't feel that way. Not to me. It feels as though they're all playing a part in something hidden and we've been left to guess what it is.'

He started the car and was pulling out of the square when she asked, 'Do you think Pascal knows that he's adored?'

'That may be putting it a bit strongly, but he can't be unaware he has an admirer.'

'If he is, he's giving nothing away.'

'I've a feeling Monsieur Dufour holds his cards close to his chest. Perhaps he's teasing Allegra, playing hard to get in the hope it will win him a wife. Marrying the boss's daughter could be a seriously good move.'

'But marrying Allegra! And he already manages the vineyard,' she objected. 'How much higher could he go?'

'Quite a bit, as it happens.'

'Don't be cryptic. You know I hate it when you're cryptic.'

'I'm not certain of the man's agenda, that's all. Mum let slip that Massimo has a heart condition. It's under control, but who knows? An early death and Dufour, married to Allegra, could inherit the vineyard. He could be thinking strategically!'

Flora stayed quiet as they drove slowly out of Vaison, taking the road back to Chateau Constantin and passing, to his surprise, several mysterious circles of stones, huge blocks sculpted from granite, standing proud in an open stretch of parkland.

He was musing on this oddity when Flora broke her silence.

'Do you think that's what this is about?' she asked. 'Inheritance? Is Allegra scared that her father might marry Sybil and deny her the inheritance she expects? Is that why she needs to frighten your mother away?'

He shook his head. 'I don't think she would – be denied her inheritance. I've a feeling that French law is the same as Italian. It's almost impossible for a child to be disinherited.'

'Are you sure?'

'Fairly sure. I was in Italy at the beginning of '44 and one of the prisoners we took at Monte Cassino spoke good English – he'd been a school teacher – and I remember what he told me.

His father had gone a bit crazy towards the end of his life, started going on pilgrimages to holy sites, giving money to neighbours when they asked, that sort of thing. When he died, he left everything he owned to the woman who lived next door.'

'And?'

'While he was away fighting, this chap Luigi heard from one of his sisters – he had a host of them – that they were off to court to make sure they all got their share. There's a law in Italy that says you can't leave your money how you like. Or not all of it. You have to leave a certain portion to your spouse, and your children.'

'You're saying that Allegra would benefit even if Massimo wanted to leave his money elsewhere?'

'Exactly. If Allegra *is* our villain, her motive may be far simpler. She's evidently a religious woman, a good Catholic, and her father's divorce must be an anathema. For her, Isabella will still be family, probably still Massimo's wife. She must hate the idea of her father having a girlfriend.'

'So, she sends a driver to kill Ruby King because she doesn't want her father to have a girlfriend? Pff!'

'Don't dismiss it too quickly. If Ruby's death was an accident, or she was in fact the target and not my mother, the other so-called threats are fairly innocuous, even if they do prove real and not imagined – losing money, pills going missing. It seems to me they could easily be Allegra's response to Sybil sharing her father's house.'

'In other words, we're still not getting very far—' Flora began, when Jack suddenly grasped the steering wheel and swung the car sideways, narrowly missing the deep ditch that ran beside the road.

A huge, yellow-wheeled harvesting machine filled the space, the driver sitting in a cab high above the large gap that ran between two enormous wheels. Giving them a cheerful wave, he trundled past.

'How on earth does that thing work?' Flora asked, recovering her breath after the near miss. For the moment, her frustration at their lack of progress disappeared.

'It's clever. I was locking the car last night – before that ghastly dinner – and talked to one of the drivers who'd just finished his shift. The machine straddles two rows of vines, a wheel on either side – that's what the large gap is for – and uses flexible bars to shake the canopy of each plant. If the grapes are ripe, they fall onto a rubber conveyer belt which then piles them into a container and leaves the grape stems on the vine. Neat, isn't it?'

Flora frowned at the explanation. Perhaps not so neat, Jack reflected, but machines were not really Flora's thing. It was people that interested her. 'There'll be a party,' he offered, as a kind of compensation. 'The harvest is nearly over for the year and the chateau holds a feast for its workers.'

'When will that be?'

'Next week, I think the chap said. My level of French and his accent didn't make it too clear.'

'Will we be here for it?'

'I'm not sure.'

He was prevaricating. For himself, he was happy to leave in the next day or so, as long as no further threats appeared on the horizon. But he was unsure about Flora. So far, she'd shown no desire to do what she'd come here for. He knew better than to remind her a churchyard still waited, but if he could persuade her to brave a search, and feel that his mother was reasonably safe, they could make a break for Paris and home very soon.

'In case we're not here for the celebration,' she said, 'I think we should talk to the vineyard workers as soon as possible. People other than the house servants. They've proved a dead end – I've got nothing out of Corinne and you've hardly done better with Pierre. Some of the workers in the winery must speak a little English and you know enough French.'

'Your confidence is touching.'

'We can do it, Jack. Dufour speaks some English, so why not the others?'

Jack kept his thoughts to himself. From what he'd seen of the area, its inhabitants were quite happy with Provençal and, if they must speak it, standard French. He was annoyed with himself; all those years at school learning the language and he could remember hardly anything.

There was no sign of Pascal Dufour when they drove into the chateau's cobbled courtyard. Was he still in Vaison? What was occupying him there? Not Allegra, Jack thought, but it must be something important to take the man away from his work in the middle of the day in the middle of the week.

They'd washed their hands and Flora had put a comb through her tangle of waves – he wished she wouldn't, he loved that tangle – and walked down the stairs to the dining room together. A buffet had been laid out on the table some time ago but left for two late-arriving visitors.

'Another spread,' he observed. 'Just as well. We haven't eaten since breakfast.'

Flora took little, he noticed, though the food on offer was as delicious as last night's meal. Maybe it was the oppressive atmosphere of this room, or the fear that Sybil might appear at any moment and trap her into thorny conversation. Or maybe discomfort over where they were headed. Fear even.

It couldn't be fear, though, could it? Nothing bad had happened to them, if you discounted the scorpion in his room, and he did, so why did he also feel this prickle of unease? A creeping sense of something very wrong in the chateau, with Flora and himself plump in the middle.

11

Flora jumped up and took their empty plates to the sideboard. She'd hardly eaten, but it felt enough; she was too full of what she needed to do.

'Dufour isn't back yet,' she said, turning to speak to Jack who had cut himself a substantial slice of Roquefort, his hand hovering over the basket of bread. 'Which means I'll have the chance to talk to people in the winery without him interfering. Find out what, if anything they know. What they might have seen over the last few weeks.'

'Do you want me with you?'

'I don't think so. One of us won't be much noticed, but two probably will. And I can play at being the silly female better than you!'

'OK. Be silly – but subtle, Flora! Once I've given this cheese the attention it deserves, I'll be in my room. Waiting to hear you've solved the mystery.'

She gave him a saucy grin. 'I just might surprise you.'

She was in luck when she crossed the courtyard to the collection of buildings that housed the wine production of Chateau Constantin, making her way first to the reception area.

It was where customers came to taste the wine and hopefully buy it, and where tours of the vineyard began and ended. A man wearing the label of supervisor, his name François Devezine, was on his way out of the door as she arrived. He was likely to be Dufour's second in command, she thought, and the right person to show her around. The right person to begin questioning.

'Hello.' She greeted him with a bright smile. 'I'm a visitor here, staying at the chateau.' The man nodded, suggesting the news of their arrival must have spread. 'I've never visited a winery before,' she went on, 'and I'd love to look around.'

'*Bien sûr, mamselle.*' He had a kind smile. 'I will take you. There is time. Please come.' It was fortunate that Monsieur Devezine spoke English, but probably essential if part of his job was to explain to tourists the mysteries of wine making.

'There is much to see. Many processes and very big equipment. We have the bottling, the warehouse, the cellar... but first,' he said, 'we visit the crushing.'

With her companion leading the way, Flora walked into the large brick-built building which lay behind the reception area. Fearsome-looking machines of stainless steel filled the area, dwarfing the men who worked on either side of long conveyer belts. Grapes were being pushed along the belt into a giant trough and from there into massive storage containers.

'Today, this is how we press the fruit,' her companion told her. 'For many years, you know, men and women they dance across the barrels. Now it is more healthy. *Hygiénique.*'

'I imagine it must be, but you still employ a good many people.' She gestured to the men who appeared to be picking out individual grapes from the conveyer belt and tossing them into a waste bin.

'For this, we need people. But the work is not very interesting,' the supervisor added, seeing her expression. 'They must throw away the bad grapes before they are crushed.'

'It's not all machinery, then?'

'*Mais non.* For rosé there is more we must do later.'

'Is all the wine making done here, in these buildings?'

'But of course.'

'So... the workers come and go from here every day? No one has a reason to go into the bastide, for example?'

'Monsieur Dufour, he is our manager, he goes to the house.'

'But no one else?'

Devezine looked puzzled but shook his head. 'Come, I will show you next the pressing.'

The pressing room offered more stainless steel. Flora stood still, staring with some awe at the enormous space the supervisor had led them to. The room, it was far too big to call a room, she thought, was filled with rows of cylinders, their stumpy steel legs and protruding levers making them almost lifelike. Shapeless humans cast in metal.

'The crushed grapes come here,' her mentor told her. 'Red grapes are pressed with their skins – the skins contain the colour, you see – and the longer they are pressed, the darker comes the wine. Next, the juice must be separated from skins and *fermentation* begins. We must always have a cool temperature for this. It preserves *la saveur*. The flavour. The wine ferments to dryness. Here, in Provence, we do not produce sweet wine.'

'How long does the process take?'

'Ten days, a month maybe, or more. *Fermentation* continues until sugar is turned into alcohol and we have a dry wine. Afterwards, we filter, but we will not go to see this. This is not so interesting. It is only for the clarification, I think you say in English. Here at Constantin we add egg whites to clear the yeast.'

'And after that, the wine is bottled?'

'We can bottle, or we can age. In Provence we drink wine young, but we can age from the best grapes. Only some grapes – a deeper colour is best. We will go to the cellar now?'

It was all very fascinating but so far had been little help. There had been no chance to talk to the men working in the crushing room and she'd learned practically nothing from Monsieur Devezine, except that it was only Dufour who regularly visited the house. Time to dare another question that had nothing to do with wine making.

'Do you live far?'

'I come from Séguret. It is a village on the other side of Vaison. A beautiful village,' he said proudly. 'You must visit.'

'And you drive here?'

'There is no other way. No bus, but yes.'

'Does everyone who works here live away from the chateau?'

He nodded. 'Not Monsieur Dufour,' he corrected himself. 'He has a house on the estate. A small villa.'

'But all the others drive here? All the men have cars?'

She was met with another puzzled look. 'Some... they share.'

'What a good idea! I haven't seen many cars at the chateau and wondered how people got to work. I did see a black saloon, though,' she ventured. 'A large car. Do you know it?'

He put his head on one side. 'Black? Maybe. Many cars are black. You like black cars, mamselle?'

'Yes, no. Shall we go to the cellar?' she finished, embarrassed at her clumsiness.

Walking down the steps to the cellar, an enormous cavern, Flora was met with an eerie glow. The space was lit by ceiling lamps placed high over each of the stone arches that stretched into the distance. Wooden casks were stored beneath the arches on either side, not as many as she would have expected, but if most of the vineyard's production was bottled, it explained the relative scarcity. At the far end, a brick wall lined with tall racking held hundreds of bottles.

'Monsieur Devezine!' A voice called down the cellar stairs. '*Le téléphone pour vous.*'

The supervisor looked harassed. 'I am sorry. I must go, mamselle. I will leave you to look, but please choose a bottle.' He indicated the tall racking. 'Make a picnic.'

Flora smiled her thanks and watched him hurry back down the row of barrels and head for the stairs that led out of the cellar. Walking up to the lined bottles, straight as soldiers, she wished Jack was with her. She hadn't a clue about wine, and he would know which bottle to choose, but it was probably best that he'd stayed away. Two interrogators would have been one too many, for certain.

Not that she'd done much interrogating. Monsieur Devezine had answered her questions willingly enough, but she'd learned next to nothing. As for the men working in the crushing room – they were the only others she'd seen, apart from a man parking a harvesting machine – it had been impossible to speak to them over the noise of machinery, while lacking any French and with the supervisor by her side. Was it worth asking Jack to return where she'd failed? She had a feeling that he would have fared no better.

She glanced across the rows of bottles, then switched her gaze up and down. Shutting her eyes, she stretched out her hand. It was as good a way as any to choose. She pulled but, instead of wrapping her fingers around a bottle, she felt the floor vibrate beneath her. Her eyes jerked open and she let out a silent scream. Part of the racking was leaning tipsily towards her, almost touching her body. There was a noise of cracking wood and suddenly it was falling, spewing bottles into thin air as though firing glass bullets, and smashing them across the stone floor in an unholy mess.

Flora was knocked to the ground by flying debris, a fortunate blow as it turned out, since if she'd stayed standing she would have been injured by shards of glass. Badly injured at that, even killed. Winded and bruised, she lay still on the floor as bottles rolled around her head and pools of wine soaked through her cotton skirt.

'Mademoiselle,' a voice called. 'Mademoiselle, are you alive?'

With difficulty, she moved her head and looked up. Pascal Dufour was looking down at her.

'Yes,' she managed. 'Just.'

'*Mon dieu, quelle catastrophe*! Please, your hand.'

Reluctantly, she held out her hand and was pulled to her feet, finding it necessary to lean against him until she felt able to take a step unaided. The strong, sweet smell of cigarette tickled her nose – Turkish? she wondered.

'Where is Devezine?' the manager demanded angrily.

'He had a telephone call.'

'He should not have left you.'

'He has been very kind,' she hastened to say. 'Shown me the winery.' She gulped down a breath, finding it difficult to get out the words. 'I was choosing a bottle.' She waved helplessly at the mess confronting them.

He tutted. 'This should not have happened.'

No, it shouldn't, she thought to herself, but I wonder why he asked if I was alive. Surely, it would have been more natural to ask if I was OK. And when did he get back from the town? It couldn't have been long ago – there'd been no sign of him when she'd walked across to the winery. Was it possible that he'd returned from Vaison hard on their heels and been hiding in the building all this time?

12

'This should not have happened,' Dufour repeated, his hand still beneath her elbow. 'I will help you to the house.'

'There's really no need but thank you.' Flora slipped from his clasp and walked unsteadily up the stairs to the cellar entrance. Very slowly, she made her way across the courtyard to the front door of the bastide. The cuts to her arm and hand were stinging, and several large bruises were already making themselves known below her knees. Goodness knows what the rest of her body must look like – she had been grazed by shattered glass and splintered wood, then landed with a thump on the stone floor.

Relieved that she'd reached the bathroom without meeting anyone, she washed the cuts in soap and water and gave the bruises an ineffectual pat. Hopefully, the tan she'd begun to acquire would mask the worst damage. Once she was satisfied she had done all she could to look presentable, she walked along to Jack's room.

As soon as he opened his door, he took in her dishevelled state and, with a gentle tug, ushered her into the bedroom.

'Dear God, Flora, you look awful! What on earth

happened? Here, sit down.' He helped her into the velvet-covered armchair, propping her against squashy cushions.

'I feel awful,' she admitted, 'but it's hardly surprising. I've just done battle with a hundred glass bottles.'

'Can I fetch you a glass of water?' She shook her head. 'Then tell me.'

After she'd related her tale of woe, Jack sat for long minutes staring down at the Aubusson rug at the foot of his bed.

'We have to take this seriously,' he said at last.

'Are you saying that we haven't already?' Flora was disconcerted. She had certainly been taking it seriously.

'I should make a confession. I guess I'd come to think my mother was letting her imagination run amok. In my mind, I'd started to label her fears as "so-called threats" rather than genuinely dangerous. I suppose it was what I wanted to believe.'

Flora studied him thoughtfully. 'I could see that was happening,' she said. 'It wasn't just your mother's fears you were keen to dismiss. You mentioned several times that Ruby King's death could have been an accident when to my mind it clearly wasn't. And you were sniffy about the scorpion, refusing to believe it was a warning. Does this mean you've changed your mind?'

'I reckon so. The scorpion must have been deliberate, after what's happened to you this afternoon. There's no way that wine rack falling to pieces could have been an accident. The shelving would have been fixed as securely as possible – the vineyard couldn't afford to have racks detaching themselves from the wall and smashing a hundred bottles of expensive wine. Someone unscrewed that racking just sufficiently that if anyone took hold of a bottle, it would collapse.'

'Not anyone, Jack. Me. It was Monsieur Devezine who invited me to take a bottle.'

Jack's eyebrows rose. 'But I can't think him guilty,' she added hastily. 'He's just too nice. Too innocent.'

'No one is entirely innocent. You should know that by now. The racking could only just have been tampered with – it would have been a danger to everyone otherwise – and Devezine was the only one around.'

'He was with me the whole time, until he was called away to a telephone call, whereas... Dufour had returned from Vaison, though I didn't know it, then miraculously appeared while I was lying amid broken bottles. He could have been hanging around all the time, waiting for his opportunity.'

'How would he have known that you'd grab a bottle?'

'I'm pretty sure that visitors are taken on a planned route, starting with the grape crushing, then taken through the various processes until they end up in the cellar. Guests probably get invited to pick their own wine and pay for their purchases back at reception. In my case, Monsieur Devezine offered me a bottle as a gift. Dufour will know the routine. He'd guess the cellar is where I'd end up, and maybe while I was being taken around the winery, he made sure the rack was triggered to fall if anyone as much as touched it. The telephone could easily have been a hoax, designed to get the supervisor out of the way.'

Jack kicked the edge of the rug in a rare sign of irritation. 'Whoever was behind it meant you harm. I don't want you trotting off on your own again. We need to stay together – from now on, we investigate as a team, Flora.'

She gave a little puff of air. 'What's the betting that you've done some trotting on your own while I've been fighting those bottles.'

'I did telephone Ridley,' he admitted with a guilty smile. 'The inheritance thing interested me. You suggested it as a motive and it very often is – and I could have been wrong about French law. Massimo's ex-wife and his two daughters could all have an interest in how the estate is left when he dies. And maybe Dufour, too, if he marries Allegra. I asked Alan to check for me. He'll come back soon enough but, in the meantime, I think we should move out. Find a hotel in the town.'

'But why? If we move to Vaison, Sybil will be left on her own. You'll be less able to protect her and we'll be less able to keep a tab on what's happening here. Particularly, what's going on with Dufour. He lives on site, I found out. He has a house, a small villa, the supervisor told me, at the far end of the vineyard, and he's a man worth watching.'

'We can keep an eye on him at a distance. It may even be easier.'

'There's Allegra, too – she needs watching as well. I'd love to get into her bedroom and have a look around, but according to Corinne she locks the door. She's the only member of the family who does which is interesting in itself.'

'Where was she this afternoon, I wonder? That's interest-ing, too. I heard Pierre mention that Clio has gone to Avignon again – called back for a second interview for the business that originally turned her down, but Allegra? Unscrewing wine racks perhaps.'

Flora gave a weary sigh. 'We're staying in a most beautiful place. I've no shop to attend to and you've left your writing at home. We should be able to relax and enjoy being here, but we can't – we have trouble hanging over us.'

A particular trouble hanging over me, she remembered miserably. A visit to the Vaison churchyard. How could she ever forget?

'OK, we'll stay, but let's get out of the chateau tomorrow. Constantin may be beautiful but it's beginning to depress me. We could take a trundle around the countryside.'

Flora gave a smile, her hazel eyes suddenly alive. 'Let's do that. Séguret – we should go there. Monsieur Devezine says it's a wonderful village.'

'A day out tomorrow, then. Don't say anything about it at

dinner tonight. We don't want anyone round that table deciding it's a good idea to tinker with the Citroën.'

Jack and his mother met on the staircase a few hours later. She was dressed for dinner and, even to his untutored eye, her frock looked expensive. How did she afford this kind of wardrobe? She'd been adamant that, after their divorce, Ralph Carrington had left her penniless and that, ever since, his father had done nothing to help her. That had been proved a lie. She'd come away from the marriage, it seemed, with sufficient funds to make a decent life for herself, but certainly not enough for the designer lifestyle she chose to embrace. Was Massimo funding it? If so, it suggested their relationship was deeper and more permanent than Jack had thought. The count seemed already to be taking on the role of husband.

'Come for a drink on the terrace,' she said. 'I've hardly spoken to you since you and that girl arrived.'

He bristled at the phrase 'that girl' but followed her out onto the broad terrace that ran the entire length of the bastide. Beneath a brightly coloured shade, wicker tables and cushioned chairs gave it a welcoming air. So, too, the servant who appeared as if by clockwork, empty tray tucked beneath his arm.

'Two glasses of Rasteau,' his mother ordered. And when she saw Jack frown, said, 'You'll like it. It's a local wine – and it's not rosé!'

Her son wasn't going to argue. There were more important things to discuss. He wondered for a moment whether he should mention what had happened to Flora this afternoon, but decided that might well send Sybil into a flurry and delay their return to Sussex. He was itching to make a start on the book that, in his mind, he'd begun to put together and for that he needed to be back at Overlay House. A writer's dilemma, he thought drily. Torture while you were actually writing and frustration when you weren't.

Once the drinks were on the table, Sybil raised her glass. 'Good luck,' she said obscurely.

'With?'

'With what you're here for.' Her tone had sharpened. 'So far, you seem to have got nowhere.'

'It's early days but I'm keeping my eyes open for anything that doesn't ring true.'

'You need to do more than keep your eyes open. You need to investigate Isabella. And Allegra. Make them your primary suspects like you do in those books of yours. It will be one of them behind the threats against me, you can be certain.'

Jack was inclined to agree but felt it better for the moment to keep his counsel. While he'd been in France, there had been no further attacks on his mother. Instead, aggression had been aimed at himself and Flora. Did that mean their villain had given up the campaign against Sybil? Or biding their time until her son had left before resuming hostilities?

Pascal Dufour was a possible suspect, he agreed with Flora, but his money was on one of the women. There'd been no sign of Isabella since they'd been in Provence, but that didn't necessarily suggest she had stayed in Paris. Until now, she had been intent on dogging her husband's footsteps, all the way to Venice if Sybil had spoken truly, and she owned a house nearby. He couldn't be certain that Isabella wasn't there, living quietly, keeping a low profile while she waited for her chance.

Allegra was the suspect who'd made her presence felt. She'd been wary of them from the outset, dug around for information, kept a watch on what they did and where they went. But if the elder daughter were the miscreant they were chasing, it was likely to be a slow business before she showed her hand fully. He might have to resign himself to a long wait, but he was certain that Flora wouldn't be waiting with him. He wanted her back in Abbeymead as soon as possible. He needed her safe from further danger – this afternoon, she'd been lucky to escape with cuts and bruises. She had a shop to look after, too, and the All's Well couldn't remain closed indefinitely, whereas at a pinch he could write here, he supposed. Might have to write here. Ideas were bubbling and if he could borrow paper and a typewriter...

He hoped, though, that while Flora was here, she would find the courage to make it to the Vaison churchyard. For a girl who was so determined and at times so foolishly brave, the question mark over her parents' deaths had become a fear to crush her. She needed to be free of the burden she carried. And the sooner she was, the better.

13

They left for Séguret shortly after breakfast. Sybil had announced that she had an appointment in Vaison at the local beauty salon later that morning, but the remainder of the household appeared to be staying put. Jack, with no wish to spend time with either Massimo or his daughters, was glad they would be out of the chateau for most of the day. They hadn't been made to feel unwelcome exactly, but the hospitality had verged on the formal, as though the count had felt duty bound to welcome Sybil's son and companion but would hardly be unhappy if they were to leave. Questions would soon be asked hinting at their departure, Jack was sure, and he wanted them away before that happened.

'Monsieur Devezine was right,' Flora said as, having bypassed Vaison, they left the village of Sablet and drove slowly towards their destination. Field after field of vines lay on either side of the road and ahead, Séguret, topped by a ruined medieval castle, wrapped itself around the bottom of a steep hill. 'It *is* beautiful.'

They pulled into a parking area just below the village. 'It looks as though we have to go the rest of the way on foot.' Jack reached over to the back seat for his straw trilby. Though not yet noon, the sun was already hot. He nodded towards the cobbled street ahead. 'It should make for an interesting walk.'

'It's fabulous! I'm so glad we came.'

Hand in hand, they climbed the steeply sloping lane and through an arched portal that had evidently once been part of the old wall guarding the village.

'They couldn't have built Séguret in a better position,' he said, looking down at the vineyards they'd left behind. 'From up here, the villagers would be safe from all but the most determined invaders.'

Flora adjusted her sunhat, attempting to scoop her long waves into a topknot beneath. 'Gosh, it's hot. Are we walking along the main street, do you think?'

The road was narrow, its cobbles lined by solid stone houses whose window sills were awash with blooms. And in ornate doorways, clouds of colour amid a jumble of pots and planters.

'I reckon it must be.' He pointed to the sign on a house wall. 'Rue des Poternes, for what it's worth.'

A few shops had found their way between the houses: a bakery, a grocer's, a fruit stall, but only one that came close to being a gift shop. Flora bent to peer through the window at the man working in the shop's cellar.

'He's a jeweller,' she announced, straightening up, 'and it looks as though he crafts his own designs.'

She started towards the stairs that led to the workshop below before Jack caught hold of her arm. 'You can come back later. Let's keep walking for now.'

'OK, but don't think you can fob me off,' she warned. 'I have holiday presents to buy and he had a tray of very pretty necklaces on display. Bracelets and brooches, too. And I have francs with me! The money I changed at Newhaven.'

She took hold of his hand again and together they continued the steep climb to the tiny main square at the top of the hill. At one end of the square stood a Romanesque church with a bell tower that Jack reckoned must be almost as old, and to one side, an equally ancient fountain. From this altitude, the view over the Rhone valley was nothing less than stunning.

'How lovely.' Flora gave a deep sigh of appreciation and walked over to the fountain for a better look. 'Fontaine des Mascarons, it says. The top seems to have been sculpted in the shape of a pineapple, but probably not. They're goblin heads gushing out the water. It's an odd mix. How old do you think it is?'

'Seventeenth, eighteenth century maybe. It would have been very important back then as a source of drinking water. That' – he pointed to an open stone structure – 'must have been the communal wash house. The *lavoir*. Look at those huge stone basins.'

'How do you know that?'

'I've seen them in the south of France before. Water was very strictly regulated. You weren't permitted to use the fountain for laundry or to wash your vegetables.'

Shading his eyes against the midday sun, he looked out across the valley. 'It's pretty special, isn't it? We could find a terrace with a view – have an early lunch. What do you think? Unless you want to see the church first.'

'You can do the church. I'm walking back to that workshop,' she said firmly. 'I might find presents for Alice and Kate and Sally.'

'Alice wearing jewellery?' He looked sceptical.

'She might do. A brooch perhaps. And Kate and Sally certainly will. Not to mention what I might like!'

'If you must, but don't spend too much! There'll be other shops to plunder. I'll be on the lookout for somewhere to eat and then come and collect you.'

Leaving Flora to her bangles and brooches, he walked through the remainder of the village, ending at the fortified

Huguenots' gate, still with its ironbound wooden shutters, that had once marked the southern entrance to the village, then retraced his steps, arriving at a restaurant with a spacious terrace that looked out over the valley below. A panorama of fields and vineyards and red-roofed buildings. Le Mesclun, he decided, was where they'd eat.

Flora was just emerging from the shop when he walked back to meet her, bouncing with pleasure at the purchases she'd made. 'Three necklaces,' she said. 'They're simple beads but very stylish, one each for Kate, Sally and me, and the most beautiful brooch for Alice in the shape of a honey bee. The jeweller told me, I think I got it right, that the bee was a symbol of Provence. And did you know,' Flora was still buzzing, 'that Séguret is the Provençal word for security? Or *sécurité* is what he said. But it's the same thing. You were right about the village being able to repel all intruders.'

'When am I not?'

That earned him a gentle poke in the chest. 'Have you found somewhere to eat?'

'I have and not before time, by the look of it. Have you emptied your purse?'

'Almost,' she confessed, 'but not quite.'

Sitting at a table beside the low wall that bounded the restaurant's terrace, they ate fresh omelettes and green salad with newly baked bread, washed down by a large glass of rosé.

'Abbeymead seems a world away,' she said, sipping the last of her wine and gazing up at the intense blue of the Provence sky. 'This is so very different from Sussex.'

'Different, but both are beautiful.'

'True, I suppose, but when you live in a place all your life, you don't always see its beauty. Or you see it, but somehow look through it. It's probably different for you, Jack – as a relative newcomer.'

'Maybe, or maybe it feels good today because for once we're

sharing it.' He smiled. 'Most often, we're walking our separate paths.'

This was dangerous talk. Any allusion, even a vague one, to a shared future rather than the friendship they presently enjoyed, was usually enough to make Flora run for the hills. Here, though, he had her captive, and it was worth the risk.

'What do you mean?' she challenged.

'Only that when you live life together, *really together*,' he emphasised, 'it offers something deeper. A richness,' he finished, not able to think of anything better.

'Perhaps.' She gave a small shrug. 'But how can you ever know?'

'By trying it.' It was an instinctive response and he waited.

'Hmm,' was all she said.

Not a categoric refusal then. He took heart. There'll come a time, Alice had insisted, when the mention of marriage won't bring Flora out in hives. Was that time coming?

As soon as they turned into the lane that led to the bastide, Flora knew something was wrong and, walking through the massive front door of the chateau, she was proved right. Sybil was in the hall, white-faced and trembling, clinging to the chair she'd sunk into. She hadn't after all made it to her beauty appointment.

Jack knelt down to speak to his mother who seemed unable to stop shaking. 'What's happened, Mum? Tell me,' he urged.

'I didn't go,' she began. There was a long pause. 'Massimo took the car.'

'Why was that?' Jack was trying to be gentle, but Flora could see he was finding it difficult to restrain his impatience.

'The doctor rang from Carpentras. Massimo had to go to the surgery... there were test results.'

'OK, so Massimo went to the doctor.'

'No... no... you don't understand. He didn't get there. The car... it went off the road into trees.'

Flora saw Sybil clasp her hands so tightly they turned blood red from the pressure.

'Where did this happen?' Jack asked, still trying to get the full story.

'At the end of the drive, at the bottom of the hill.'

'We didn't see anything when we turned into the driveway.'

'The man from the garage... he came. He's taken it away. It's a big mess.'

'Were any other cars involved?' The question was asked cautiously.

'No, thank the Lord. Just Massimo.'

'And the count? How is he?' Flora bent towards the still shaking woman to hear her answer.

'They took him to hospital.' Her voice cracked. 'They just phoned. He's bruised very badly, and his shoulder is dislocated.'

Jack straightened up. 'It will be painful, but bruises disappear and the shoulder will mend. You shouldn't be too worried.'

She shook her head more vehemently. 'That's not it. It's his heart... it's not good.'

'Then Massimo is in the best place,' he said practically. 'In the Vaison hospital?'

She nodded.

'You can't do much at the moment, but as soon as the doctors say it's OK for you to visit, I'll drive you there.'

'You've had a bad shock,' Flora put in. 'Why don't you take a rest? I'll ask Corinne to bring some sweet tea to your room.'

Without another word, Sybil dragged herself to her feet and made for the staircase.

'Corinne should be in the kitchen,' Flora said, as they watched his mother make a slow progress up the stairs. 'I'd best go and find her.'

When Flora had disappeared, he walked into the main

sitting room, the salon as it was known by the household. Three people stared at him as he came through the doorway. Clio, her face wet with tears, looked up from her seat on the Bergère sofa while Allegra stood by the open French window, clutching at Pascal Dufour's shoulder, her face etched with unhappiness. Dufour himself wore a stoic expression, as though this drama was one he had to get through before he could move on to more interesting stuff.

Jack gazed at each of them in turn. It might be that the threat to his mother's safety was far from over. Massimo must have driven down that hill a hundred times before, so why today had he crashed the car? Had someone tampered with the vehicle – someone who knew Sybil would be driving herself to Vaison this morning? Could it have been one of these three?

14

In the early evening, he knocked on Sybil's door. Flora had offered to pay her a visit but Jack felt it incumbent on him to check how his mother was coping. Not at all well when he'd seen her last.

'How are you?' He put his head round the bedroom door, careful not to cross the threshold.

'Frightened,' she said, but her voice was stronger. 'You can come in, you know. You don't need to dance around in the corridor.' A lot stronger, he thought sourly.

'Frightened because you think you were meant to be driving that car?' He sat down in one of the velvet-covered Louis the Fifteenth chairs.

'Well, wasn't I?' she demanded, lying back against the pillows.

When he didn't respond, she said in a quieter voice, 'Frightened for Massimo, too. I don't know what the doctors will say. I don't even know the results of the tests they ran. He never got to the surgery.'

'You'll find out very soon. Tomorrow maybe – I'm sure you'll be able to visit.'

She said nothing and Jack thought it best to spill out what he'd decided. 'I'll drive you into Vaison, as I said. Flora, too. I think it's best that she and I find a hotel in town.'

His mother sat bolt upright, pushing her hair roughly from her face. 'You're abandoning me!'

'Not at all. I'll be only a few miles away. And at a distance, it might prove easier to find out what's going on here.' He was remembering Flora's words.

'I can't see how,' she said combatively.

'If we stay, we can be watched. I'm pretty sure we *are* being watched. I can't talk freely either to you or to Flora without the risk of being overheard. And maybe whoever is responsible for these attacks, if it is someone at the chateau, will relax once I've left. They'll drop their guard. And that can lead to mistakes.'

His mother gave a dismissive snort, evidently disagreeing. But Jack was adamant. It was the right thing to do, he was certain.

'In any case, Mum, with our host in hospital, we shouldn't be here.'

'I can't see that either.'

Unwilling to argue further, he got up to go. 'Get some more rest,' he advised. 'I'll make sure the maid brings you supper and I'll see you tomorrow.'

Dinner that evening was a scratch affair. The household was in turmoil, knocked sideways by the news of the count's accident. There was no sign of Dufour and neither sister had appeared by meal time; it seemed they were locked in private conversation upstairs. When Flora joined him in the dining room, Jack took one look at the empty table and suggested they make their way to the kitchen. The servants appeared to have gone to ground as well and, in their absence, he raided the refrigerator for cold meat and salad while Flora sandwiched their spoils inside two large baguettes.

'If the house remains quiet, I'm going to purloin Massimo's study,' he said, wiping the last crumbs from his fingers. 'But I think you should make yourself scarce.'

'Why and why?' Flora collected their plates and ran them under the hot water tap.

'I want to telephone Ridley again – without anyone listening. By now, he should have the information I asked him for, but I don't want you involved. If anyone is on the watch this evening, it won't be you they see.'

'So much for investigating as a team!'

'Only one of us can make the call,' he said reasonably, 'and I'll tell you what he says as soon as I'm done.'

Flora stored away the china, brushed the floor of stray crumbs and straightened the linoleum tablecloth. 'There! Who would know we'd ever been here? Are we really leaving tomorrow?'

'I think it's best.' He switched off the lights as they left the room. 'Do you mind going?'

'Mind? Goodness, no. I'll be glad to get out of here. The chateau may be luxurious but I find it oppressive. I feel I have to be careful in what I do, what I say. I have this sense that people are hiding behind doors – I know it's stupid – that they're spying, waiting for us to leave or calculating how they can get rid of us.'

'In that I don't think you're too wrong.'

Once he'd seen Flora climb the stairs to her room, Jack padded silently along the hall to where he'd noticed Massimo working. Moonlight filtered through the unshuttered window and, quietly closing the door behind him, he left the lights off and walked towards the desk and the black outline of the telephone. The phone boasted an outside line which meant he could dial the international operator directly. Perfect. No going through the local equivalent of a Dilys Fuller, the postmistress of Abbeymead, a woman with a penchant for listening in whenever she was bored with serving her shop's customers.

He rang Alan Ridley's number, crossing his fingers the inspector would be home, and was in luck. The inspector was not only there but had done his homework.

'French inheritance law?' he said. 'Didn't take too long to find out. It's much the same as Italian apparently. A wife and children can't be disinherited no matter how much a chap might wish it! They get a set amount each and only then can the bloke divvy up the rest of the property. What's this all about, Jack? Or need I ask?'

'I imagine you needn't. My mother is in a bit of trouble and I'm trying to help. I wondered if inheritance might be the motive behind the threats she's faced, but from what you've said, probably not. It will likely be something much simpler – she's intruded into a family that don't want her.'

'Sounds like you've got your work cut out. And here was me thinking you and little Miss Steele were enjoying an idyllic holiday together!'

'Thanks, Alan,' he said caustically. 'I'll see you at the Cross Keys once I get back. The beer's on you!'

As Jack replaced the receiver, he was conscious of a slight movement of air and spun around. There was no one. He walked into the hall and its emptiness looked back at him. Had he imagined it? Was life at Constantin turning him paranoid? As he started for the stairs, the sweet smell of a cigarette came wafting towards him. He frowned, trying to grasp a memory but then gave up.

'I was right,' he said, flopping down on the one easy chair Flora's room boasted. She swung her legs off the bed and sat facing him, her expression expectant.

'Inheritance isn't a motive after all?'

'It can't be. French law is almost identical to Italian, so

wherever Massimo made his will or whatever he gave as his place of residence, he would have to leave two thirds of his estate to his daughters.'

'What of the remaining third?'

'It's for him to decide. He's free to leave it as he wishes.'

'So, he could leave that to Sybil, even if they never married?'

'He could, it's true. But there would be others he'd want to remember, I imagine. Isabella, for instance. As a divorced wife, legally she's entitled to nothing, but Massimo might still want to leave her money or property. They were married for many years, after all. That one third would have to stretch a long way.'

'And if the count married Sybil?'

'As his wife, she would be entitled to a quarter of the estate with the daughters sharing a half between them.'

'That means they'd get less.' Flora pounced. 'Isn't that significant?'

'Not that much less that it's worth killing for.'

Flora bounced off the bed and put her arms around him. 'It would still be in their interests to prevent their father marrying again. And you know what Inspector Ridley always says,' she murmured into his ear. 'Where money is concerned, nothing should surprise you.'

15

When Jack knocked at her door the next morning, Flora wasn't in her room but, walking down the stairs, he heard her speaking to someone at the front door. She was in determined mood, nothing unusual in that, but this morning her voice held an unfamiliar coldness. Reaching the bottom of the staircase, he glanced along the hall and saw her figure silhouetted in the open doorway. It was stiff and straight.

'I've promised, haven't I?' Her words were clipped. 'I'll meet you this afternoon – I'll be there at three. But right now, I think you should leave.'

Jack couldn't see much of the visitor, a scrap of blue linen shirt, a pair of shiny brogues, but he reckoned it had to be Richard Frant. Why was the man here? Why had he travelled down from Paris?

'Listen, Flora—' Frant began, his voice raised. But at that moment, it seemed, he caught sight of Jack hovering in the background and stopped speaking. Whatever objection he'd been about to make was abruptly terminated. With a glowering face, he wheeled around and stomped across the courtyard to a silver sports car parked untidily beneath the dusty plane trees. Jack made a face. Too showy, he thought, and not a patch on my red Austin.

'Frant, I presume?' he asked, as she turned from the door. 'And in Provence?'

Flora's lips had formed a tight, thin line. 'He's followed me, Jack. Would you believe that? Followed me all the way from Paris.'

'How did he know...' Jack began.

'I was stupid, that's how. When I phoned to thank him for his offer and tell him I wouldn't be taking it up after all, I was foolish enough to mention I was staying near Vaison at a Chateau Constantin. It wouldn't have taken much checking for him to discover where that was, then set off to track me down.'

Richard Frant was certainly a shady character, Jack thought, and he was glad Flora had sent him on his way. By the look of it, though, the man was forcing her hand, making Flora confront her demons whether she liked it or not, and that was all to the good. The sooner she did, the sooner she could be on her way back to Abbeymead.

He wanted her far away from whatever mess was likely to unfold. And he was pretty certain it would. Whoever was intent on harming his mother hadn't stopped, and wasn't going to. The crash yesterday was just the latest attempt. Massimo's accident might be genuine, a case of an experienced driver losing concentration, but it was much more likely that the car had been tampered with in the expectation that Sybil would be driving. Yesterday, they'd hurt the wrong person, but next time they might not. Jack couldn't forget that this was someone who, in all likelihood, had killed before. The hapless Ruby King. Next time, it could be his mother as victim, or Flora, or himself. He was determined it wouldn't be Flora.

'Are you packed?' he asked cheerfully, trying not to let his thoughts show. 'We can leave after breakfast, if that's OK with you, and drop my mother at the hospital. As long as she's been told she can visit.'

Sybil, it turned out, had been told she couldn't. At least, not yet. Massimo was currently in a sedated condition and she would have to postpone her visit until later that afternoon or maybe not until the following day. She was not best pleased with the news and sat silent and sullen throughout breakfast.

'Phew. Thank goodness we're out of there,' Flora said, once they'd packed the car and were speeding down the steep hill towards the main road. To the junction where Massimo had come to grief. 'Did you check the brakes?' she asked suddenly.

He grinned. 'I did. It was my first thought, though I doubt anyone would try the same stunt twice. It would be a little too obvious. At the moment, Massimo's crash is being talked of as "an accident", but if it happened again...'

Conversation dwindled as they navigated a roundabout and took the main road to Vaison, until Flora said suddenly, 'I hope we've not burnt our boats by moving out of the chateau. Hotels in the town could be full – have you thought of that?'

'I'm sure there'll be space somewhere. I rather fancy a hotel in the *haute-ville*, if we can find one. Unless you have other ideas. I like the thought of sitting on top of a rock!'

'Fine by me. I've only seen it from a distance, but it looks pretty special. And it's a short walk into the centre of town.'

Once they had crossed the Roman bridge, the Ouvèze meandering peacefully below, Jack halted the car outside the first inn they came to. It was a large square stone-built building, with faded blue shutters and window boxes red with geraniums. A brilliantly painted sign told them that this was Hostellerie le Beffroi.

'What do you think? There's parking opposite.' Jack pointed towards a small space that had been cleared of vegetation, sufficient to take three cars.

'It looks charming.'

'Good. If they have rooms, I'll pull over.'

The hotel had rooms. The crowds from Paris that descended every summer on this sleepy Provençal town had returned to the city and, now as the nights drew in, holiday-makers from abroad were also thinner on the ground.

Flora was delighted with the room she was given. Looking out over the river and the modern town beyond, it was spacious and well-furnished, its terracotta floor tiles covered in bright cotton rugs. She felt immediately at home.

'We're so high up, it's as though I'm halfway to heaven,' she said, throwing open the window and glancing down at the panorama of rock and water and red-roofed buildings below.

'*And*,' she walked over to the bed and gave it a few experimental bounces, 'the mattress is soft – bliss!'

Jack was happy enough with a smaller room at the front of the hotel overlooking the narrow street they'd driven along. From here, he would have a good view of their parked car. In light of recent events, it seemed important.

'Let's get some lunch,' he said, coming to stand beside her at the window. 'We've time to eat before you need to meet Frant.' He glanced down at her. The tightened lips had reappeared. 'Do it, Flora,' he urged. 'Get it over with and it will be a weight you won't have to carry.'

'I could end up carrying an even heavier one,' she retorted. 'I've said I'll meet him, and I will. He can show me what he thinks he saw, then get in his flashy car and drive himself back to Paris. I don't want to see him again. How I ever...'

'Ah, the foibles of youth,' he teased.

'What will you be doing while I'm trying to keep my temper? Sleeping?'

'How cruel! I'll be paying a visit to a garage. I found out from Pierre who it was that collected Massimo's car. It was a Vaison garage, the one the count most often uses. From the valet's description of the accident – not that I'd take that as

gospel, I think you'd call his report excitable – it was the brakes
that failed and sent Massimo hurtling across the road into that
copse of trees. I'll have to be careful with my questions but I'd
like to find out from the mechanic what it would take to tamper
with the brakes without the driver knowing until it's too late.
I've only a vague idea of how technically competent you'd need
to be, and it might help to narrow down our suspects.'

'Are you thinking that a woman couldn't do it?' She jumped
off the bed and dragged a comb through hair that was lighter
now from several days of sun. 'It's annoying to agree with you,
but I do. Dufour would be my choice, or Dufour at Allegra's
behest. I'm beginning to think they could be working together. I
know he seems antagonistic to her but that could be a charade –
his indifference comes across as a bit obvious, a bit overdone,
don't you think? It could easily be a front.'

After they'd eaten a quick lunch at a nearby café, they walked
together down the steep incline to the river, across the Roman
bridge, and along the same street where they'd seen Allegra and
followed her into the church. At Place Montfort, they said goodbye, Flora to walk on to Notre Dame de Nazareth and its cemetery and Jack to search out the road at the northern corner of the
town square, where he'd been told Massimo's garage could be
found.

Garage Charavin was a slightly run-down building, its
triple doors badly in need of paint and the living quarters above
showing several cracked window panes. A Monsieur Alain
Frossard was named as the proprietor.

It was likely to be Monsieur Frossard that Jack glimpsed, on
his back beneath a sleek grey Renault, since he seemed to be the
garage's sole mechanic. Frossard must have seen Jack's legs
appear in the entrance because he pushed the creeper free of
the car's underside and scrambled to his feet. Wiping his hands

on a dirty rag, he came forward asking, if Jack translated correctly, what he could do for this new customer.

'I'm sorry,' he apologised. 'My French is not good.'

The mechanic waved his piece of rag in the air, dismissing the problem. 'We have the English here.'

Jack took this to mean he had permission to use his own language. 'You collected a car recently that had been in an accident,' he began. He looked around the garage. 'That one, over there, I think. The one by the wall.'

'Ah, *oui*. It comes yesterday.'

Together they walked over to the saloon that Jack had recognised by its colour. The deep maroon was unusual. One wing had been crushed almost completely, the front bumper torn off and both headlights smashed.

'It doesn't look too good,' he said.

Alain Frossard spread his hands. 'I can make better.'

'Do you know how the accident happened?'

The man looked puzzled and Jack tried again. 'How do you think Count Falconi crashed the car?'

'Ah! Maybe he is not well.' He rolled his eyes to suggest dizziness.

It was possible, Jack supposed. If Massimo's heart condition was serious, the man could have blacked out and momentarily lost control.

'I was staying at the chateau at the time and wondered... if it wasn't the brakes at fault?'

'The brakes?'

'*Les freins*?' That was the one car-related word Jack knew.

'*Non*! I see the car two weeks.' He held up two fingers to make it clear. 'Everything good.'

'So, nothing wrong with the mechanics?' If that was the case, there was no point in questioning the man on how difficult it would be to mess with the brakes.

'This only.' Frossard stroked the damaged front panel. 'But I make good, fit new lights, fit new number. All OK.' The man beamed.

Jack was disappointed. Left with little to say, he was about to thank Frossard for his time when the telephone rang and the mechanic, abandoning his greasy cloth, hurried over to the shabby desk that sat in the corner. Voluble French poured down the line. From where Jack was standing, it sounded like a dissatisfied customer at the other end and it took Monsieur Frossard some time to calm his caller.

While he was talking, Jack took the opportunity to inspect the engine – the bonnet had been left propped open. He knew only the basics of what a combustion engine should look like but, as far as he could see, there appeared to be no problem. Was it possible that the mechanic had worked on the car already, had made good whatever damage there was? If he had, it would mean that he'd lied about the brakes. And why would he have done that?

Alain Frossard was still speaking when Jack's glance fell on his desk. Below the obligatory calendar, this one displaying scenes from the Provençal countryside, and to one side of a clutter of invoices, a small group of framed photographs huddled together. One of them stood out. The face looked familiar. A pretty face, the face of a young girl. She must be monsieur's girlfriend, his wife maybe. Jack judged him old enough to have been married several years. But why was it so familiar? Where had he seen the girl?

Suddenly, it came to him – it was a photograph of Corinne, Flora's maid. Sybil's maid. Allegra's and Clio's, too. A raft of new possibilities unfolded as he stood gazing silently at the girl's photograph. Then, thanking Monsieur Frossard, he retrieved his hat and walked out.

16

Leaving Jack in the main square, Flora walked on alone. A difficult walk, her heart and head at odds. The meeting with Richard Frant felt a penance, a punishment she'd inflicted on herself, but one that her head was telling her she had to see through. It wasn't Richard that bothered her unduly. Meeting him again after so many years had made her feel... nothing, in fact. His proprietorial attitude irritated, the fact that he'd followed her to Provence was an annoyance, but other than that he'd had no noticeable effect. It was what she was about to discover, or not, that was causing her heart to beat a little too loudly and her breath to come a little too quickly.

Notre Dame de Nazareth, the parish church of Vaison-la-Romaine, was a surprise. Its expanse, as she approached, made it seem more of a cathedral than the modest church she'd been expecting. An avenue of dwarf cypress lined a path across the gravel forecourt and led her to the main entrance. Seeing no sign of Richard, she walked into the church and was surprised again. Despite its size, the building possessed a beauty that could only be described as simple: a central nave, its ceiling barrel-vaulted on beams, led the eye towards a plain stone altar standing proud within its own semicircular space. There was no decoration to speak of, no brilliant paintings, no extravagant statues – merely a quiet peace.

She glanced across the rows of empty wooden pews, wondering if this was where they should meet, but there was still no sign of Richard. Daylight flooding through an open doorway on one side of the church persuaded her to venture further. A small cloister lay beyond, secret and hidden from general view. A place of the utmost serenity. A low wall enclosed an inner garden, the greenery of its formal beds adding a burst of colour, while arched columns of shining marble supported each long gallery – the marble likely, she thought, to have been cannibalised from the ruins of older monuments. In walking into Notre Dame de Nazareth, she had walked back centuries.

A movement ahead had Flora suddenly alert. A flash of blue linen and the figure of a man rose from the wall and began to walk towards her. As he neared, she saw Richard's hands were outstretched.

'Flora! At last!'

Stiffly, she held out one hand, offering a businesslike hand-shake. The smile on his lips faltered. 'I should have said where to meet,' he blustered. 'I didn't have time to think at the chateau, you were so keen to see me gone.' He was trying to make a joke of it, she could see.

'I'm a guest there, Richard, and your arrival was unexpected. I'd no wish to disturb the household.'

'Unexpected maybe, but not unwelcome, I hope.'

'Not particularly welcome,' she said truthfully. 'When I telephoned you in Paris, it was clear I was travelling with Mr Carrington. There was really no need for you to follow me. I had a lift and I knew where I was going – there could only be one church in Vaison.'

'Ah, but that's where you're wrong.' He wagged an annoying finger at her. 'There is one other in the *haute-ville*.'

'I know. I've seen it,' she said flatly, 'but it doesn't have a cemetery. This one, I'm presuming, does. Now we're both here, it would save time if you took me to it and showed me the graves you mentioned.'

Flora couldn't bring herself to speak of her parents in those graves. She still clung to the faint chance that Richard had been mistaken.

His slightly podgy cheeks flushed. 'You are in a hurry! What is it? Can't wait to get back to your travelling companion?' There was an unpleasant sneer in his voice.

'Mr Carrington has his own errands to run. Why don't we get on with mine?' she asked briskly, her mouth set.

There was a small huff before he said, 'There's no way through from here to the cemetery. We have to go back into the church.'

'Then, please, lead the way.'

He glared at her, silently storing up his animosity, she was sure. He would get his revenge, he must be thinking, with the painful revelation to come.

The cemetery was small and very old. Here and there a more recent addition showed its face, but in the main the grave-stones were pitted and weathered. Richard stopped at the entrance, seeming unsure. It would have been months ago, Flora reflected, that he'd last been here.

Furrowing his hand through sandy hair, he pointed ahead to the stone boundary. 'They were by the far wall, if I remember rightly.'

'Surely you must remember. It was such an important find for you!' Richard, she'd come to realise, had deliberately used his discovery to entice her back into his life, to trap her into a relationship she didn't want, rather than from any sense of altruism. He had not wished to help a once close friend, a former sweetheart, only himself, perhaps desperate as a still single man, to recover a love affair he'd once despised.

He turned away, ignoring her remark, and began to weave his way around dozens of lichen-covered gravestones, half-fallen angels and memorial plaques that leant drunkenly towards the lumpy grass. Flora followed slowly, her heart again running unpleasantly fast. He'd stopped once more and another furrowing of his hair followed. Was this theatre, she wondered, a way of showing how necessary he was to her? She could have screamed with frustration.

But at last he was moving again and this time came to a halt close by the boundary wall. 'Here,' he said. 'Here they are.'

The gravestones he indicated were markedly newer than anything surrounding them. Out of the corner of her eye – Flora hardly dared look – she glimpsed the word 'Steele'. Taking a deep breath, she looked across at him, smiling as best she could but determined to see him go. She had to be here alone.

'Thank you, Richard. I can manage from now.'

'What?'

'I'd like you to leave,' she said sweetly. 'I'd like to be on my own. But thank you.'

'Is that it? Is that all you can say?'

'Is there more?' There was a glint in her hazel eyes that challenged, causing his plump cheeks to flush more deeply.

'You always were a cold fish,' he said angrily.

Flora stood her ground, staring him out, until defeated, he wheeled around and tramped from the cemetery, his low muttering clearly audible. For a while, after he'd gone, she did nothing, allowing the warmth of the September sun to loosen the tension in her shoulders. Birdsong came to her as she stood there; for the first time, she realised the cemetery was bounded by trees. Beech trees. Looking up at a sapphire sky, she watched as a flight of swallows swooped and dived in happy freedom. Then, finally, she turned to read the inscription.

Erected by the commune of Vaison-la-Romaine in remembrance of our English visitors who tragically lost their lives far from home.

Falling to her knees, she bowed her head. Then slowly reached out her hand and touched the carved letters. It was true. This was where her mother and father had lain all these years since that dreadful day when their Highgate neighbour and very good friend had collected her from school with the words, *You're going to have to be a brave girl, Flora.*

How could it be that she'd been left in ignorance? How could her aunt, dear Aunt Violet, have kept this from her? Had she suspected her brother of causing the accident and been determined to keep it from his small daughter? Flora would never know. It would have been from the best of motives, that she did know, but if only... She wished the tears could come, tears that she had never shed, but all she felt was emptiness. Drearily, she got to her feet, dusted down her cotton skirt and, without looking back, walked from the cemetery into the road beyond.

Her mind elsewhere and seeing little but the pavement in front of her, she barely noticed the woman standing to one side of the cemetery entrance. A woman who looked sad. A woman who had been watching her.

17

Jack was still pondering what his discovery of Corinne's photograph might mean, when he caught sight of Flora walking into the main square from the direction of the church. She looked dazed rather than distressed and he wondered if it had been an abortive visit. He'd wanted very much to be with her but had thought it best she deal with Richard Frant on her own. His presence would not have helped matters, he was certain.

Cutting diagonally across the square, he was within inches of her before she realised he was there. For a long moment they looked at each other, neither it seemed wanting to break the silence.

At length, he said, 'How was your visit?'

'They're there,' was her answer.

It might be brief but it told him all he needed to know. Taking her by the arm, he steered her towards the nearest café, ordering two glasses of kir royale before they had taken a table.

'So... Richard wasn't mistaken?'

'About me, yes. About my parents, no.'

Their drinks arrived and Jack clinked glasses. 'Drink up,' he urged. 'It might make you feel better.'

'It couldn't make me feel worse,' she said morosely, but after a while roused herself to effort and reached out to take his hand.

'Jack, I'm sorry. I've no right to burden you with my misery, but I'd hoped Richard's claim was all flim-flam. And it isn't.' She paused. 'I suppose I hoped that if it should chance to be true, knowing would make me feel better.'

'And it hasn't,' he finished for her.

She shook her head, but when he nudged the glass of kir towards her, she was persuaded to take a sip.

'It might do – eventually,' he added hopefully, 'when you've had time properly to absorb the news.'

Her expression suggested otherwise, but he could see she was trying hard to shake off her unhappiness.

'Tell me what *you've* been doing,' she said. 'Did you find the garage?'

'I did, and Massimo's car inside. On the surface, the vehicle doesn't appear to have been tampered with.'

'On the surface?'

'From my limited knowledge, everything beneath the bonnet appeared undamaged, but I've a suspicion the mechanic had already worked on the car, although pretending he was just about to start – panel beating, replacing the lights, and so on. In other words, repairing the external damage caused when Massimo powered into those trees.'

'But the brakes? You think he might have repaired them beforehand? Why, though? What makes you suspect him?'

'I have a hunch,' he said slyly.

'Stop it, Jack. I'm not in the mood for teasing.'

'No, really. It is a hunch, or maybe just a sense that he sounded a little too casual when he spoke of the accident. He must know the count well, he's been servicing his car regularly yet, even taking into account he was speaking in a language not his own, there was no handwringing, no expressions of sympathy, no worry even over his customer's condition in hospital.'

'OK, but—'

'And then I saw the photograph.'

Her eyebrows shot up and in response he said simply, 'Corinne.'

'He has a photograph of the maid? He knows her!'

'Not only knows. I reckon he's her boyfriend, maybe even her husband.'

'She doesn't wear a ring,' Flora pointed out.

'She's a maidservant. She may think it more politic not to.'

Flora mused for a while, slowly sipping her drink, and noticeably relaxing. Jack was glad to see it. 'The garage has a link then to the chateau,' she said, 'other than a purely commercial one, but does that have any significance? Unless you're thinking—'

'I'm thinking that Alain Frossard knows Massimo's car inside out and no doubt holds a set of keys for it. That he has a contact in the chateau who could make it easy for him to gain access to the estate, to a locked garage, say, without being seen. And that he must own a car himself, one with a Provençal number plate. Perhaps a large, black saloon.'

Flora took a deep breath. 'That is quite some hunch! But it fits, doesn't it? Except...'

'Except what?'

'Motive? Why would Frossard be involved? What's in it for him?'

'Money, would be my guess. Garage Charavin looks shabby, run-down. In need of cash.'

'Someone is paying him to murder?' She sounded doubtful. 'That's quite a leap. One of our suspects at Constantin, d'you think?'

'There's no one else, is there? And now we have Corinne, able to move without suspicion between the chateau and Frossard. She would be a very useful go-between.'

'It's still a huge risk for the man. As a murderer, he'd face the guillotine. Even if his garage isn't doing well, he'd need to be desperate.'

'Perhaps he is. Until we do a bit more digging, we can't know. I need to find out where he lives and where he keeps his car. If I can find that, we may be on the way to solving the mystery.'

'Were you able to look around the garage?'

Jack shook his head. 'There was no sign of it there. Nor in the surrounding area. After I left him, I went on a small tour of the neighbourhood. There were no cars that came close to matching the admittedly sketchy description we have. He could garage the vehicle elsewhere, of course, or he could be deliberately hiding it, which if it *was* the murder weapon would be sensible.'

'Or he hasn't got a car and is happy to walk to work. Do we have any way of finding out where he lives? I could try asking Corinne, I suppose.'

'Too obvious. It might be better to ask Massimo. It's possible he might know. He must have been dealing with Frossard for years.'

Flora shook her head. 'It's not likely he will.' She put down her glass. 'I don't think the count concerns himself over much with his underlings and, in any case, he's probably too unwell to answer questions.'

'Then we'll wait – tomorrow is another day. For now, let's wander back to the hotel. We can sit in the garden and enjoy the sunset. It's quite a show!'

'Monsieur Carrington, a message.' The receptionist came bustling onto the breakfast terrace early on Monday morning as they were finishing their coffee.

Spreading out the sheet of paper she'd handed him, Jack fished in his pocket for glasses.

'You've changed them,' Flora said, delighted, catching sight of his new spectacles. 'Tortoiseshell frames at last! Now you look a proper writer!'

He let her enjoy the old joke, but frowned as he read the note. 'A telephone call from my mother, demanding as always. Well, at least we had Sunday free. I'm to collect her from the chateau at ten o'clock sharp! The hospital is now allowing visitors.'

'Massimo must be feeling better.'

'Good news for us. He might be well enough to answer a few questions. Are you coming with me?'

'Why not? Unless your mother objects.'

Sybil did not look best pleased when she spied another woman in the passenger seat, but after Flora made a play of getting out of the car and offering her the place, she appeared mollified.

'How is your hotel?' she asked, once they were on the main road and making their way back to Vaison.

Sybil asked questions, Flora felt, without any real wish of having them answered. It was a routine mechanical politeness, learned early in life, but now largely without meaning.

'It's very comfortable,' she responded. 'The views are wonderful.'

'They would be,' his mother said, already bored. 'You're on a hill.'

Flora subsided into silence. Conversation really wasn't worth the effort. 'I'm thinking of moving into a hotel myself,' Sybil suddenly announced from the front seat.

Flora saw the back of Jack's head twitch. Hadn't his mother made the point in Paris that she was too poor to pay for a hotel and had no option but to return to Provence with Massimo?

'Why is that?' he asked.

'I don't like living at the chateau, not without Massimo.

There's an atmosphere there; brooding, I'd call it. Clio didn't get the Avignon job, by the way, even after a second interview – I'm not surprised, the girl simply doesn't know how to present herself – and that eldest daughter is an absolute horror. She's wretchedly unpleasant and I don't trust her.'

'Has something else happened?' There was worry in his voice.

'Not yet, but I've been watching Allegra like a hawk – ever since you ran out on me.'

Jack made no response. He couldn't be bothered to argue, it seemed, and Flora could only agree. Sybil was a tiresome person and the best way to deal with her was to ignore most of what she said.

Their curmudgeonly passenger consulted her watch. 'We're going to be too early,' she pronounced. 'Visiting hours are eleven to twelve.'

'You were the one who insisted on leaving at ten,' Jack said curtly. 'Right now, I could be reading a newspaper on the hotel terrace and enjoying a second pot of coffee.'

'You can broaden your education instead.' His mother had no intention of apologising. 'You can look around the Roman ruins. They're worth a visit, so I'm told.'

'I passed them yesterday on my way to the church,' Flora put in somewhat unwisely. 'They looked interesting.'

'Church? What were you doing in the church?'

'Just sightseeing,' she said casually, castigating herself for once more speaking too hastily.

'You would have passed one of the Roman sites then. There's two – both in the centre of town near the tourist office, one on either side of the road.'

'I'll leave the car here, I think.' They were in the main shopping road and Jack brought the Citroën to a halt outside an estate agents.

Flora peered out of the car window and caught a glimpse across the road of the deep dip she'd bypassed yesterday.

'That's La Villasse,' his mother said, waving her hand at where Flora was looking. 'Puymin is up there.' She jerked her head in the opposite direction and Flora could see a cluster of ruined pillars climbing the hill to the left of where they sat. 'You can buy a ticket for both at the booth over there.'

'We'll do the nearest,' Jack said. 'We've only half an hour before you have to be at the hospital.' Clambering out of the car, he walked over to the booth to buy their tickets and, within minutes, they were strolling through La Villasse.

Flora was entranced by the ruins of what must have been the very heart of the ancient town. Vestiges of once beautiful patrician houses were everywhere – sumptuous homes such as the House of the Silver Bust and the Dolphin House, which according to the sign had originally been a farm, then converted into a magnificent urban villa. It had taken its name from the small marble dolphin found buried in one of its rooms. La Villasse had evidently been an affluent neighbourhood, full of shops and life. And money.

'Over on the Puymin site, there's an amazing theatre,' Sybil drawled. 'Built by some Roman emperor, I believe.'

'Tiberius,' Jack offered.

'Someone like that,' she said offhandedly. 'The ruin was unearthed in the 1900s and then rebuilt. The last few years, it's been used for concerts. It makes quite a venue!'

'It must do. But this is special, too.' Flora paused, looking along the paved road that ran through the centre of the site, the marks of chariot wheels still visible. 'We have to be walking on what must have been the main street.'

Sybil looked blankly at her, then down at her watch. 'I must go,' she announced. 'I want to be with Massimo for as long as I can.'

Even before she'd stopped speaking, she had started off

towards the exit at such a pace that both Jack and Flora were left bemused, only seconds later pushing themselves into a jog to catch her up.

Halfway to the exit, Jack came to an abrupt stop – he'd seen something, Flora realised – and before she could work out what, he had launched himself forward, reaching his mother in a few strides and pushing her roughly to one side. Landing in a heap together, they were spreadeagled across a square of grass which sat between enclosing pillars.

'What on earth—' Sybil began angrily, her voice drowned by the crashing of stone a few yards away. Part of a pillar, an enormous chunk of stone, had tumbled earthwards. Without Jack's swift reaction, his mother would have been severely injured. Or worse.

Flora looked up, trying to judge from where the stone had fallen and was rewarded by seeing the figure of a young boy. He was peering down at them but, seeing her eyes on him, he wheeled around and ran at full pelt towards the main street.

'That boy,' Flora called out urgently, as a head of bright red hair melted swiftly into the medley of shoppers. But Jack had already seen him and was on his feet and chasing.

Sybil was pale-faced and breathing heavily, and Flora turned to help her to her feet. 'They haven't given up,' the woman stuttered.

'No, they haven't,' she agreed grimly.

With her arm linked to Sybil's, she walked the older woman slowly to the exit and found Jack by the roadside, looking perplexed and angry.

'I lost him – among all that.'

Amid the crowd of shoppers, a large number of vans were disgorging their contents onto the road: a jumble of wooden stalls, canvas awnings, and numerous handcarts and barrows. No wonder Jack was looking perplexed.

'What's going on, do you think?' But even as she spoke, Flora smelt a familiar aroma. A strong sweet smell of tobacco.

'They're getting ready for market day. It's tomorrow,' Sybil told her. 'What did you mean, you lost him?' she asked, turning to her son.

'A boy. A young boy. He was the one who sent the pillar tumbling.'

'That's ridiculous.' Sybil had regained her abrasive manner. 'A child! Whatever next?'

'Whatever next,' he muttered to Flora, as they trailed after his mother on her way to the hospital several streets distant.

'Did you smell the tobacco?' Flora asked quietly.

'I did and I've smelt it before. At the chateau, when I used Massimo's phone.'

'I've smelt it before, too. In the cellar at the winery. Whenever there's an "incident", Pascal Dufour seems always to be there. Is he our villain, do you think? Is it possible he paid that boy today? Possible he paid Frossard to go to Paris and drive at your mother?'

'Anything is possible in this place.'

Jack was sounding shaken but then so was she. A beautiful morning, a delightful stroll through the ancient world, and then what? Death or near-death had come calling again.

18

With the hospital visit imminent, there was little chance to discuss what had happened at La Villasse. Sybil, herself, kept a strained silence, hurrying along the road and seeming intent on pushing the incident from her mind. Her primary concern was clear: Massimo's health and how well he was recovering. Unwillingly, Flora resigned herself to a long wait until she could talk over with Jack this last brazen attack.

The Vaison hospital was unusually quiet when they arrived, the first rush of patients having been seen earlier in the day. At Sybil's mention of the Falconi name, a nurse waved them through to the south side of the building where the few private wards were located.

Approaching the closed door of Massimo's room, they heard voices from within, a low murmur on one side of the conversation, a more staccato tone on the other.

'The count has visitors.' Jack sounded disappointed. 'I think it's best that Flora and I leave you to it, Mum. We can come back another time.'

'Nonsense!' Sybil railed. 'You're here now. You should say hello.' The thunderous look with which Flora was becoming familiar had made another appearance. 'I've a good idea who's in there, upsetting Massimo, making him ill again. And she can go!'

Jack looked questioningly at Flora. Neither of them was sure what exactly was going on and Sybil didn't wait to tell them. Striding forward, she opened the door with a bang.

Flora stood in the open doorway and peered around Sybil's furious figure to gain a view of the count's visitor. She wasn't surprised, she realised. It had to be Isabella Falconi. As they'd expected, she had followed Massimo back to Provence. But when? When had she arrived from Paris? In time to supervise the tampering of his car? In time to persuade a young boy into launching a lethal block of stone? Or had that been Dufour, with or without Isabella's connivance? He had been close to the Roman site, the cigarette smoke proved that. Close by, yet invisible.

Isabella had plumped herself down on the bed rather than taking one of the chairs supplied for visitors and was leaning so close to her former husband that he was barely visible. As she spoke, her hands chopped at the air in emphasis, her brightly streaked knot of hair bobbing in unison.

'Haranguing the poor man again,' Sybil said angrily. 'I won't have it!'

'You will stop me?' Isabella slewed around, her strange light eyes holding fire. 'I do not think so. He is my husband. He is ill and I will see him. I have the right.'

'He is not your husband and you have no right. No right to stalk him in the way you've been doing. You've followed us again, back to Vaison this time.'

'So? Why not? My home is here. I live where I want. You cannot stop me.'

Sybil advanced determinedly to the bed. 'I can stop you from making Massimo more unwell. You need to go. Now!'

'Go!' Isabella screeched. 'You go. You are the one who do

not look after him. He is bad, his heart is not good and what do you do?'

'Give him peace. Unlike you.'

'No.' She wagged her finger in Sybil's face. 'No peace. This man is mine. I look after him. Not you. You give him accident. You hurt Massimo.'

'*Signore, per favore,*' the count implored. 'Please not here.'

Flora was unsure what role she and Jack should be playing in this decidedly awkward drama. Would it add fuel to the blaze if they turned and went? She glanced across at Jack and had a shrug in response. He was as uncertain as she.

'You are insane,' was all Sybil said and turned away.

At that moment, Isabella jumped off the bed and advanced on Jack's mother, pushing her into the wall, her hands outstretched as though she would strangle her enemy. Flora stepped forward, seeing Jack do the same, but Massimo had rung the red bell attached to his headboard and, almost instantly, a nurse arrived.

It took the nurse a few seconds only to size up the situation. 'Madame,' she said, grabbing hold of Isabella's shoulders. 'Please. You are in a hospital. Come with me.'

Isabella shrugged off the nurse's hold and stomped to the door. 'You' – she pointed a finger at Sybil, glowering by the wall – 'you will not win. I am the wife. I will win.'

There was a long and uncomfortable silence after the nurse had ushered the angry woman from the room. Massimo, looking pale and drawn, shifted beneath the bed covers.

'We should go,' Jack said.

'No, please.' Massimo held up his hand. 'I am happy to see you. Sybil tells me on the telephone that you are not at the chateau now. I am sorry for that.'

'In the circumstances, we thought it best to find a hotel,' Jack said.

'But our time at the vineyard was wonderful,' Flora put in, grappling to remember her manners.

'And you, Sybil.' The count turned to her. 'You are not at the chateau now.'

'I will be – as soon as you're better,' she said rousingly. 'While you're here in the hospital, it's easier for me to stay in town.'

The count seemed happy to accept her reasoning. 'I am better now. Much better. Soon I will be out of this bed.'

'And back in your own home,' Sybil said warmly.

There was another silence, until he said, 'I am sorry about Isabella.' His voice was weak but the note of apology plain. 'She can be a little...'

'Violent?' Flora said.

'She has a temper and sometimes...' He left the sentence trailing. 'Today she came here – I did not ask. Then she would not go.'

'If she comes back, Massimo,' Sybil said firmly, 'ring your bell straight away. The nurse will have her out of the door in an instant.'

He passed a weary hand over his forehead. 'Poor Isabella. She has the temper but really she is harmless.'

'Is she?' Sybil's voice had sharpened. 'Let's hope so. From my experience this morning—' She broke off.

'What experience? What has happened?' In a flurry, he attempted to lever himself up from his pillows.

'Nothing.' She gave a pale smile, pushing him gently back to rest. 'Nothing of any importance.'

Sybil wasn't going to tell but it was clear she believed Isabella was behind this morning's attack at La Villasse. Her reticence surprised Flora. From what she'd seen of Sybil, the woman was inherently selfish but here she was putting Massimo's health before her own safety. Perhaps she genuinely loved the man.

'You see,' the count said, addressing Jack who had remained standing by the door, 'I am happy with your mother.'

'I'm glad to hear it.' To Flora's ear, Jack's words didn't carry conviction. She had seen, too, the faint grimace that accompanied them.

'And she is happy with me.'

'I am,' Sybil said staunchly. 'If that woman would only leave us alone...'

'Isabella cannot accept I do not wish her for a wife. She should. She knows what she has done.'

Flora chanced a look at Jack. He was alert, too. What *had* Isabella done? they wondered. It must have been something drastic, for it to bring to an end a more than thirty-year marriage.

'We have a problem with Isabella,' he said, his eyes sad, 'but I will fix it. We will move house and she will leave us alone.'

'Move from France?' Flora asked.

He nodded. 'I will sell the chateau. It will not be difficult. Our rosé is very appreciated and the house it is comfortable. But no match for Italy. I have a beautiful palazzo in the Veneto. It is beautiful, yes?' he asked Sybil.

Her face lit up. 'It is. A masterpiece.'

'And my vineyards there produce the very best white wine. I have a good manager, he does things well, but the palazzo needs an owner. I need to be there. All the time I worry I will be invaded. I have security but also many things to steal. On the wall a rare Giorgione mural. It is without price. Also many antiques.'

He paused for breath and seemed, for the moment, unable to go on. But as Flora was readying herself to say goodbye, he began to speak again. 'The estate in the Veneto is important. It is worth many millions of lire and must be cared for. When I die much will go to my family, but I want that Sybil is well looked after. She may not wish to live in Italy for ever, but she must have money. Then she lives where she wishes and lives well.'

'You shouldn't be talking of dying,' Sybil scolded. 'You should be thinking of our future – together.'

'I am, my dear one. But it is always good to be prepared. My heart is not the same as a young man's.'

'We were very sorry to hear of the accident,' Jack put in. 'It must have been a frightening experience.'

At last there was a chance for him to ask his questions. They might even learn what they'd come for, Flora thought hopefully.

'Not frightening at all! Much too quick.' Massimo laughed aloud at his joke, sending him into a prolonged fit of coughing.

When he'd recovered, Jack said cautiously, 'Do you remember nothing at all?'

The count shook his head. 'The car, it went faster and faster. I had no control, I think. Then I was here in bed, in the hospital. That is all I know.'

'The car must have sprung a mechanical fault.'

Flora saw Sybil frown at her son's words. His mother must know that Jack thought differently, but she seemed determined that nothing was to impede Massimo's recovery. She would make sure that any hint the accident had been deliberately engineered was silenced.

'"That must be it,' the count agreed. 'Something mechanical, but it should not be. I go to Frossard always and he makes a big check two weeks ago – before we leave for Paris. He should notice something is wrong. I will have words with him when I am home again.'

Flora doubted he would get much satisfaction. The mechanic would swear there had been nothing wrong with the vehicle when he last serviced it and, if he had been guilty of tampering with Massimo's car – and she was feeling surer of it every minute – there was nothing to prove it. He had repaired the damage before Jack appeared on his doorstep.

'Does Monsieur Frossard live locally?' Jack asked.

'But, yes, a village near us – Crestet, I think, or maybe...' He looked towards Sybil for help. 'Maybe Sablet?'

'It doesn't matter.' His mother glared at Jack. 'It's not something you need worry about, Massimo.'

Jack took the glare in his stride. There were questions to be answered and he wasn't to be deterred.

'Wherever Frossard has his home, I imagine he'll be at the Vaison garage most days,' he said easily, 'if you wanted to discuss the problem.' When Massimo gave a tired nod, he went on, 'Was that the first time you had driven the car since you returned from Paris?'

The count thought about it. 'No. I took your mama for lunch in Avignon. The day before you arrived.'

'And since then the chateau garage has been kept locked at all times?'

'Of course. Why, what do you mean?'

Alain Frossard must have messed with the car in the last few days, Flora deduced. He would have needed to gain access to the estate and to this locked garage, which made Corinne invaluable to him. But were they conspirators together, or was she an innocent dupe and it was only Frossard being paid to do harm? And by someone at the chateau.

'The garage is of no importance,' Sybil said quickly, looking even crosser. 'Massimo must concentrate on getting well.'

'I will, you can be sure.' The count reached out for her hand. 'I will be well for the harvest feast. Sybil, I think... I think this will be when we make the big announcement.'

Her face flushed with pleasure. 'If you're sure,' she said, her voice shaking slightly.

'Absolutely. That is what you English say, no?'

'And the big announcement?' Jack murmured as he and Flora walked out of the hospital into blinding sunshine.

'It has to be a wedding.'

'Oh, God,' he groaned. 'That will create a touch paper just asking to be lit. Whoever is our villain – Alain and Corinne, Isabella, Allegra, Dufour, they're almost too numerous to count – whoever we're looking for, will be waving a match, for sure.'

'A whole box of matches,' Flora agreed.

19

That evening after dinner, they took a glass of wine onto the terrace at the rear of the hotel and found a secluded table. At last there was time to talk through the day's events and what, if any, progress they'd made.

Wrapped in the large shawl she'd packed at the last moment, Flora hugged it closer. Without the sun, a slight September chill had crept into the air.

'I'm really disappointed,' she said, her glass now half-empty. 'Quite despondent, in fact. When we first arrived, I thought we'd knock this mystery on its head within days. Allegra had to be our mastermind, it was obvious. When Dufour popped out of the woodwork – he keeps turning up at the most suspicious moments – it wasn't so obvious after all. Then, yesterday, we had Alain Frossard joining the gang and today it's Isabella who is suddenly back on the scene. Too many people. Too confusing.'

Jack took a long drink, watching the horizon's glow mutate into streaks of pink and mauve and settle finally to a luminescent grey. 'I guess we have one firm lead. We need to hang on to that.'

Flora huddled further into the shawl. 'I'm sure we do. But what is it?'

'The car, what else? The vehicle that drove into Ruby King. It has to be somewhere in Provence and I reckon it's not a million miles away. In Crestet or Sablet or—'

'Or half a dozen other villages whose names Massimo can't remember.'

'At least a finite number to search.'

'You honestly mean to drive around half of Provence looking for Frossard's house,' she said testily.

'Not his house, his garage. And it will be much less than half of Provence.'

Flora's shoulders gave an irritated jig. 'What if you do miraculously find his garage? Is it likely to contain what, after all, is a murder weapon? Or will he have been a clever chap and moved the vehicle well out of sight? And if, by some stroke of genius, the car *is* there, what's the betting that by now Frossard will have repaired any giveaway damage – as he has with the count's?'

'You *are* despondent!'

'I don't mean to be a grouch, Jack, but I hate the feeling that we're being made fools of. And, while we're being laughed at, the threats are becoming more serious. A lot more serious. Did you see the size of that boulder aimed at Sybil? If you hadn't been so quick...'

'I'm not minimising the danger,' he said gravely, 'or puffing off our chances of discovering who's behind this bedlam. But finding the car that killed Ruby will lead us to the driver who, in turn, will lead us – if my guess is right – to the mastermind, as you call him.'

'Or her,' she said quickly.

'Or her.' He smiled. 'Look, it's been a difficult few days for you. Why don't you take tomorrow off and leave me to hunt alone?'

'I should be with you. Remember, we said we'd only work as a team.'

'I know we did, but tomorrow will be wearisome. A trail around garages, and I can't see you finding that too exciting. There won't be enough time to enjoy the villages themselves. Take the day off and go to the market. You know you'd love it. My mother tells me it's a traditional French market, which means it sells just about everything.'

'It's tempting, but—'

'No buts. The receptionist was singing the market's praises, too. It's brilliant, she said, and we should definitely visit. Apparently it's been held every week in Vaison for over five centuries and takes up the greater part of the town. There are literally hundreds of exhibitors. But you have to get there early – by three o'clock in the afternoon, everything is packed away.'

Flora continued to look uncertain. 'I don't know. I feel I'd be abandoning you.'

He shuffled his chair nearer to hers, then leaned across to kiss her. 'You couldn't do that if you tried,' he said softly.

Flora woke to a sky of the deepest blue and the ever present hot sun. It was mid-September and in Abbeymead the winter clothes would be being pulled from suitcases and shaken free of mothballs. Christmas plans would be taking shape and committees formed to raise the necessary funds for whatever village activities had been agreed. The coal merchant would be busy delivering his wares and people's stores of wood gradually replenished, ready for evening fires. For a moment, Flora smelt the apple wood she would soon be burning and a wave of homesickness took hold. For the past week or so, she'd barely thought of the All's Well, she realised guiltily. How could that be when Abbeymead and the bookshop were her entire life? She would ring Alice this evening, she vowed. Rather than use the cramped kiosk in the hotel, she had seen a telephone box just this side of the Roman bridge.

Stretching herself lazily between the sheets, she remembered that today she'd been given permission to indulge herself: with her love of markets. Aunt Violet might have been an expert at auctions – her aunt had loved her afternoons at the sales that occasionally took place when an old house in the district was sold and the new owners wished to create an entirely new library, or no library at all – but Flora was the connoisseur of local markets.

Jack had warned he was making an early start and she'd resigned herself to eating breakfast alone. Their fellow guests had been settling their accounts when she'd walked through reception and the breakfast room was empty except for herself. She made a brief meal: orange juice and a croissant followed by several pieces of fruit and two cups of coffee. She was ready now to do battle in the town.

At ten o'clock, the streets were already crowded, people walking six deep between stalls and beneath sunshades, in a market that appeared to spill across the entire centre of the town, cars having been barred for the morning. Flora decided she would begin in Place Montfort, and from there wander through the surrounding streets. Every inch of the main square had stalls crammed with goods. And on all sides the colours and the scents of the Midi.

Walking through the square, her eyes brightened. Amid the bric-a-brac, she'd spied a dozen or so stalls of handicrafts: paintings, posters, pottery. And beautiful household items carved from olive wood: salad servers, cheese boards, bowls... if only. But their prices had her walk on quickly; she would need to look for something more modest. Turning left, she saw that Cours Taulignan had become the main food market, the boulangerie today competing with a dozen stalls selling bread, rolls and croissants. Beyond the bakery were the cheese, fish and meat sellers, along with overflowing stalls of fruit and vegetables.

She ignored the cellophane-wrapped pigeons and a display of dainty jars of honey. They would be a disaster in the making if she carried them home in her suitcase. A pot of fat black and green olives from Nyons to eat with Jack on the terrace? Possibly. But then she saw the apricots, small baskets of golden beauty and, digging into her pocket for loose francs, she chose one of the largest punnets. The luxury of it – fresh apricots!

The zigzag of Cours Taulignan came to an end at the junction with the town's main thoroughfare. Yesterday that same street had protected a young boy from capture, a boy intent on murder, but today it could not have looked less sinister, brimming as it was with painted china, patterned tablecloths of bees and grapes, even a stall selling straw hats. Only men's hats, but in every colour of the rainbow. Dare she buy one for Jack? The pale pink, she thought, with a black band, and smiled to herself, imagining his expression.

Finally, encircled by a wall of perfume, she reached a stall she knew she would buy from. Laid out, tray by tray, in a cloud of sweetness, were shining ovals of soap: olive, honey, lemon, almond, rose. A bewildering variety. Choosing three – the lemon and rose were favourites – she tucked them into her bag. One each for Kate, Alice and Sally to accompany the jewellery she'd bought in Séguret. Even in this very different world, her friends were never far from her mind.

It was as she was packing her purse away and deciding that next she must look for an inexpensive cotton frock that she caught sight of a head bobbing through the crowd. A head of bright red hair. She craned her neck and could just make out the figure of a boy, weaving his way through the jumble of stalls. It was him! The murderous child! He'd returned to the scene of his crime. Either he was too naive to realise how foolish that might be or he was stupidly audacious. Clicking her handbag

shut, Flora ducked beneath the stall's awning and sped in
pursuit.

She'd soon caught up with him, but was unsure of her next
move. Should she accost the boy here in the street, or hope he
was making for a quieter part of town where she could question
him more easily? It was a heaven-sent opportunity. Unless the
boy was a delinquent and enjoyed endangering strangers for
fun, he must have been bribed, been paid, to hurl that rock. If
she could get him to name his benefactor...

Deciding in seconds that she would keep following him, she
stayed some paces behind. The boy seemed perfectly at home
in his surroundings – a local child quite evidently – and seemed
to know exactly where he was heading. Was that to return home
or had he an appointment to keep?

A hundred yards further on, he stopped and looked around,
then crossed the road to a café next to the post office. Ducking
behind a telephone box, Flora kept watch. The boy had
approached a table where a woman, floppy sunhat shading her
face, sat nursing a glass of fresh orange. Edging from her shelter,
Flora was quick to lose herself among the crowd of strollers,
trying to get as close to the café as she could without revealing
herself. It was then she saw the woman's face. A face she knew.
And heard herself groan aloud. Clio Falconi! Surely not
another name to add to their list of likely villains.

Clio, she saw, had handed the child something. An enve-
lope? A parcel? It looked like a small box. Wooden and decorated – it was difficult to make out – but the boy looked pleased
with his present and in a few minutes had said goodbye and
walked away. She needed to speak to him. Now.

Ensuring she couldn't be seen from the café, she crossed
back again to the other side of the road to resume the chase. The
boy had increased his pace and, wherever he was going, he was
in a hurry to get there. Flora herself sped up and, within a few
minutes, had been forced to break into a run. It was

approaching midday and the sun's heat was intense, turning her cheeks an uncomfortable pink and sending trickles of sweat down her neck. Still, the boy ran on, darting in and out of stalls as he crossed the main square to reach one of the few roads that remained open to vehicles.

A large white van hove into view and, in that instant, Flora lost sight of him. The vehicle was agonisingly slow and, once past, revealed – nothing and nobody. She looked hopelessly around. Where had the boy gone? He could have taken any one of the three streets in front of her.

As she hesitated, wondering whether to continue or give up the pursuit as hopeless, a voice sounded at her shoulder.

'*Êtes vous perdu, mamselle* Steele?'

She wheeled around. It was Allegra Falconi asking or pretending to ask if she was lost. Did she know the boy? Did she know what he'd done? And had she seen Flora following him?

'Enjoying a stroll,' she stumbled out, unable to think of anything better.

'*Il fait sûrement trop chaud pour une promenade.*'

Flora detected a decided smirk on the woman's face. 'Yes, you're right,' she said, 'much too hot to walk,' and muttered something inaudible about finding a drink. It was a feeble excuse, but she was desperate to escape from a humiliating situation.

Walking away, she felt only despair. She'd lost the child and, with him, lost the best opportunity she was likely to have of discovering who was behind the evil that stalked Chateau Constantin. And adding to her wretchedness, there was now another name to join their list of suspects. The box Flora had seen handed over could have been an innocent present for a child that Clio knew well. Equally, it might easily have constituted a pay-off, a bribe, for services rendered. Was every one of the Falconis involved in this campaign of terror? Were they all in it together?

All except Massimo. But why then had he been in conclave with Isabella when they'd arrived at the hospital? What had the two of them been discussing so urgently? Perhaps not even Massimo could be exempted now. The chateau was that veritable pit of snakes that Jack had described.

20

Jack's day had been no more successful, Flora discovered, when she met him that evening. He had driven to both Crestet and Sablet, the two villages Massimo had mentioned, and had spent hours asking anyone he could find if they knew an Alain Frossard with a business in Vaison-la-Romaine, but not one enquiry had produced a result.

'I'll try again tomorrow,' he said over dinner.

He'd returned late to the hotel and this was the first opportunity they'd had to exchange news. Having found a small restaurant by the river on the far side of the bridge, they were enjoying plates of chicken Dijon accompanied by a spread of fresh vegetables. For a moment, Flora stopped eating and stared at the river below. Jack was wedded to a lost cause, she considered, and wondered what she could say that might dissuade him from wasting any more of his time.

In the end, she went for brutal. 'Is it really worth all this effort? Frossard could have sold the car by now, or repaired whatever damage there was. Even if you found the vehicle, how useful would it be in building a case against him?'

'It's the only clue we've got,' Jack said gloomily, 'and we

need to hang on to it. So far the search has been discouraging, I admit, but if I find that car, I'll make sure I persuade the police to authorise a forensic examination – luminol will reveal blood stains, no matter how well the bodywork is repaired. I have to keep going, Flora.'

'If you must, I suppose. But – there might be something easier for us to pursue. Another clue.'

He looked up, his fork suspended mid-air. 'Another clue? Have you been busy?' There was suspicion in his voice. 'The market was due to finish early, wasn't it? What did you do for the rest of the afternoon?'

'I came back to the hotel and read.'

'How peaceful,' he said drily.

'I needed peace,' she retorted, then told him how she'd seen and chased the red-haired boy. 'He disappeared into fresh air,' she said. 'Puff, and he was gone. If only I could have talked to him... he could be far more use to us than your black saloon.'

'Or, to play devil's advocate, he could just be a mischievous child who didn't understand the seriousness of what he'd done.'

Flora shook her head, wiping her hands on the linen napkin. 'It was deliberate, Jack. That rock was aimed at your mother and meant to cause harm. The boy knew what he was doing, even if he didn't realise he might actually kill.'

She folded her arms, determined to make her point. 'Everything we've learned so far has been deliberate. The vehicle on the Rue de Rivoli was driven at those women. It wasn't an accident, and neither was Massimo's crash. Your mother was meant to be in that car. And yesterday, she was a target again.'

Jack finished eating and sat thinking for a while. 'And why would a child do such a thing?'

'He was being bribed,' she said confidently. 'I'm almost sure of it. Or maybe threatened. And the Falconis, or some of them, are behind it.'

'Did you see any sign of Dufour?'

'Not today, no. But it was Clio Falconi who gave the child his present and Allegra who mysteriously appeared beside me at the very moment the boy vanished.'

'And he'll stay vanished would be my bet. He'll be even more difficult to winkle out than Frossard's car. Why don't you forget the boy and come with me tomorrow? You might bring me luck.'

'I think I'd rather stay in Vaison,' she said diffidently. 'The boy was walking around quite openly. It's plain he's not expecting anyone to nab him any time soon and, if I'm watchful, I might see him again.'

Flora saw the shadow of disappointment in his face and felt guilty. He was right that she had little chance of seeing the boy again, but the hope wasn't entirely futile. And there was another reason she preferred to stay in town. A reason that was more important to her, one she didn't feel able to discuss right now – not even with Jack.

When she'd met him after Richard had taken her to the cemetery, she'd given him only the briefest account of her visit there, been grateful for the glass of kir and for his company, and content to let the matter rest. Since then, Jack had avoided any mention of her parents. He possessed a delicacy, she'd come to realise over the months she'd known him, that somehow always told him when it was right to say nothing. Flora valued his silence – she had first to make peace with herself before she could talk. And tonight, though he might suspect there were other reasons she'd turned him down, other reasons she'd wanted to stay in Vaison, he didn't press the matter.

An *île flottante* served as a delicious end to the meal, followed by a coffee each, and they were ready to retrace their steps up the steep hill of the *haute-ville* and back to the hotel.

'*Jusqu'à demain,*' he said, kissing her good night outside her bedroom door.

'Until tomorrow?' she hazarded, kissing him back.

.   .   .

So it was that after breakfast the next morning, she waved him off to Carpentras, his first port of call, then returned to her bedroom to change. She would dress carefully for her visit to the graveyard. She was meeting her parents, this time alone, for only the second instance in twenty years, and it seemed essential to Flora to look her best.

She had been keeping the rainbow silk for something special, not that the whole trip to France hadn't been special – in more ways than one, she thought wryly – but today was destined to be the frock's first appearance, a swing dress with cap sleeves and square neck that she'd spent far too much money on the previous summer. Every time she'd opened her wardrobe door this last year and seen it hanging from the rail, the price tag still attached, she had felt wickedly extravagant. Calculated to send tongues wagging, it was not the dress for a Sussex village but she'd bought it all the same.

In the event, it was a French village that would be blessed with its first appearance. Glancing in the mirror minutes before she left, Flora was pleased with the image reflected back at her. After days of constant sunshine, her cheeks were slightly tanned and her hair had lightened considerably, the reddish-brown waves now streaked with blonde. It was an expensive look, matching the elegance of the printed silk. As she walked down the hill towards the Roman bridge, she was conscious of the admiring glances that came her way and felt warmed. Somehow it made her decision to return to the cemetery feel the right one.

She was halfway across Place Montfort, her mind on the moment ahead when, out of the blue, she was buffeted heavily on the shoulder and found herself falling, unable to stay on her feet. It was a girl who'd cannoned into her and who lay similarly sprawled inches away. Flora was the first to stumble to her feet, being careful to brush down the precious dress before she walked over to the prone figure.

'Corinne!' For a moment, she was taken aback, then offered her help.

The girl took Flora's hand and pulled herself unsteadily upright. 'Miss Steele! I am sorry.'

'It was an accident,' she reassured the maid. 'At least, neither of us are badly hurt.'

Corinne gave a nod but there was no answering smile. 'Are you all right?' Flora had noticed for the first time the tell-tale sign of recent tears.

'Yes, yes,' the maid said hastily.

'But you're upset?' she pursued. 'You were running like a banshee.'

Corinne was unlikely to know any banshees but she understood the gist of Flora's message and said, 'Today not good.'

'I can see that. By why are you so upset? What has happened?'

The girl seemed to cast around for inspiration before she spoke. 'Trouble at the house. Nothing to worry. I do something wrong. But OK now.'

It was plain she had concocted an excuse and Flora didn't believe her. She hadn't seen Corinne before she'd been sent flying but calculated the girl must have entered the square from the opposite corner, and that corner led into the narrow street that housed Frossard's garage. That was it, she thought excitedly. It was nothing to do with the chateau; Corinne had fallen out with her boyfriend. There had been an argument, she was almost certain, but why? Had it been a simple lovers' quarrel or had they disagreed over something far more dangerous? If Corinne had learned for the first time that Frossard had been responsible for killing a woman...

The maid had turned away and was repacking her basket, its contents strewn across the square. Flora bent to help her. A magazine, *Europe Échecs*, a chessboard its featured image, lay crumpled on the tarmac.

'Do you play chess, Corinne?' It seemed an unusual hobby for the girl, but then why shouldn't a maidservant play in her spare time?

Corinne straightened up, hugging her basket to her chest. 'Yes,' she said uncertainly.

'That's impressive. How well do you play?' She gave the girl a warm smile. 'I was pretty hopeless when I tried.' She remembered only too clearly the evenings she'd spent with Richard, constantly the loser in their games. Until one day she'd had enough of his crowing and abandoned the chessboard for good, refusing to be browbeaten a minute longer.

'I begin. I learn.'

There was a defiant note in the girl's voice and Flora wondered why. Wondered, too, why there was something about Corinne playing chess that nagged at her. It was an odd discovery and she knew it would prey on her mind.

'Well, good luck,' was all she said, however, and set off once more for the church.

Notre Dame de Nazareth stood proudly in the sunshine, its ancient stones warm and smooth. Ignoring the avenue of cypress and the church entrance, Flora walked around the massive building to the gate that led into the cemetery. In a matter of minutes, she'd found her way back to the double grave where the inscription on two stones of shining ebony marked the spot where her parents lay. She should bring flowers, she thought, it's what people did, but somehow she couldn't.

For a long time, she stood looking at the gravestones, hardly conscious of what she was seeing. Free of Richard's irksome presence, she could take time, allow the buzz in her mind to settle. She would never know, she thought sadly, why her mother and father had ended here, so far from home. Never know why her aunt had refused to tell her the truth. For years, she had been gripped by the suspicion that her parents' marriage, her parents' fate, had been too dreadful for Violet to speak of. It was something she must learn to live with. Still. Must learn to accept and walk away, as she'd accepted and walked away from the shame of Richard's disloyalty. This was the most peace she would ever enjoy.

Turning to go, Flora found herself looking into the face of an unknown woman.

'Mademoiselle?'

'Yes,' she said uneasily.

'I see you here before.'

'Yes,' she agreed, feeling an even greater unease. Had this elderly woman been sent to spy on her? Had she been bribed or threatened by the Falconis or Pascal Dufour?

'You know them?' The woman nodded towards the gravestones.

'I do,' Flora said quietly. And then, for some unknown reason, felt impelled to speak, to share the burden she carried. 'They were my parents,' she said, in a rush of words.

'Ah!' The woman gave a long sigh. 'We find the money to bury here, but not to send home. *Quel chagrin*. They were good people.'

Flora gaped at her. 'You knew them?'

'But yes. They stay with me. My home is by La Villasse.'

'Why were they staying with you?' The mystery had become more mysterious still.

'They take a holiday and pay for a room with me. I always have people then. To pay *les factures*. The bills. Now, I have *pension* and have no need.' The woman had kind eyes, Flora thought, kind eyes and a gentle face.

'I see... though not really. They were in France for a holiday, yet they left me behind...' It took a while before Flora could bring herself to ask, 'Why did they die?'

'It was sad. Very sad.' The woman shook her head. 'They leave you in England for a little holiday together before—'

'Before what? What happened?'

'You do not know?'

Miserably, Flora studied the grass beneath her feet.

The woman reached to touch her arm, patting it softly. 'Your mama must go to hospital – in Avignon. No hospital here in Vaison then. There was a very bad storm, much rain, and the car' – her hands flew into the air – 'it leave the road, hit a big tree, and it roll' – she circled her hands, one round another – 'down into the ditch. Very deep.'

'But to travel in such weather... was my mother very ill?'

'Very ill. The baby not good. Your father desperate.'

'The baby? My mother was having a baby?'

'But yes. And you are the big sister. They talk about the big sister when the baby arrives.'

Flora felt her throat contract and her lungs lose whatever air they contained. Through blurred vision, she asked, 'The baby...'

Her companion again shook her head. Touching Flora's arm once more, she said, 'I leave you now. It is good that you have found them.'

She was hardly conscious that the woman had walked away. Her head was full. Her heart overflowing. Her parents had loved her and loved each other. They had died together, her father trying to save his wife's life and their baby's, the brother or sister she had never known and would never know. It was a story filled with love. Real love. To risk everything for the person most precious to you!

A strange wave of euphoria burst over her and for a moment she rode it with a smile on her lips. Then shrugging it away, she stood completely still and listened to her thoughts. Was this the way she felt about Jack, the way he felt about her? That whatever fate had in store, they would face it together? That whatever sacrifice had to be made for each other, they would be willing to make it?

When Jack arrived back at the hotel, tired and hungry from a day of fruitless searching, Flora was waiting for him. He had barely extricated himself from the Citroën when she wrapped him in her arms and showered him with kisses.

'Whoa, what have I done to deserve this?' He returned her kiss with enthusiasm.

'Everything,' she told him and, walking back into the hotel, spilled the whole incredible story she'd been told.

'You know what happened,' he said, cupping her cheeks in his hands. 'At last. You know why they ended here.'

'I do, and I can hardly believe it.'

'So... you didn't stay in town to go looking for red-haired boys after all?' he mocked, letting her go.

Flora had the grace to look shamefaced. 'I was never going to,' she said truthfully. 'I just needed time to think, to be alone, to visit them again, and... Jack' – a sudden thought had grabbed her – 'do you play chess?'

'I used to in the army. The regiment had several good players and it whiled away the hours when we weren't fighting. It was a way to forget what you were there for.'

'When you were in France, did you ever come across a magazine called *Europe Échecs*?'

He frowned, searching his memory. 'A chess magazine? Yes... that's right... I remember... my best pal found a pile of them when he went to check on a house that had been abandoned.'

'Was it a magazine for beginners?'

'It was in French for a start, so difficult to say. There was a section that looked pretty easy, but most of it would have appealed to someone who'd played for a while. It gave instructions, I think, on how to follow through on different moves.'

'Were they difficult to understand? Apart from being in a foreign language.'

'The text was fairly simple, if I remember rightly. The diagrams were more important. What's this about, Flora?'

'It was just a thought.' The thought was too vague at the moment to share. 'Come on, let's find a cup of tea.'

'Tea?' He grimaced. 'French tea will not be something I'll miss. Think of that first wonderful cup when we get back to Abbeymead!'

21

Jack was glad to have Flora's company when, the following morning, he resumed an increasingly frustrating search. In the face of so little other evidence, finding the large, black saloon responsible for Ruby King's death had assumed an unexpected significance. From the outset, Flora had been sceptical of his quest, thinking the search impossible and a needless effort, but today she seemed happy to make one last attempt with him and fail together.

And fail they did. Late that afternoon, as Jack drove across the Roman bridge and began the long climb to their hotel, he felt as though he'd been wedged behind a steering wheel for at least a month. This morning, they had visited a clutch of villages, some no more than hamlets, then grabbed a baguette for lunch, and driven on to at least another four places large enough to get a mention on his map. All without success.

He was disappointed but resigned. If he were honest, there had always been doubt in his heart that he'd find the car that killed Ruby and final defeat had been softened by sharing it with the woman he loved. The day had been tiresome, but their mood had stayed buoyant. The mystery of her mother and father no longer cast a shadow over Flora nor, he dared to imagine, over their future together.

Today, there had seemed a new ease between them, an acceptance that their bond was solid and unbreakable. Jack didn't think it imagination. She had found her parents again and, more importantly, discovered that her worst fears and imaginings had been false. It was a sad story, exceedingly so for Flora: losing her mother, father and only sibling had plunged her into facing the world alone. It had been Aunt Violet who'd saved her from an orphaned childhood spent with strangers. Flora's discovery in the Vaison churchyard had brought sorrow, but one tempered by joy – he could see that in her eyes. She knew now that she'd belonged to a warm and loving family, knew that her parents' marriage had been true and she a cherished daughter.

Tired and slightly dusty, they walked into the hotel to be greeted by the receptionist waving a scrap of paper in their direction. While they'd been meeting one dead end after another, there'd been a telephone call from Jack's mother to tell him that Massimo had been discharged from hospital and that they were both now back at Constantin.

'There's a party at the chateau the day after tomorrow,' Jack read out. 'A feast to celebrate the grape harvest – and we're invited. Fancy going? I can't say I'm keen but it would be a good opportunity to snoop, I guess.'

'We must go,' she agreed. 'Definitely. And you have to be there for the big announcement. You're her son.' When he looked blank, she tapped a tattoo on his chest with her finger. 'Have you forgotten? Massimo and Sybil are getting married. Probably.'

'Oh, that.' His mother's personal affairs had ceased to interest him years ago and, though he felt strongly that she'd be better to steer clear of the Falconi family, Sybil was her own woman and would do as she pleased. She always had. 'The note says that we can stay the night,' he continued. 'Our old rooms will be made ready for us.'

'I'd rather not,' she said quickly. 'Maybe we can come back to the hotel once the excitement is over.'

Although Flora was hoping they would return to the Beffroi that evening, the bedroom at the chateau offered a comfortable setting in which to make ready for the party. It was the same room she'd slept in previously and, glancing around its familiar furnishings, she had mixed feelings. There had been a definite lowering of spirits when she'd walked through the front entrance of the bastide again, but this room was pleasant enough and she had always loved the view from its wide windows – of the hills rolling into the distance, awash with trellis after trellis of vines. She would be here for one night only, she told herself, and then they could be gone.

And, in a few days, gone from Provence and France. Surely, once the marriage was announced, Jack's mother would be safe and he could leave with an untroubled mind. Flora had thought initially that any plans for a marriage might provoke further attacks on Sybil, but had changed her mind. Massimo was now restored to health. He was a powerful man, the patriarch of the family, and his protection would ensure that continuing the campaign against a woman he was pledged to marry would be pointless. Allegra would have to swallow her chagrin if she were to continue living under the same roof, Isabella forget her mad campaign to reinstate herself as the count's wife, and Pascal Dufour would be forced to judge Sybil afresh. As the future wife of his employer, he would know he must tread carefully.

It would be fascinating to see their reaction to Massimo's announcement. And not just fascinating, but telling, too. This evening's big event offered a chance, perhaps the last chance, to discover who had killed Ruby and nearly killed Sybil. Flora could see as well as Jack that their investigation had run out of steam and unless tonight provided at least some clues, they would be returning to Abbeymead in large part defeated.

Except it didn't feel like defeat. Not entirely. Flora hugged her new discovery close, feeling its comfort, its warmth. Since meeting the woman in the cemetery, she saw differently, her entire perspective changed: on her past, on her life, on Jack. But that was something she didn't want to think too much about. Not at the moment. Not yet.

She had packed a straw basket with the rainbow dress and her best sandals along with clean underwear, night clothes and a wash bag, and could only hope she would pass muster. Sybil was bound to be decked in yet another designer outfit and the Falconi women would no doubt pull out all the stops. She hoped what in reality was a simple dress, despite its expensive material, would meet Jack's approval and not attract too many pursed lips from her hosts.

It took only a short time to wash and change, dab some crème puff on her cheeks and try the rose-coloured lipstick that she'd bought on their travels. Pleasingly, it echoed the pink of her dress. Her often unruly waves were scooped into a topknot and fastened with a hair clip in the shape of a sunflower. A nod to Provence, she thought happily, taking a last look in the mirror and feeling satisfied – she'd done as well as she could.

Expecting Jack to meet her on the ground floor, she shut her bedroom door and made for the staircase. A little way in front of her, on the opposite side of the corridor, she became aware of Allegra leaving her own room. The woman was dressed in deep purple, a long billowing gown, almost Eastern in appearance, and Flora stood looking at the retreating figure wondering what had encouraged the young woman to choose such an extravagant garment.

Then she realised that for once Allegra had not locked her bedroom door. On impulse, with a swift glance to right and left, she opened it and darted inside. She felt slightly bad at invading the woman's privacy but not that bad. A dive into Allegra's retreat was something Flora had wanted to do from the first day she'd arrived at the chateau.

The room itself felt scrubbed and bare, a monkish cell though ten times as large. The floor was plainly tiled without a rug in sight and the whitewashed walls held only a crucifix, large and imposing, hanging opposite the bed. It would be the last thing Allegra saw at night and the first she saw in the morning.

Pulling open the dressing table drawers, one by one, Flora was met with nothing more interesting than a pile of scarves, a heap of gloves, and a jewellery box containing a single ring. Oddly, it was a man's ring. Had Allegra bought in advance for the husband she hoped to have? In the bottom drawer, another anomaly: a collection of heavy make-up, hidden away at the back, as though the woman could not bring herself to own it. The wardrobe, too, contradicted the general asceticism, being crammed full of clothes most of which, Flora reckoned, were extremely expensive. The whole room felt a testimony to the conflict that must rage within Allegra – a self-denying piety pitted against the desire to break out and enjoy the plenty of life.

As a last hope, Flora crossed to the bedside table, though she need not have bothered; a copy of the Bible stared up at her, rebuking her for the invasion. Annoyed that she had found nothing, she turned to go, hoping her absence downstairs had not been too marked and, in her haste, stubbed her toe against the iron bed frame. She was hopping in pain when she spotted something white beneath the bed. A letter. Drawing it from its hiding place, she saw it was addressed to Allegra and strangely, entirely in English. But Allegra didn't speak English, did she? Or had that been a pretence, like so much about Chateau Constantin?

The letter was contained in a single page, written on both sides. At the top was an address in Paris that Flora didn't recognise, but that was hardly surprising. Quickly, she scanned the text. It seemed innocent enough: a thank you for a present, an observation on the weather, a complaint about the writer's living quarters. Flora turned the page over, her eyes travelling from line to line before the signature bounced out at her. A neon-lit name – Ruby King!

Allegra knew Ruby. And not just knew her, but from the tone of the letter was a regular correspondent. Someone who could be called a friend: exchanging news, sending gifts, and doing so in Ruby's native language. The complaint about where she was living – that wouldn't have been Monsieur Michon's apartment, but the woman's real home. The place she retreated to after making false phone calls to Sybil. Had the gift she mentioned been one of money? Flora wondered. Money to pay Ruby for making friends with Sybil, for luring her to the Rue de Rivoli so that Alain Frossard could kill her? Flora felt herself grow hot and her heartbeat race. Things were beginning, at last, to make sense.

She must find Jack. Speak to him urgently. But how was she to do that, surrounded by people the whole evening? Could she curb her impatience until they returned to the hotel, when it might not be until tomorrow? She would have to try. Slipping out of the room, she started once more towards the staircase, gliding silently along the corridor, only to turn at a noise behind her. It was Corinne.

The last time she'd seen the maid had been in Place Montfort when, along with Flora, the girl and her basket had gone flying, its contents spread wide. The chess magazine! That was something she'd forgotten. Flora had never got to the bottom of the puzzle, but she knew as certain as the sky outside was still blue that Corinne did not play chess, had never played chess, and that the magazine was destined for someone else. Someone

Flora wasn't supposed to know about. As a present? As a bribe? Like the parcel Clio Falconi had handed to that murderous young boy.

Had Corinne seen her coming out of Allegra's bedroom? She hoped fervently that wasn't so and looked cautiously back over her shoulder. The maid appeared to pay her no attention but was going into the room Flora had just vacated. It was too early for her night-time duties, so what was Corinne doing there?

Flora was on edge. Apprehensive. Sensing connections she couldn't make but that were nevertheless vital. She must find Jack, she repeated to herself. Even if she couldn't tell him what was on her mind, she needed his steady presence.

22

'I wondered where you'd got to.' Jack smiled up at her. He was looking particularly smart this evening, she saw, in pressed grey slacks and a new short-sleeved shirt he'd bought in Paris. 'I've been having a look around and there's a huge table been set up in the courtyard. Fairy lights, too. And so much food I can't imagine where the staff will find a place for it all.'

Still trying to quieten a heart that was jumping uncomfortably, Flora fought to stop herself from grabbing hold of him and spilling out everything she'd learned.

'Can we be any help, do you think?' Anything to distract, or she would surely burst.

'We'd probably be in the way if we tried the kitchen. Let's walk outside. There may be something we can do in the courtyard. Let's go via the garden.'

Taking hold of her hand, he walked with her towards the rear of the building and the open door that led directly into the garden, but the undoubted sounds of a confrontation had them pause their steps. Rapid-fire French lost Flora from the second sentence, but through the doorway she recognised the sparring couple: Allegra and Pascal. Against the woman's flowing purple, the robe rising and falling as she gesticulated, Dufour's dark suit and waistcoat looked ridiculously formal, even funereal.

'What's going on?' she whispered to Jack, hoping he could translate.

'He's turning her down, I think, but at that speed it's not easy to understand.'

'Turning her down? From what?'

'He wants out. Something about plans? They haven't worked and he doesn't want to be involved. He's tired of her attention. Oh, that was brutal.' Jack squeezed her hand. 'We should go, Flora. We can find another route to the courtyard. I don't want to be caught eavesdropping.'

'What plans?' she asked, as they wheeled around and made for the front entrance.

'Search me, but it sounded pretty final. Whatever Allegra has been plotting with him, Dufour is no longer interested.'

Flora couldn't stop herself from bobbing up and down. 'I can't wait to say this!' she said breathlessly, standing on tiptoe in an effort to speak into his ear. 'I have to tell you! I think I know what plans Allegra—'

'Ah, there you are.' It was Sybil, with the count a few steps behind. 'I was sure I saw your car parked outside, Jack. Were your rooms ready for you?'

'They were and we used them. Thank you,' he said. 'Though we'll probably be driving back to Vaison tonight.'

When Sybil looked affronted, Flora was quick to add, 'It was a brilliant idea to have a room in which to change.'

'Brilliant,' Jack echoed with what, to Flora's ears, sounded feigned enthusiasm. 'But how are you feeling?'

His question was addressed to the count who, though still pale, looked tonight every inch the smart host, his upright figure gracing a sharply cut suit and his silver hair brushed to shining.

'Better, thank you,' Massimo said. 'Better every day, but I must not have too many shocks, the doctors tell me.'

'No, indeed,' Jack's mother said scoldingly. 'And there won't *be* any shocks tonight. It's a party we're throwing after all.'

Flora hoped the comment wouldn't prove a hostage to fortune. 'It's very kind of you to invite us,' she said to Massimo.

He spread his hands in a gesture of bounty. 'So much food – we need you to eat! Come. We must find our seats.'

When Flora caught sight of the table set up in the court-yard, her eyes popped. Alice would be in her element, she thought, massively excited by the sheer range of food on display. Kate, too. For a moment, she felt horribly homesick again – for her friends, her shop, her village. Abbeymead seemed so far away and suddenly very precious.

The table stretched halfway across the courtyard, some twenty feet in length, Flora calculated, and was covered end to end with bowls, dishes, plates, filled with every delicacy she had seen on her travels and some she hadn't. The vineyard workers and their wives and girlfriends, some twenty people, had arrived a while earlier and now stood waiting for their employer to take his seat. Flora became conscious of other figures standing to one side. Allegra, fresh from her quarrel, and her sister, Clio. Dufour, an angry scowl on his face, his hair more red than blond tonight, an echo of his mood no doubt, and behind Allegra, was that... yes, it was. Isabella! Why had Massimo invited her, and how would Sybil view this unwanted guest? Were the daughters responsible for the invite but had kept the count in ignorance?

Massimo must have seen his former wife, but made no sign that her presence perturbed him. Nodding to his assembled guests, he waved at them to take a seat around the candlelit table.

'Please,' he said and sat himself down at its head, indicating that Sybil should sit beside him.

Allegra, her face stony and expressionless, took a chair halfway down the table, her sister opposite. Dufour, Flora noticed, chose a place well away from either, staring fixedly at the brightly coloured tablecloth in an effort, she presumed, not to catch Allegra's eye.

Flora's gaze moved on, amazed to see that Isabella, of all people, had plumped herself down at the foot of the table as though she were the hostess. Had Massimo noticed? Would he challenge her? But there was silence from him and Flora wondered what on earth was going on. Presumably, this was the evening he was to announce Sybil as his new wife, yet everything suggested that was unlikely. Was Massimo as much a deceiver as everyone else in the family? It was a thought Flora had had before and never quite forgotten.

Her eyes travelled on again from the count to Sybil. Jack's mother was sitting rigid in her chair, swallowing her anger, it seemed, unwilling to make a scene in front of so many people, and at an event billed as a celebration. She was wise, Flora decided. It would be time to take Massimo to account when all this was over.

For the next half hour, she was too busy eating to take much part in the conversation, most of which was in French and, without Jack to translate – he was separated from her by several chairs – it was a hopeless task to understand more than a few words. She was reduced to smiling vacantly at her neighbours' comments, hoping it was the right gesture, while continuing to eat: crayfish canapés to begin, then fluffy cheese soufflés, followed by a massive ham and Lyonnaise salad, and a chicken course with ratatouille and potatoes au gratin. Multiple glasses of rosé accompanied every dish, Flora's glass refilled until she had laughingly to ask the server to stop. Time to stop eating, too. True, there were some delightful pots of crème brûlée just inches away and what looked like a fig tart, but really...

It was while she was hesitating that the count stood up,

wine glass in hand. The toasts had arrived and Flora was glad of
the pause. Massimo was speaking, she thought, as she struggled
to understand the language, of how well the vineyard had
performed this last year. There was a toast to all his workers,
followed by one to his supervisor, Monsieur Devezine – Flora
smiled across at him – and one to his brilliant manager. The
workers didn't look too keen at that, but raised a reluctant glass
to Pascal Dufour.

'*Et à ma famille...*' Massimo was coming to his close. Easy
enough to understand that, and it should be interesting. Would
Isabella be included in the family? But as far as Flora could
make out, there was no mention of her in the speech that
followed. At least Sybil had been spared that insult. Strangely
enough, no mention of Clio either. Instead, it was the elder
daughter who appeared to be showered with praise for her hard
work – at least that's what Flora took from the smiles and nods
in Allegra's direction.

She turned her head slightly to look down the table at Clio
while Massimo was still speaking. The girl's face was blank and
Flora learned nothing, but caught Jack's eye and they
exchanged a look. Both of them were wondering, she knew,
what Clio had done to upset her father so badly that she'd been
omitted from Massimo's speech. At a family occasion such as
this – in a sense, the chateau and its workers were as much a
family as the Falconis – it was understandable he would pay
tribute to his elder daughter. Glossing over his ex-wife was
understandable, too, but Clio?

It was then that Flora became aware of the girl staring down
the table at *her*. Staring very hard. Hastily, she reached out for a
pot of crème brûlée and began to eat, waiting for Massimo to
announce his forthcoming marriage. But no announcement
came. Bewildered, she abandoned what was left of the crème –
she really couldn't eat another mouthful – and tried to work out
what exactly this evening had meant. On the surface, a

bonhomie: she'd heard the compliments, seen the smiles, but below? Something very different. A seething anger, it seemed, a bubbling resentment.

It was with relief that she felt able at last to leave the table and join those guests who were mingling in the courtyard while they drank their after-dinner coffee. Flora had no wish for coffee, no wish for more wine, and she had eaten far too much. What she needed was a walk.

'What do you think?' she asked Jack, when he joined her by the coffee pot.

'About the marriage that never was?' He shook his head. 'No idea, but no doubt I'll soon have my ears bent.' He looked across at his mother who had remained at the table, sitting stiffly in her seat.

'You should talk to her, Jack. I need to walk. I am absolutely stuffed.'

'How disgracefully inelegant, Miss Steele. I'll come with you.'

'No. Stay with Sybil. She must be very upset and I won't be long.'

'Don't be! There's a limit to how much furious mother I can bear.'

Setting her face to the cool night air, Flora walked out of the courtyard and through the archway that led into the garden and the lake beyond. It felt good to be on the move, good to leave the chatter behind and walk in silence. She had no need of a torch tonight, the moon riding high in the sky had silvered the lawn and everything it touched, sending shadows dancing as trees and bushes rustled in a breeze that was growing stronger. The lake itself wore a soft sheen, the moon dappling its surface in ceaselessly shifting patterns of light.

It looked so calm, so fresh, that Flora couldn't resist.

Bending down, she paddled her fingers in the water. It was surprisingly cold but delightful. She cupped her hands together and splashed a little water on her face. After too much rosé, it felt a cooling balm. Bending to take another handful, she heard behind her what sounded like a swish of the grass. She turned quickly to see what it might be, only to feel a fierce push in her back. A push that sent her teetering on the rim of the lake. Frantically, she tried to regain her balance, but yet another hard push had her lose what little footing she had. And she was falling, falling into the waters of the lake, unable to save herself.

In an instant, she had sunk to the muddy bottom, long fingers of weeds wrapping themselves around her limbs. Enmeshing her, suffocating her, the attentions of an unwanted lover. With a ferocious kick, she broke from their tentacles, forcing herself upwards to break through the water's surface, only to feel a hand push hard on her head. Push her down and down. Once again, she kicked out, struggling to free herself, and once again she was thrust beneath the waters and, this time, held there. Someone had decided to kill her. Flora was in a fight to save her life.

23

Jack took a seat next to his mother, unsure what to say or whether to say anything. Massimo had moved to stand among a crowd of his workers, seeming happy to spend time talking and laughing with them. The count's speech, if Jack had translated correctly, had celebrated a bumper year for the production of rosé and been effusive in its congratulations to the workforce. Among the vineyards of Provence, Chateau Constantin had maintained its position as a premier winemaker.

But for Sybil, the speech must have counted for nothing. As they sat together, Jack could feel his mother's anger seeping from every pore and was nervous. Should he even attempt to broach the subject of a marriage that wasn't and, if he dared, how should he do it? In the end, Sybil did it for him.

'He couldn't announce we were getting married,' she said airily. 'Not with Isabella sitting there.' The stiffness in her limbs, the deepened lines on her face, belied her words. His mother was suffering, Jack could see, and he trod carefully.

'Do you have any idea why she was invited? Or' – he'd had a sudden thought – 'did she invite herself?'

'Massimo asked her to come,' Sybil said in the same nonchalant tone. 'You probably think it odd, but he felt it was the right thing to do. She knows many of the workers personally and their wives, too. He didn't want them to feel uncomfortable if she was excluded.'

Jack could see no logic in that, but he kept his thoughts to himself. His suspicion was growing that Massimo had developed cold feet and at the last moment avoided making the announcement. It would have taken some bravura, he guessed, to do so with his ex-wife seated at the foot of the table, outstaring him. Unless, of course, the man had never had any intention of making the announcement. No intention of marrying his mother and Sybil had been duped. He was wondering what he could say to lighten the mood when she changed the subject. It seemed she had no wish to probe Massimo's motives too deeply and Jack was grateful.

'This Flora girl...' she began.

There was a prickling along his neck. An annoyance at Sybil's casual disregard. Too often he'd heard Flora spoken of as though she were a giddy girl, a shallow scatterbrain, when he knew her for anything but. Their friendship had been a lesson to him in the way, even now, society so often dismissed women – at best queens of the kitchen and, at worst, fluffy nonentities. His mother, though neither fluffy nor a kitchen queen, had proved no different.

'You said she was a friend,' Sybil said, 'that she was visiting Provence for a particular reason.' She had modified her tone somewhat and he wondered if she'd felt his froideur, suppressed though it was.

'That's right. She had business of her own here.'

'And?'

'It's been successful. She's done what she came to do.' He might sound curt but he had no intention of confiding how greatly her family had troubled Flora.

'How much of a friend is she?' Sybil asked, leaning towards him.

'A good friend.'

That was as far as he'd go. Apart from his very young child-hood, he had never felt close to his mother. As an adolescent, she had made his life a misery, either smothering him with kisses or screaming at him for looking too much like his divorced father. He'd left home as soon as he could and, since then, had adopted a calm neutrality towards her. One entirely free of emotion.

'You don't trust me, Jack,' she said, watching his thoughts chase their way across his face. 'But I'm not stupid. I've seen the way you look at her. You love her.'

He didn't deny it, but maintained a silence.

'And Flora – how does *she* feel?'

She was forcing him to speak when he'd no wish to, but for once his mother sounded genuinely interested.

'She cares for me,' he said after several minutes.

'And love?'

'I don't know,' he confessed, surprised to hear himself continue the conversation, surprised to be talking in this fashion to his mother of all people. Perhaps in the emotion of the evening, Sybil had become more of the mother he'd never had.

'Don't be too slow in finding out.' She wagged her head knowledgeably. 'There'll be a time when it feels right. Make sure you take it when it comes.'

How strange to hear her echo Alice Jenner's very words. Months ago, as peace had returned to Abbeymead after the turmoil of Birds Acre Farm, Flora's old friend had offered him the same advice.

A noise from inside the house, loud voices engaged in a quarrel, had Sybil's eyebrows arch. 'Allegra,' she said definitely. 'That woman is such a bully. I feel for Corinne.'

'She seems an angry young woman,' was his only comment,

to which his mother gave a derisive snort. She had other names for a woman she hated.

This evening, Allegra had been angry in spades, he reflected. By the look of it, whatever plans she'd been nurturing had been scuppered, first by Dufour and now by her maidservant. Jack would have given a lot to know the nature of those plans. He could guess and probably be right, but only hard evidence would bring Ruby King's murderer to justice. Or expose the villain threatening his mother. And hard evidence is what he and Flora lacked.

At that thought, he got quickly to his feet. 'I'd best go looking for Flora. She said something about walking to the lake. I don't want her falling in!'

It had been a joke, but as he walked across the lawns, now shadowed by a passing cloud, and towards the spread of water, Jack thought he could hear sounds. A splash? A thrashing in the lake? He began to run, in his ears another noise, a rustling, a thudding, beyond the lake this time. The noise of running feet.

Fighting for breath, he reached the lakeside and scanned its expanse. Nothing. Then as the moon reappeared fully from behind the cloud, he saw hair. Long, russet-coloured strands of hair.

Without hesitation, he jumped. The lake was cold and deep, colder and deeper than he'd expected and there were weeds, a mass of weeds, to fight through. Within seconds, though, he was by her side, his arms beneath hers, and dragging them both to the surface.

'I'm here, Flora,' he said into her ear with the small amount of breath he had left.

Keeping her head above water, he swam with her to the side of the lake and with an almighty effort lifted her clear of the water and onto dry land. It took another almighty effort to haul himself out of the lake, weighed down as he was by saturated clothes. Clutching at clumps of grass for any kind of purchase, he slowly dragged himself free of the water, and crawled to his feet, shaking from wet and cold.

Immediately, he tugged Flora further on to the grass and turned her on one side to allow water to drain from her nose and mouth. The Heimlich manoeuvre, he thought. That must be next. He'd learned it in the army. It was the only way he knew to rid her lungs of liquid. It took several attempts but, with what appeared to be the last drop of water, he felt his pulse slow in relief. It was a while, though, before she could speak.

Reaching out for his hand, she said shakily, 'I'm OK, Jack.'

'You're very far from OK.' His face was set hard, the sweat beading his forehead. 'Don't try to speak but when you feel you can stand, I'm taking you to the house. One of the maids can find us towels, then it's back to Vaison as quickly as I can drive there. And neither of us, Flora, neither of us, are ever coming back to this haunt of vipers.'

His limbs felt weak from tension and it took some time for them to stumble back to the bastide, Flora leaning heavily on his arm, and both of them leaking water from their sodden garments.

'An accident,' he told a passing maid when they finally made it to the chateau's entrance hall. 'Can you find us extra towels and bring them to Miss Steele's room?'

The maid looked slightly scared but was prompt in doing as she was asked. That was the easy bit. Tugging dripping clothes from their backs was torture, for Flora in particular, weak as she was, but at last shirt, slacks, dress and underwear had been bundled into a spare pillowcase the maid had thoughtfully supplied, and they were able to towel themselves dry. By the time they'd pulled on the clothes they'd worn to come to the chateau, Flora's face was white, all vestiges of her tan disappeared.

'Let's hope the Beffroi has a good laundry,' he said, pointing to the pillowcase already blotched by water stains. 'Ready to go now?'

'Your mother? Massimo? Shouldn't we say goodbye?'

He shook his head. 'We'll phone from the hotel. Tomorrow. Right now, I want you out of here.'

Flora smiled limply. 'Believe me, I want to be out of here.'

They were fortunate in meeting no one on their way to the front door. The maid who had found them towels was busy in the kitchen, most of the vineyard workers had left for home and Sybil and Massimo had disappeared – maybe to discuss their future, Jack thought, or what there was of it. As for the daughters, they had vanished into thin air, and a calm that felt slightly sinister prevailed. It was as though behind closed doors no one would admit to knowing, while everyone did, that Flora had faced acute danger and murder had come close.

In the courtyard, a very few of Massimo's employees had stayed talking together, too engrossed in their conversation to notice Jack and Flora as they made their way to the Citroën parked beneath the plane trees. They were almost at the vehicle when a figure rushed past the remaining workers, then veered to one side of them, and disappeared into the dark. It was Pascal Dufour and he was in his shirtsleeves. The detail startled Jack. The man was always so correctly dressed, formal in every aspect, that to see him in casual attire sent an alarm ringing. Where was his jacket? He had been wearing it during the meal and, now the evening air had cooled considerably, why had he taken it off? The bell rang louder. Was it possible it had become unwearable? Possible that his jacket was drenched in lake water?

At Hostellerie le Beffroi, Jack explained their bulging pillowcase by mentioning an accident but it was done so vaguely that the receptionist was left bemused.

'Brandy, please,' he said before she could ask for further enlightenment. 'Two glasses of brandy, if you would. And a pot of coffee. We'll be upstairs.'

He waited until the drinks had been delivered and Flora encouraged to sip the brandy before he mentioned Dufour.

'I noticed the shirtsleeves.' She shivered slightly, whether from the cold or the sudden punch of brandy, Jack wasn't sure. 'He's never without a jacket.'

'Exactly. It suggests... do you... do you have any idea of the person who attacked you?' He was loathe to remind Flora of the terror she'd endured, but he needed her to recall the moment before it lost its sharp outline.

'Not really. I was bending to ladle water into my hands and there was a terrific push from behind. In the small of my back. I lost my balance and fell in.'

'And then?'

He saw her grip the glass tighter. 'I went to the bottom. It seemed a long way down and it was sandy and gritty, the water wasn't clear, and there were trailing plants that grabbed hold of me and...'

She broke off and took a large gulp of the spirit.

'Take your time, but try to remember as much as you can.'

'I kicked up to the surface but whoever was there pushed me down again. They had their hand on my head.'

'A man's hand? Could it have been Dufour? He could easily have left the courtyard without being noticed.'

She gave a little shrug. 'Maybe, but it could equally have been Allegra or Corinne. I think the maid saw me coming out of Allegra's room and she was bound to have told her mistress.'

'One of the women tried to drown you for poking around in Allegra's room? It doesn't seem likely.'

'It does to me. It was what I found there. I haven't been able to tell you, Jack, but – Allegra knows Ruby King! Knew Ruby King. She was in correspondence with her.'

'Are you sure?' He was stunned. That was quite a claim.

'I saw a letter from Ruby. It read as though they knew each other well. Ruby was writing from Paris, from the flat we never found.'

'What did she say?'

'The letter was innocuous enough. Nothing at all incriminating, but the fact that they knew each other – surely that *is* incriminating. Someone paid Ruby to make friends with your mother, we decided that, to manoeuvre her into a situation where she could be attacked and her death made to seem an accident. That someone has to be Allegra. There was even a mention of a present. And Allegra must know Alain Frossard – he services her father's car. She could have used Corinne as a go-between and bribed him to go to Paris. Bribed him again to tamper with Massimo's car.' Flora finished her brandy in one swallow. 'No wonder she looked so sick when it was her father not Sybil who suffered the faulty brakes.'

'OK, but if it's a cosy little trio of Allegra, Corinne and Frossard, why was Dufour in shirtsleeves and why the row between him and Allegra that we witnessed tonight?'

'The jacket is a mystery, but as for the quarrel – maybe she used him, too. And he was fed up with being her poodle.'

'So he goes rogue and decides to murder you for himself?'

'We don't know what their quarrel was about,' Flora pointed out. 'It could simply be that he was fed up with being adored. Being followed around. We saw them arguing before – do you remember? He might have decided that after all Allegra was too great a price to pay for a vineyard of his own.'

Jack was unconvinced. 'Dufour is involved in a way that goes far beyond personal feelings, I'm sure.' He gestured to the tray. 'Shall I pour? A hot coffee should do the trick.'

'I'm feeling better already.'

'You're looking a bit less peaky, I'd say. Perhaps I should have ordered two glasses of brandy.'

'Definitely not. Coffee is perfect.' As he filled their cups, she asked, 'How would you describe the colour of Dufour's hair?'

He was mystified. 'Blond? A kind of pinkish fair?'

'Strawberry blond,' she said. 'It's unusual for a Frenchman. I thought that when I first saw him, fair hair and blue eyes.'

'So his ancestors came from some Nordic country.' He handed her the coffee, the smell making him feel hungry. How could that be after so much food?

'Pinkish fair isn't too far from red,' she said hopefully.

'Red? The boy, you mean?'

She nodded, clutching her cup in both hands, her face wearing the look he knew from old. Intrigue, excitement, a puzzle being solved. 'The child who attacked Sybil in the ruins wasn't picked at random. He has to have been someone the conspirator knew and could trust to keep quiet. Someone who could be given a bribe without alerting suspicion in his parents.'

'You're thinking the boy is a relative of Dufour's?'

'Not a brother or a son, if Dufour has any children, which seems unlikely, but someone related to him. Fairly closely related.'

'If so, that makes our band of villains a quartet rather than a trio.'

'And Corinne could have acted as a go-between for all of them. She knows the boy, I'm sure. The chess magazine wasn't hers, I'd swear, it had to have been for him. Then there's the box Clio gave the boy – her sister may have asked her to do it – it could have been a chess set, I've been thinking. It was the right shape.'

She pulled at a strand of hair, still damp from lake water, her frustration evident. There were dark rings beneath her eyes, he noticed, and her cheeks were pinched. Jack felt a burst of protectiveness and began making plans.

'Overall, it makes for a muddy picture,' she grumbled. 'There are just too many people involved.'

'And not enough time to investigate every one of them.'

An unspoken question lay in his words and he fortified himself with another coffee before she could ask it. 'You're going home, Flora,' he said. 'Back to Abbeymead as soon as I can book a ticket for the ferry.'

'That's amazingly high-handed,' she protested.

'I agree, but I want you safe and if you stay here I can't be sure.'

'And what about you? Can you be sure you'll be safe? Or are you leaving your mother to cope alone with whatever comes her way? And she will be alone, now there's been no mention of a marriage.'

'You must know I wouldn't do that. I'll drive you to Paris, stay for the night, then see you onto the train to Dieppe the next morning and drive back. You'll have to get a cab from Newhaven, I'm afraid – unless you fancy driving the Austin to Abbeymead.'

'Actually I would,' she mused. Then seeing his face, said, 'I won't, of course. And I won't leave you here alone either. We'll face this quartet of bandits together.'

Jack let it go. They wouldn't be facing it together, he was adamant, but it wasn't the time to argue. He would see Flora on her way home no matter how much she protested, but right now it was quiet she needed. And a peaceful night's sleep.

'Into bed,' he said, 'and I'll see you in the morning.'

24

Jack closed the bedroom door quietly, making sure he took with him the tray of empty cups and glasses – he wanted Flora to sleep without interruption. The foyer was in gloom when he emerged from the staircase, the night porter not yet on duty and the receptionist enjoying a late supper, he guessed. He was sliding the tray onto her desk when he became aware of a figure sitting in one of the two armchairs the foyer provided. The chair was in deep shadow, but the waspish voice aimed in his direction made its inhabitant clear.

'What kind of behaviour do you call this?' his mother asked. 'You and that girl. You were guests at the chateau. Invited to a party at my request. The least you could have done was to thank Massimo for his hospitality and say a civilised goodbye.'

Jack walked over to her, taking his time to settle himself in the companion chair. He'd had more than enough of the civilisation Chateau Constantin offered.

'I had to get Flora back to the hotel,' he said calmly. 'We were both in need of hot showers and a new set of clothes and you were nowhere in sight. Neither was the count.'

'Hot showers!' Even in the gloom, he saw Sybil's face flush

an angry red. 'You couldn't wait to say a decent goodbye because of a hot shower?'

'Not after being half drowned in Massimo's lake. Let me tell you what happened.'

And he did.

Once he'd finished speaking, his mother sat for a long time staring at him, seeming unable to take in what he'd told her. 'Someone tried to drown her?' she asked at last. She sounded incredulous. 'Are you sure?'

'I couldn't be more sure. She was unconscious in the water when I reached the lake. She would have died if I hadn't left you when I did and gone looking for her.'

'But... but couldn't she just have fallen in? She'd had wine. Actually, quite a lot. And it was dark.'

'Flora drinks little, the moon was full and the sky clear except for the odd cloud. And no, she couldn't have fallen in. Someone pushed her into the lake and then held her down. She was supposed to die. It was attempted murder.'

There was a quick intake of breath, his mother wrapping her arms close around her body. A form of self-defence, he supposed, but it would be no protection against the evil that permeated the chateau.

'Was it the same person who has tried to harm me?' she managed to ask after another long silence.

'I'm pretty sure of it. And this person isn't going to stop. Flora isn't safe here and I want her back in Abbeymead. As soon as I can buy a ferry ticket to Newhaven, I'm driving her to Paris.'

'*She* isn't safe!' The flush had deepened. 'What about me? You're leaving me on my own to cope with this mad woman, and it is a woman, I've no doubt. She's still on the loose and becoming more brazen by the day.'

'I'll be gone for two days at most. I'll stay in Paris overnight, then head back here.'

Sybil looked slightly mollified, although not completely. 'That's still two days I'll be alone with this monster watching me. What if they decide to strike immediately you leave?'

'I have to see Flora is out of danger,' he said implacably. 'Once she's safe, I'll be back. And I'll get to the bottom of this conspiracy. If it makes you feel better, stay in your room and lock the door.'

'I'm not living at the chateau.'

'What?'

Sybil lowered her head, studying the pleats of her silk skirt. 'I've moved out. I've checked into the hotel where I stayed before.'

Jack directed a steady look at her. 'That seems a sudden decision.'

'We had a row,' she said baldly. 'You might as well know. I felt slighted, humiliated. After Massimo promised he'd make an announcement at the party, tell everyone who mattered that we were getting married, then nothing. I tried to forget it, brush it off as unimportant, but I find I can't.'

He reckoned they must have been quarrelling at the time he and Flora had walked out of the front door of the chateau. No wonder their host had been nowhere in sight.

'I see,' he said, unsure just how to respond.

'Do you? Somehow I doubt it. How can you possibly understand? I felt humiliated enough when I was married to your father. Married! I use the word advisedly. Married when Ralph chose to remember he was a husband, but more often than not left to one side while he caroused with his gambling buddies or flirted with his latest conquest.'

Sybil leaned forward and took hold of his arm. Her grip was fierce. 'Massimo was a man I could trust. A man who loved me. That's what I thought. With him I'd know a settled life at last. He'd been married for years and proved himself to be a good husband.'

Jack's brow wrinkled. There was something wrong with that statement. 'He divorced Isabella, Mum. Is that being a good husband?'

'There was a reason for that,' she said defensively. 'There must have been.'

'So... what was it?'

Sybil's expression returned to its familiar resentment. 'I don't know, but I do know it wasn't his fault that the marriage fell apart.'

Jack couldn't see how that was so. To him, it felt more like wishful thinking, but it was never wise to argue with his mother. And certainly not tonight after a monumental row and an indignant walk-out.

'So where does it leave you both?' he asked tentatively. 'The quarrel?'

Sybil twitched her shoulders in irritation. 'He was full of excuses, of course. The party hadn't been the right time to make the announcement. He'd been stupid to suggest it. It would be better if it came later when he could tell his family privately. After that, he'd inform his workforce. I didn't believe a word of it. An excuse, all of it, and a rubbish excuse at that. I won't be returning to the chateau until he makes good his promise.'

'And if he doesn't?' Jack dared to ask.

'I'll move on,' she said defiantly.

He was unsure how his mother was to do that. She was at an age when new beginnings were difficult, and over the last year had entrusted her future exclusively to the count. He wished he could help her.

'Is Massimo scared of Isabella, do you think? Is that why he backed out?'

'Why would he be scared?'

'I'm just trying to figure it out. Get into his mind. At the hospital, he seemed so sure he would marry again.'

That produced another irritated twitch but Jack persevered. 'What about his daughters?'

'What about them?'

'Is he fearful of their reaction? It's evident he wants to talk to them before telling anyone else.'

Sybil pursed her lips. 'He idolises Allegra. Clio less, I think. She's not a favourite with him, but he's not scared of either of them. He has no reason to be. Once Allegra knows, she'll be poisonous, for sure, but he won't let it stop him doing what he wants.'

'Even so, it seems to me a pretty murky family, Mum. Do you really want to be part of it?'

His mother thought before answering and when she did, Jack heard the sincerity in her voice. 'Massimo isn't just a safe harbour, you know. I respect him. And I love him – genuinely. I think we could be happy together.' She paused, her lips twisted into a grimace. 'Your father will be laughing for weeks if he hears of this latest calamity. Do you ever see him these days?'

'We've met up once or twice over the last year or so.'

'When you see him again, don't tell him what's happened. He's amused himself finely with mocking my Italian count. I don't want to give him more ammunition with which to hurt me.'

'Why on earth would I tell him?'

She looked at him thoughtfully. 'No, you wouldn't. You don't have his cruel streak.'

'Come on.' He got to his feet and held his hand out to her. 'It's getting late. I'll walk you back to your hotel and we'll talk tomorrow once I've organised Flora's ticket.'

'Walk me back? You think I'm in danger here?'

'Not tonight, but it's always good to be careful.'

. . .

At breakfast the next morning, Flora heard the tale of Sybil's late-night visit. She couldn't bring herself to like Jack's mother – for much of the time, her own son didn't, so perhaps she shouldn't feel too bad – but the sudden collapse of Sybil's cherished marriage plans made Flora sad. It also made her wary. The possibility that Massimo might take a second wife had to be behind the attacks on Jack's mother – there seemed no other motive – and, if the count had begun to waver over his decision, another outrage might tip him into rejecting the idea entirely. If he was to dither, whoever was behind the violence could decide to go for broke.

Why the proposed marriage mattered so much left Flora struggling to find a reason that made sense. Was it Isabella's campaign to regain her position as the count's wife? That would certainly come to a grinding halt if Massimo married again. Allegra's hatred of the divorce? She was a deeply religious woman who would believe in the sanctity of marriage and who loved her mother. Pascal Dufour's scheming for position and money? His ambitions could well be curtailed by a second wife. Any or all of these were possible, she supposed, but somehow none of them seemed grave enough to explain multiple murder. And it would have been multiple if Jack hadn't decided to come looking for her last night.

'If there's a monster at the chateau, as my mother believes, my money is on Allegra,' Jack said, finishing a glass of fresh orange and pushing to one side the basket of warm rolls.

'I can't decide on the monster,' she admitted, 'but I hope Allegra hasn't won.'

'If winning is getting what she wanted – ousting Sybil – then she's won.'

'And to do that, she's implicated her maid and made Frossard a murderer. Have you thought, Jack? It could have been Frossard last night at the lake. He wasn't at the feast, but Corinne could have smuggled him onto the estate, watched me walk to the lake and told him where he could find me. If the maid *did* see me come out of Allegra's room, it was another reason to get rid of me. To make sure I couldn't broadcast what I'd discovered.' She dusted her hands off on the linen napkin. 'On the other hand, I don't want to forget Dufour's missing jacket. He was definitely at the celebration, and quite legitimately.'

'I'm like you – unsure.' Jack tapped a teaspoon along the saucer rim. Trying to tap his way through the miasma, Flora thought.

'I reckon Allegra has tried to involve him in her machinations,' he said, 'but it seems that he's walked away. The brush-off the day we saw her go into the church looked personal to me, as though he was turning his back on the idea of ever being a husband. And the quarrel last night? Possibly a refusal to be involved in whatever she was plotting – your demise maybe. I'm not counting him out completely but... What about Isabella? She was at the party, too.'

Flora wrinkled her nose at the suggestion. 'She might know what's going on, she probably does, but I don't feel she's had any active part in it. She's all noise and fury but no real gumption.'

He grinned.

'What?'

'The idea of Isabella and gumption. The two don't go together. Gumption suggests resourcefulness, a willingness to persevere, to put in the hard graft, while Isabella seems prone to an on-the-spot kind of violence.'

'That's exactly what I mean. She's as wicked as the rest of them but, unless something instantly triggers her anger, she'll stay a bystander for the most part, waiting for her moment.' Flora bent to pick up her bag. 'Time to go? What are we doing today?'

'*We* aren't doing anything. *You* are having a rest. Go back to bed and sleep. Or find a sunny spot in the garden and take a book with you. I'm off to make enquiries about how best to get a ticket for the Dieppe ferry. I want to book your passage today – at the latest, tomorrow.'

Flora bit her lip. She didn't want a ticket. She didn't want to leave, though that wasn't strictly true. She longed to be home again, back in Abbeymead, but Jack should be with her. Leaving him to face goodness knows what danger felt cowardly and Flora wasn't a coward. But he'd sounded adamant and, though he was usually amenable – at times easy-going to a worrying degree – Flora knew she wasn't going to win this tussle.

And perhaps he was right. Her presence was confusing matters, she could see. Rather than being the investigator she'd hoped, she had become the pursued – first a target for flying bottles, then a victim to be drowned. Maybe the picture would become clearer if she weren't here; one less distraction, one less complication. Maybe without her, Jack would have a better chance of discovering the killer they were after.

Still feeling drained from her ordeal at Constantin, Flora had been happy enough to take Jack's advice and spend most of yesterday in her room. The day had been particularly hot and to stretch herself out on the cool white counterpane, her window open to birdsong and whatever breeze was going, had been an attractive option.

Jack, on the other hand, had spent hours on a fruitless hunt for a travel agency either in the town or nearby. Nowhere locally boasted such a luxury any longer, he'd learned – he would have to go to Avignon – but, after a long search, a shop-keeper he'd consulted had found a telephone number that would allow him to contact the Dieppe ferry directly. By then, it had been too late in the day to ring, but this morning immediately after breakfast, he hurried off to do battle with the French telephone service, leaving Flora to wander into the garden.

It was another day of piercing blue sky and a sun that bathed the town in a shimmering heat from early in the morning. The hotel's garden was small but provided sufficient shade for a few hours' reading. Flora found a wooden bench tucked into one corner between giant lavender bushes, now past their bloom, and a deep pink bougainvillaea, and settled herself to begin *The Darling Buds of May*. It was the novel she'd chosen from the All's Well's shelves as her travelling companion, but so far had stayed unopened.

Halfway through the morning when she'd laid aside her book and was dozing in the garden's warmth, Jack appeared at her side. He looked frazzled.

'I can't seem to get through to anyone. The number rings but either the booking office is closed for some reason or the number I've been given is wrong.'

'Oh dear. I'll have to stay in Vaison,' she said brightly.

'No you won't. I'm ringing Alan Ridley.'

'The inspector? But why?'

'I thought I'd ask him to book your ticket from the Newhaven end, if he's willing. I've been meaning to call him for the last few days, in any case. It's possible he has contacts in the French police and if push comes to shove, that could be useful.'

'What do you mean, if push comes to shove?' she asked, avoiding any mention of the ferry. Even if Alan Ridley managed to book from Newhaven, it would take days before the ticket arrived. Her spirits lifted but almost as quickly drooped.

'As long as you're on the passenger manifest...' He was frowning as he took a seat beside her. 'It won't matter that you haven't a paper ticket.'

'Push comes to shove?' she asked again, still refusing to think of ferries and tickets.

'If there's trouble,' he murmured vaguely.

'Of course there'll be trouble. How could there not be? And you won't let me share it.' Jumping to her feet, she slammed *The*

Darling Buds of May down onto the seat. 'I'm going out – you don't need me here. And there's something I have to do.'

'Flora!' he called after her.

She turned as she reached the paved terrace and gave him a mischievous smile. 'Relax. I'm walking into town. There's something I must buy, but I'll be back by the time you've had your boys' chat.'

25

Jack watched as she whisked herself through the French doors on her way to the hotel entrance. He wished Flora had stayed with him or stayed where she was sure to be safe, but there was little he could do to stop her.

Trying hard to put his fears aside, he followed her into the hotel and walked to the small booth leading off the main foyer that housed the telephone for public use, hoping that this call would be more successful. He gave the hotel operator his room number and, with surprising efficiency, she dialled straight through to the Brighton police station. His luck continued to hold – the inspector, he learned, had just this minute walked in. Jack glanced down at his watch and was annoyed with himself for forgetting the one hour time difference. It took a while for Ridley to come to the phone, Jack's hotel bill increasing by the second. The telephone might be for public use but it wouldn't be free.

'Jack, old chap!' After what seemed an age, the inspector's voice came loud and clear. 'What are you doing ringing me again? I thought you were on holiday. Or have you got yourself tangled in that case you asked me about?'

'I'm still on holiday. Sort of,' he hedged. 'But I need a bit of help. There's been some trouble here.'

'Isn't there always when you're around?' A loud laugh crackled down the line. 'I'll bet you anything it's about your young lady. She's trouble with a capital T.'

'Yes, it's about Flora I'm ringing,' he said stiffly. 'I need to get her back to Newhaven but for some reason the ferry office at Dieppe isn't answering the telephone and I can't buy a ticket. I was wondering if you could do me a favour and book her a place from your end?'

'It shouldn't be too difficult. When is she leaving?'

'As soon as possible. She'll stop the night in Paris and take the train to Dieppe the next day, so the afternoon boat any time from around three onwards.'

'You sound a bit distracted, old man. What kind of trouble are you in?' Ridley sounded reluctant. He didn't want to know, Jack suspected, but force of habit had made him ask. 'And why aren't you travelling back together?'

Jack resigned himself to telling the inspector the whole story or most of it. 'It's my mother that's in trouble, Alan,' he concluded, 'and we've both been trying to help. But that's meant Flora has attracted some very unpleasant attention. I want her out of here and safe in Abbeymead.'

'Your mother, you say? That's not good.' He could imagine the inspector shaking his head. Mothers had a special place in Ridley's heart, Jack remembered. Mrs Ridley still cooked her son a roast dinner every Sunday.

'It isn't good. Someone in this place doesn't like her or doesn't like the fact she's intending to marry the count. I think she's in danger which is why I've decided to stay for a while.'

The inspector gave a tut. 'You be careful, Jack. You're in a foreign country and you're on your own.'

'That's one of the reasons I wanted to talk to you. Apart from the ferry, I mean. Do you have any contacts in the

French police? Someone I could call on if things got desperate.'

There was a short silence. Jack imagined the inspector was reviewing any dealings he'd had with France over the years.

'Nobody I can think of. Nobody who'd be of any real use to you. Like I say, you need to tread carefully.'

'If I can nail the person who's behind these attacks – not just on my mother but on Flora, too – I'll be on my way home and feeling happy. So far, though, we've no real clues. Just hints, suggestions of who it might be.'

'It sounds like you've got suspects at least.'

'Plenty of those. Too many, in fact.'

'Then go for the weakest link. Remember? Hammer the one who's going to break first. Even if they're not guilty, they'll know something that will lead you to the right place.'

The maid, Jack thought. Corinne had to be the weakest link, although not that weak. The chateau's servants appeared loyal to their employer and were no doubt paid well to keep their mouths shut. When he'd tried questioning Pierre, the valet had pretended not to understand him – his French wasn't that bad – and Flora had so far failed to persuade the maid to say anything useful. But loyalty could be overstretched and, if he could ensure Corinne felt intimidated, she might disclose whatever secrets she held. As Frossard's girlfriend, she would know something at least of what he'd been up to and with whom.

'Are you still there?' the inspector asked.

'Yes. Sorry, Alan. I'm working out our weakest link and how best to tackle them.'

'I'll wish you luck, old chap. Go slowly but if you're in a real mess, ring me. I might be able to pull strings.'

In half an hour, Jack had left a note for Flora at the reception desk, and was driving out of Vaison towards Chateau Constantin. He'd sworn that he would never come near the place again, but here he was less than forty-eight hours later revisiting the scene of attempted murder. Flora's murder.

The estate lay snoozing peacefully in the September sun as he drove along the gravelled lane to the chateau at the top of the hill. It was difficult to imagine it as a setting for violence, yet Constantin had witnessed two attempts on Flora's life and possibly two on his mother's, if he counted the tampering with her medicine.

The air of serenity that had lain across the estate as he drove to the house was broken abruptly when, turning into the court-yard, he was confronted by a sight that startled. Two police cars were parked sideways across the cobbles, leaving him to inch the Citroën into what space was left.

There was no sign of a police officer; it was Pascal Dufour who came hurrying across to the car. Jack had barely opened the driver's door, when Dufour put out a detaining hand.

'Monsieur Carrington, it is best you go.'

Jack looked at him with widened eyes. 'Really? Why is that?'

'Your mother, she is now in Vaison. There is no reason for you to be here and we are... we are...'

'In a mess,' he suggested. 'I can see that.' He looked across at the police cars. 'And I know that my mother has gone. I've come to speak to Corinne, in fact.' He watched for a reaction on Dufour's face, but the man's expression was impossible to read. 'Mrs Carrington left behind one or two items she needs at the hotel,' he went on, 'and I promised to collect them this morning. Corinne could help me find them.'

He'd thought of the excuse on his drive over and was rather proud of the way it slid off his tongue without hesitation.

Dufour didn't look as pleased. Instead, he looked aghast. 'Corinne? But you cannot.'

'She may be busy at the moment,' he said amenably, 'but I'm happy to wait for—'

'No!' He interrupted Jack. 'You do not understand. Corinne is dead.'

'Dead?' he repeated, the shock sounding in his voice.

Dufour nodded. 'You must go, Monsieur.'

Jack had no intention of going anywhere, not until he'd discovered just how a young woman in full health had suddenly lost her life. In that, he was lucky. A policeman had emerged from the front door of the chateau and was striding towards them. He looked as if he meant business.

'*Bonjour*,' he greeted Jack. '*Vous êtes...?*'

'Jack Carrington. My mother has been staying here,' he replied in English. 'I've come to collect a few of her belongings.'

The police officer frowned, maybe trying, Jack thought, to make sense of the language. He hoped the man could. The conversation he wanted to have would be laughable if he had to use French.

'You were here Saturday night?' the officer asked. Jack was relieved. Once more his schoolboy lessons could be consigned to the cupboard.

'I was. There was a party to celebrate the harvest.'

The policeman nodded. 'I understand this. Did you see the maid, Corinne Moreau?'

'For a few minutes only.' He remembered the quarrel she'd had with Allegra. Now he thought about it, that was the last time he'd seen the maid. The only time. His mind wandered around the long table they'd sat at, right here in the courtyard. Had Corinne been there, enjoying the feast? Or serving at the table?

'She wasn't at the meal,' he said, now sure of his facts.

'What time did you see her last?'

'I'd say around seven o'clock.'

The man nodded. 'Do you know why she did not stay for the party?' The policeman looked at him intensely.

'I'm sorry, I have no idea.' He thought quickly. The quarrel with Allegra perhaps? Should he mention that? 'But Corinne – Monsieur Dufour tells me she is dead.'

The officer nodded gravely.

'But how? Where?' Would the man reveal these details or were the police keeping the information close to their chests?

'She has been murdered, monsieur. Her body was found last evening in Le Jardin des Neuf Demoiselles. A lady walking her dog saw the poor girl. A bad business.'

The Garden of the Nine Damsels, the park where he and Flora had seen the circle of granite blocks. It was a fair distance from Chateau Constantin. What had Corinne been doing in the park, and how had she got there? Some form of transport would be needed which meant that Allegra was unlikely to be involved in any kidnapping.

'It is a strangle,' the policeman said almost apologetically, gesturing towards his neck. 'A very bad business,' he repeated. 'But you are staying where?'

'Hostellerie le Beffroi in the *haute-ville*.'

'I know it. If we need to speak again, we will come to you.'

There was little Jack could do other than nod his agreement and drive back to Vaison.

Walking down the hill from the *haute-ville* to the Roman bridge, Flora was still bristling. She would leave Jack to his telephone call, she fumed. He was trying to protect her, she understood that and, after her rescue the night before last, his fears would be intense. But she hated to be told what to do. Had always hated it, she thought crossly, and she wasn't about to change. It took a stomp along the winding street that flowed into the main square before her annoyance abated.

Compromise wasn't something she was good at but sometimes, she recognised, it was necessary. Particularly necessary if
you had made a binding promise. As her parents had. They
must have learned to compromise; they had been happy
together. Truly happy, the lady had said.

Flora had been honest when she'd told Jack she was going to
the shops. She had something to buy, something precious that
she needed to do alone. A simple action that thousands, maybe
millions, of people performed every day and would do today,
but for her it held all the meaning in the world.

The day she had chased the unknown child, she'd glimpsed
a florist's tiny shop tucked away in one of the smaller streets of
the town and it was there that she made her way. A bunch of
flowers or a potted plant, she asked herself, standing beneath
the shop's striped awning amid a collection of bucketed dahlias
and sweet-smelling roses. Pressing her forehead to the window,
she could see flowers banked high to the ceiling, and every inch
of floor space covered in blooms. It was going to be a difficult
choice.

With the owner's help, she emerged some quarter of an
hour later with a bouquet of delphiniums and pale pink roses,
tied with the bright blue ribbon she'd chosen especially. A
vague memory had Flora recall that many of her childhood
dresses had been blue – her mother must have liked the colour.

Walking slowly towards Notre Dame de Nazareth, she was
glad there were few people about. It was the time of day when
most were at their place of work or were busy with household
chores. She hoped the lady who had spoken to her was busy,
too. She had been a kind woman, someone who had liked her
parents and grieved for them, but today Flora wanted to be
quite alone.

She knew her way now and walked directly into the cemetery, tracing a path through lichen-covered memorials to find
the two headstones of shining ebony. Bending low, she placed

her bouquet between each gravestone and, as she did, said a silent prayer for the two people who should have been dear to her but whom she had barely known. This time the tears came. The first tears she had ever shed since that terrible day when she'd been told she would never see her parents again.

First tears. And the first time she had brought flowers to a cemetery – not even to Violet, lying in the graveyard of St Saviour's. There had been a barrier, almost a physical obstacle, that she'd never managed to overcome. Until now. She might not return here for a long time – though she would return – but she would leave flowers for Violet as soon as she was home in Abbeymead.

Brushing the tears away, Flora got to her feet and, with a final backward glance, said goodbye to the family she'd hardly known and would never know.

26

Driving towards the Roman bridge on his way back to the hotel, Jack saw Flora a little way ahead. He gave a soft toot on the horn and pulled in to the kerbside.

She looked up, and hurried to meet him. 'Where have you been?' she asked, once he'd extricated himself from the car and joined her on the pavement. 'I left you at the hotel. I thought you had an important call to make.'

'I had and I did. I've been to Chateau Constantin,' he said briefly. 'What about you?' Her hands were empty, he noticed, and suspicion took hold. If she hadn't been shopping, what had she been doing? 'Nothing in the shops that you liked?'

'I went to buy flowers.' She slipped her arm in his and, when he still looked uncertain, added, 'For my parents.'

'Right.'

It was an underwhelming response, but she'd taken him by surprise. Behind those few simple words lay a huge sea change. Flora had never bought flowers for the dead, not even for her aunt Violet whom she'd adored and who had loved and cared for her most of her life. For years, she'd refused even to visit the cemetery at Highgate where she'd been told, falsely as it turned out, that her parents were buried. A monumental change of mind driven, he was sure, by what she'd learned from a woman she hadn't known. Their encounter in the cemetery had proved a hundred times more significant for Flora than her meeting with Richard, rendered a nonentity by the intervening years.

The accident in which her parents had died had been just that, not the fault of an angry, controlling husband driving headlong into a storm he should have avoided, but his attempt to save the woman he loved. Flora's fears had been quelled, the change in her thinking profound. Might other things change? Jack wondered. Her avoidance of commitment, her staunch determination to remain single?

'Why did you go the chateau?' She nudged at the arm he'd linked in hers. 'You swore you'd never cross its threshold again.'

'And I meant it. But something the inspector suggested on the phone made me think again. In the absence of hard evidence, his advice was to go for our weakest link and extract whatever truth we could. For me, that had to be Corinne.'

Falling into step, they walked towards the bridge and the river. '*Was* she the weakest link when you spoke to her?' Flora asked, and when he didn't answer, 'You did see her?'

Jack shook his head, unsure of how to break the appalling news.

'Was it Corinne's day off?' Flora persevered.

'Let's walk by the river,' he said.

A pair of hazel eyes scanned him anxiously. 'What's happened, Jack? Tell me!'

He said nothing but crossed with her to the other side of the road and took the steps down to the riverside walk.

'Corinne is dead,' he said at last.

Flora dropped his arm, her lips parted in shock. 'How can she be?'

'Murdered.' There was no way of softening the fact.

Her hand flew to her mouth and she sank down on one of

the benches lining the river. 'Murdered. I can't believe... I mean who, why? She was just a maidservant. Allegra's, Clio's, your mother's maid, too, when she was at the chateau. She may have been a go-between, but why did she have to die?'

He spread his hands wide. 'I don't know. The police are on the case, though they're not saying much. I was lucky to get an officer to talk at all, to tell me she was dead.'

'That was it? He told you nothing else? How she died?'

It was the inevitable question and Jack had hoped he wouldn't have to answer it. 'She was strangled.'

Flora sat looking straight ahead. She wasn't seeing the river, he knew. 'Did he say where... where Corinne died?' she asked at last.

'She was found yesterday evening by someone walking their dog. Whether that was where she was killed, I don't know. She was by the circle of stones we saw in the park. The one that runs alongside the road out of Vaison towards Sablet.'

'The poor, poor girl.' Flora was silent for several minutes until she said in a decided voice, 'If I was to guess *why* Corinne was killed, it would be because she knew too much. She knew who killed Ruby King, knew who tried to kill your mother. Maybe even who tried to kill me at the party. And it's not too difficult to guess who did it. The man who was supposed to care for her – Alain Frossard.'

'But as his girlfriend, Corinne must always have known too much,' he objected. 'Why would he kill her now?'

'Maybe she didn't know. Maybe she'd only just put two and two together. Or if she did know what he was doing, even perhaps helping him do it, she couldn't bear the idea any longer and decided to confess.'

Flora fell silent again, then quite suddenly grabbed at his arm. 'They had a quarrel. I must have told you. It was the day you drove to Carpentras looking for Frossard's car. I was on my way to the cemetery for the second time. I wanted to visit my parents' graves on my own and I was crossing the square thinking about it, not noticing much around me, when someone cannoned into me. It was Corinne and we were both sent flying. She'd been rushing blindly across the square and hadn't seen me. And she'd been crying, I was sure. From the direction she'd come, I reckoned she'd been at Frossard's garage and had a row with him.'

'The row could have been a lovers' tiff.'

'It could. Or it could have been something far more serious. Corinne might have told him she wanted out of whatever he was planning. Might have threatened to tell the police if he didn't stop.'

'I went to Carpentras on Wednesday, didn't I? But it was only yesterday or the night before that Corinne was killed.'

'So, a gap of a few days. Perhaps Frossard hoped he could persuade her to keep quiet, but when he realised she was definitely going to spill the beans, he decided to save his skin by killing her.'

'You're certain in your mind that it is Frossard?'

'I can't see who else it could be. He was the only one who wasn't at the party.' She took hold of his hand. 'Jack – let's go to the park. The one where Corinne was killed.'

'The police will be all over it. I doubt we'll be allowed anywhere near.'

'Maybe not, but let's try.'

'What good will it do?' It seemed pointless to Jack. If the police were searching, how could they do any better?

'Perhaps no good at all. But you went to the chateau to see Corinne for information. Information you never got. Why don't we follow the trail she left? It's probably our last hope of discovering anything.'

It was a depressing thought but true, and he found himself reluctantly agreeing. 'I'm fairly sure it will be a wasted trip, but we'll go. We're walking, I suppose?'

'A walk is fine. I think we can cut across to the park from further along the river. If we pick the right road to turn down, we should end up close by.'

Flora was almost right, he realised, as they emerged from a side street and saw to their right the dusty expanse of the Garden of the Nine Damsels, the grass in places withered by the summer's sun and pockmarked by bare brown patches. As he'd predicted, a large area had been roped off and blue uniformed police were swarming over the site and beyond.

'See what I mean?' He stood by the roadside, gloomily surveying the activity.

'The whole park hasn't been cordoned off. There's plenty left to explore. We can still poke around.'

Flora's poking around inevitably led to trouble, but he could see the sense in what she suggested. There was no getting near the spot where the body had been found but it was possible, if unlikely, that somewhere else in the park might hold a clue. After his phone call to the inspector, Corinne had seemed to be the way ahead and perhaps she still was. If they could learn more about her death, it might take them a step forward. Even small progress would be welcome.

Several police officers stood at the entrance to the park and, saying a polite good day to them, he waved a hand towards the acre of grass beyond.

'*Nous pouvons marcher?*'

There were a few French shrugs which Jack took to mean permission and, taking hold of Flora's hand, he skirted the roped area, walking as slowly as he dared. Beside him, Flora's head was bobbing furiously as she tried to make out what exactly the men in white were doing – by the look of it, a forensic team had joined their uniformed colleagues.

'I bet they don't find much,' she said dismissively, when they were well past.

'Maybe there's not much to find. There's little chance of a weapon.' Not if the killing had been strangulation, he thought.

'But footprints?'

'Too dry. There hasn't been rain for weeks.'

'Fingerprints on the stones?'

'If they showed up, which I'm not sure they would, there will be literally dozens. It's a public park. And whoever killed Corinne—'

'—Frossard.'

'OK, Frossard. He'll have worn gloves if he had any sense. And he seems pretty cute. He was very quick to fix Massimo's car after the crash – if he *was* the guilty one. And very quick to disappear from Paris along with his murderous saloon. He must have travelled back immediately after Ruby King was killed.'

'Should we tell the police about Ruby, do you think? Or would that just complicate matters? They'd probably dismiss it as speculation and tell us to go away.'

'Sure to, I would think. Ruby mowed down, Massimo's car losing control, a falling pillar from a ruined site – all easily explained as accidents.'

'And the attempt to drown me?'

'They'd want to know why you didn't report the incident as soon as you could. Why not on the night it happened? Why come up with it now, once a woman has been murdered?'

'I could give them a few reasons.'

'None of which they're likely to believe. Come on, now we are here, let's look around.'

They had walked past what was left of the grass and into a greener landscape where clumps of tall bamboo-like grasses proliferated and, behind them, a thicket of birch. Overhead, the sun had reached its zenith and the path they glimpsed unwinding through the trees offered a welcome shade.

'It's rather lovely,' Flora said, as they walked beneath a lace-work of branches, shuffling through the russet of fallen leaves, the first sign that autumn was on its way. 'Do you think it's here that Frossard arranged a tryst with Corinne?'

'It's possible. We heard her quarrel with Allegra around seven the night of the party but nobody appears to have seen her after that. And nobody seems to have worried that she was absent from the chateau.'

Flora chewed it over for a moment. 'Sunday could have been her day off, I suppose. And if not, Allegra either knew what had happened to her maid or she thought the girl had flounced off in a temper after their quarrel.'

'Let's assume then she was killed the night of the party but not found until yesterday evening. The stone pillar must have hidden her well – her body would have lain in deep shadow and it was only when someone walked their dog nearby that she was found. Frossard could have picked her up from Constantin at the bottom of the hill on Saturday night without anyone being the wiser – the party was in full swing but, in any case, he didn't need to drive up to the chateau. No one would know he'd been anywhere near the estate.'

'He picked her up, brought her here and strangled her. How horrible!'

He stopped walking, a frown on his face. 'When you think of it, it's a strange place to choose if your intention is murder. When the police make their enquiries, I'll be surprised if they don't find someone who saw something. It's dark by eight o'clock but a main road runs along the side of the park and it's well lit. You can see the stones from the road. You'd certainly see two people struggling.'

'Frossard might not have killed her there, just dragged the body to the stones as a way of covering his tracks. The post-mortem will probably be able to say, but maybe it's here, beneath these trees, that he killed her.' Her shoulders hunched at the thought, but she kept walking and Jack fell into step beside her.

They had reached the outer limit of the park and turned to walk back along the pathway when she asked, 'What's that?' Her eyes had narrowed and her expression grown intent.

'What?'

'That. Just ahead to one side of us. It looks like material, caught in one of the branches. I'm not tall enough...'

But he was. Reaching up, Jack disentangled the square of silk from a mass of branches and handed it to her. 'A scarf and it looks posh.'

'It is posh.' Her voice wavered slightly. 'It's not any old scarf, Jack.' Flora leaned back against a tree trunk, looking as though she'd had the breath punched out of her. 'It's an Hermès and I've seen it before. It belongs to your mother.'

'What the hell—'

'You're allowed to swear. It has to be the weirdest find.'

A mix of emotions coursed through him. Bewilderment. Disbelief. Fear. 'The scarf was used to strangle Corinne?'

'It looks that way. Has Sybil turned murderer, do you think?'

He couldn't raise even a glimmer of a smile.

'Corinne must have taken it.' Flora gave him a reassuring hug. 'Stolen it to wear for the evening, perhaps. She knew about the Hermès and knew your mother had left clothes at the chateau when she moved to the hotel. She could easily have slipped the scarf into her handbag. Or...' She paused. 'It could have been someone else who took it – stole it in the hope of implicating Sybil in the murder.'

Jack felt his head clear. 'That's ridiculous. Who is going to believe my mother is a killer?'

'Eventually nobody, but it gains the murderer time, doesn't it? It muddies the investigation. Encourages the police to follow a non-existent trail. And, of course, it hurts Sybil which is what this is all about. If suspicions are raised and it gets into the local paper, can you imagine what that will do to her and to any chance of her marrying the count? No smoke without fire. You know how it works. I certainly do. I had enough of it when Kevin Anderson ended up dead in my bookshop.'

Jack hesitated, but only for a moment, before he took the scarf back from Flora. 'I don't want to but I'll have to give it to the police,' he said miserably.

It would involve his mother in questioning that she didn't need, make her life awkward and uncomfortable, probably for weeks, but he had to do it. There was a possibility the police could find fingerprints. Silk, he knew, was a fabric with a high thread count and if any material was going to reveal who'd handled it, silk would be the one.

They walked back towards the park entrance and, stopping in front of the policeman who stood guard at the cordon, Jack offered him the scarf. The officer frowned but gestured to them to stay where they were and approached a man in plain clothes standing in the shadow of the largest damsel. The man in charge, Jack presumed.

The detective sauntered over to them. 'You found this?' he asked in English, fidgeting with a moustache that had colonised much of his face.

'In the trees over there. It was caught in the branches.'

The man nodded. 'Name, address, telephone number please.' He barked at his junior colleague to take down the information. Then, giving his moustache another tug, a sign of dismissal they assumed, he walked away. The formalities were over; they were allowed to leave.

'Well, that was exciting,' Flora remarked as they strolled back along the river bank to the parked Citroën.

'Exciting it may have been, but it's got us nowhere,' he muttered, disheartened by the turn of events. The police might have new evidence but their own investigation had moved not one step forward.

'I wouldn't say nowhere,' she objected. 'If the scarf provides the police with sufficient evidence to charge Frossard for Corinne's murder, they're likely to discover the rest of the story.'

'You honestly think the trail could lead all the way back to Ruby King?'

'Why not, if their investigation is thorough? Frossard could be charged with double murder. And thinking of Massimo's car and the flying rock at the Roman ruins, attempted murder. Your mother's. Does Frossard know that young boy, I wonder? I'm fairly certain that Corinne does – did,' she corrected herself quietly.

'I don't understand the man.' He thrust his hands deep in his pockets and gazed moodily at the pavement. 'I can see he might have killed Corinne if she threatened to talk, but why get involved in this dirty business in the first place? What was in it for him?'

'Money. It has to be. You said his garage looked run-down which suggests he needed cash and there's no other motive that I can see. Someone paid him to kill, Jack, the someone we've been after. The police will have to nail them, too.'

He suppressed a sigh. Flora was a good deal more sanguine than he. He could only hope the Avignon police – the detective must be from the city – were good at their job. His fingerprints were on that scarf, Flora's, too, and the police would soon come calling. It wouldn't only be his mother in an awkward situation.

27

That evening after dinner in the old town, Jack suggested they walk to the castle, its ruins clearly visible from the Beffroi. Clinging to a rocky promontory high above the town, the fortress meant a strenuous but exhilarating climb.

'It will blow the cobwebs away before we turn in for the night,' he said confidently.

A narrow pathway wound its way to the top, the entrance hidden behind tall hedges. Only a battered wooden sign marked *Le Château Comtal*, a few yards from the hotel, showed the way. Hand in hand, they began the climb.

'I thought I was taking a delightful evening stroll.' Jack's breath was coming unevenly, as they turned yet another corner on the zigzag pathway. 'How wrong can you be?'

'It *is* delightful. I can smell lavender in the air and the view when we get to the top will be spectacular. Notice that it's not me who's panting – I don't like to boast but... fitter?'

'Not fitter. Just ten years younger,' he retorted.

Flora tended to forget the years that stretched between them. Jack was such a comfortable companion, someone who shared her interests and her humour. And, ten years older or

not, he *was* very attractive, she thought, watching him now as he
strode ahead, trying to pretend he was breathing easily. His face
and neck had caught the sun and there was a tell-tale mark just
below his shirt collar. When he turned to smile, his changeable
grey eyes were almost silver in the evening light.

Flora reached out and grasped him round the waist.

'No dirty tricks! No trying to stop me beating you!'

She laughed, but fired by competition, put as much energy
into her legs as she could and spurted past. Surprised, he stood
still for a moment, then he was striding after her.

The tall hedges were soon left behind, the path turning
stony with a rocky escarpment on one side and a steep dip, filled
with cypress trees, on the other. The ramparts of the medieval
fortress had survived, but little else, and Flora felt the castle's
eyeless windows follow their progress as they struggled to the
top, arriving at the ruins barely able to speak.

'All I wanted was a cuddle,' she said, still laughing, though
she, too, was struggling to regain her breath.

'And a cuddle is what you shall have.'

His arms wrapped around her and stayed there for a long
while, until she broke free to walk through the first crumbling
archway. Entranced, she stood looking out at the spread of red
roofs and white walls below, houses and roads fading slowly
into the dusk as she watched. In the evening light, the river
flowed indigo, past banks of scrubby grass and through clusters
of bush and tree.

'The view is as splendid as I thought.' She turned to smile
back at him. 'And look! That's the path we took. Like a coiled
snake, only white. It was steep.'

Her glance drifted across the rocks that cascaded down-
wards on every side of the castle, some smooth and weathered,
others jagged, poking sharply through the trees that grew on the
lower slopes. In the far distance, the blue-green blur of the
Dentelles.

'I can just make out the Roman site we visited.' She pointed to what from this distance appeared a jumble of honey-coloured stone.

'I see it, too.' Jack had joined her. 'Though it's difficult to make out the main street. For some reason, the site across the road is clearer. The oval of the amphitheatre really stands out. It's a shame we never got there. It looks impressive. Perhaps we can squeeze in a visit before we leave – maybe get tickets for a performance.'

'I won't be here to see it, will I?' Flora tried to keep the tartness from her voice, but it was difficult. 'Inspector Ridley will ensure that. Probably at this very moment he's buying my ferry ticket.'

'Not at this very moment. Possibly at the Cross Keys eating one of their truly disgusting pork pies!' There was a pause before Jack said slowly, 'Of course, if Frossard's arrest comes off, it could change things.'

'In what way?' She perked up a little.

'With the mechanic behind bars, Provence will be a good deal safer, for one thing. Whoever's paying Frossard would need to find another pair of hands willing to get dirty, and that might not be easy.'

'So... I wouldn't have to leave?' She stood looking out at the darkening view. 'Or maybe we can leave together.'

'It would be good, but...' He found a seat on what remained of a dry-stone wall and pulled her down beside him.

'But?'

'If we're right, and I think we are, that someone has been paying our mechanic, that person will still be around after the man's arrest and, if they're determined enough, they'll still be planning on murder. Frossard might talk or he might not, and if he doesn't, it will take the police a long time to find the villain who's skulking in the shadows. If they ever do. Which means that my mother is still vulnerable. And so are you.'

'And you,' she pointed out.

'All three of us. If one of the Falconi family, or possibly Dufour, is who we're after, he or she is not going anywhere, though I suppose Frossard's arrest, if it happens, might scare them.'

'It would do more than scare. I reckon Frossard would talk. And if he did and pointed the finger at whoever's been pulling his strings...'

'That's an awful lot of ifs and we can't risk it, not until there's a clearer picture. Much as I want, I can't travel home with you. I'll have to stick around until the police get to the bottom of what's going on.'

'And while you're sticking around, what happens to the new book? Arthur won't be too happy, will he?' Arthur Bellaby was Jack's London agent.

'I'll square it with him, don't worry. Unlike you, I don't have a business to run. I can write pretty well anywhere if I have to and, luckily, I brought work with me – several chapters are more or less complete. I'm fairly sure I could hire a typewriter in Avignon.' He frowned. 'I'll have to wire Arthur for a loan, though. The hotel won't keep me for nothing.'

Flora wondered silently how thrilled Arthur would be to learn he was to fund one of his authors on what must seem an indefinite holiday. She kicked moodily at a stray pebble.

'You could be here for months, you know.' When he said nothing, she burst out, 'I don't want to be without you for months.'

He turned to her, a question in his eyes. 'That's quite an admission, Flora Steele.'

It was, she thought. She'd surprised herself. But surprising or not, it was how she felt. The idea of travelling home alone, of carrying on life in Abbeymead without Jack close by, a few snatched telephone calls their only communication, brought a painful lump to her throat. Not even returning to her beloved bookshop could make up for it.

In an attempt to shake herself free of thoughts she didn't want, Flora jumped to her feet and walked across to what was left of the outermost wall of the castle, in places barely a foot high.

'It's a precipitous drop.' She leant over, gazing down at the rocks below.

'Which is why you should step back right now.' He swooped on her from behind, dragging her away from the edge. 'Rather than dicing with death, can I tempt you?' he said into her ear. 'A nice red wine perhaps? Let's go back to the town, find a bar and drink to success, no matter how unlikely it seems.'

They'd drunk a very good red wine in a small bar they found at the far end of the *haute-ville* and stayed late talking into the night. Walking hand in hand back to the hotel, beneath a sky full of stars, the evening felt to Jack as though it signalled a new beginning for them both. He shouldn't count chickens, he knew, but Flora's unguarded remark, that glimpse into feelings she was so determined not to acknowledge, suggested their future together was more secure than it had ever been.

At breakfast the next morning, though, the talking had stopped, both of them cradling sore heads.

'We could walk to the amphitheatre after breakfast.' Flora's tone was hardly enthusiastic. 'Ask if there are any tickets for a performance tonight.'

'Good idea.' He tried to sound keen but failed. Offering her the basket of croissants that had arrived at their table, he tried again. 'Perhaps we should walk over later? I'd better stay around the hotel this morning. Ridley should be ringing with details of the ferry.'

He noted the clamped lips. Flora was still unhappy about

leaving and he wasn't jumping for joy either. The hotel was comfortable enough but it wasn't Overlay House. It wasn't his favourite writing room where he had everything to hand. And the thought of eating alone each night, of dealing every day with a recalcitrant mother as the police investigation ground on, wasn't exactly enthralling.

'Monsieur Carrington, your mother has called.'

As if in tune with his thoughts, the trainee receptionist was at their table handing him a note. What now? he thought wearily, feeling his mind tire and his body sag. Who had Sybil quarrelled with now? Or was she frantic because the police had called to question her? If she knew he'd handed them her scarf, he could be in for a drubbing.

'She telephoned?'

'No, no. She call here.'

'At the hotel?'

The girl beamed. 'But yes. I tell her you are at breakfast and she says not to disturb you.'

'Right, thank you.' He took the note and read the few scribbled lines.

'What does she say?' Having rejected the croissants, Flora fidgeted with a slice of toast, but couldn't bring herself to eat. 'I really must never drink that much wine again,' she said. 'Or drink that late.'

'Look at this. What do you make of it?'

Flora scanned the note he handed her. 'Massimo wants to sort things out. That's good, isn't it?'

'I suppose.' He felt a shadow of uneasiness that he couldn't explain.

'She's meeting him in the *haute-ville*, she says. At the castle. That must be why she called on us, we're on the way there. He wants to show her the view – I'm surprised she's never visited the fortress before. Then they're taking us to lunch. What a treat! A restaurant Massimo knows in Nyons. Well, that's a surprise – but in a good way.'

'A big surprise. Almost too quick... and the fortress?' The uneasiness was still there.

'Do you think they've been sobered by Corinne's death? Life is too short, that kind of thing, and they've decided to forget their quarrel and patch things up.'

'Perhaps,' he said uncertainly.

'But I agree, the fortress is a strange place for a meeting. It will be a tough walk for your mother.' She put down her coffee cup and looked across at him.

'And a precipitous drop when she gets there,' he said grimly. A sudden cold took hold of him. 'Those were your words, weren't they?'

Flora's mouth fell open. 'You don't think ... you do think! Jack, we have to get there!'

He jumped up, sending his chair crashing onto the paved terrace. Grabbing her by the hand, he rushed them through the hotel and out of the front entrance to the path they'd taken the night before.

How long had the note lain in reception? he wondered feverishly. How far ahead of them was his mother? He prayed he was wrong, he prayed this was a simple trip to sightsee and an opportunity for Massimo to make amends, but if it wasn't, if he wasn't wrong, would they get there in time?

28

Jack had sprinted ahead and was already on the path and disappearing around the first corner when Flora passed the signpost to the castle. There was no way she could match his speed, but it didn't stop her trying. The snaking path seemed endless as she pounded after him, her mouth dry and her heartbeat thrashing in her ears. A tragedy could be unfolding ahead and it heightened every one of her senses. The hedges seemed taller and more suffocating, the bird song louder, the rocky escarpment when she reached it raw and sharper, and the sky above a blue so intense that it filled her entire vision.

Somehow, she made it to the top, the shaking in her limbs forcing her to slump against the castle's ruined entrance for precious seconds before she could thrust herself through the archway into the open space beyond.

At the far edge of the courtyard, where the castle looked out onto open countryside, she was aware of movement, a confused mass that shifted this way and that. Running forward, Flora tried to make sense of what she was seeing. Her pulse was tumbling still and her head dizzy from lack of breath but slowly, as her eyes focussed, the mass separated into three separate figures. Three people. Fighting. Silently.

One was Jack. She would know his lanky form anywhere. He had his arms around a smaller shape – his mother, she realised – and seemed to be hauling her backwards. To safety? Silhouetted against him, a third figure, hooded and clothed in black, had Sybil's arm clenched tight and was wrenching her from Jack's hold, dragging the woman towards what was left of a broken arch framing the chasm below.

Flora was within feet of the battle before she could see properly. Then stopped mid-stride. The black hood had slipped and Sybil's assailant was revealed. Clio Falconi! Of course. It had to be. The Hermès scarf.

The girl seemed crazed, filled with a supernatural energy that resisted all Jack's efforts to wrest his mother free. Without pausing to consider, Flora rushed the last few feet and grabbed the girl's skirt. There was a loud renting of material, eerie in the unnatural silence and Clio, looking down, was momentarily distracted. In that second, Jack hauled his mother free of the girl's grasp and pushed her to one side. Baffled and angry, the girl swivelled round, her raised fists landing straight into Jack's face. He staggered back and Clio, seeing her chance, bounced forward, intent on making an end to her quarry.

Except that Flora had rejoined the fray. The girl's plait had escaped her hood and was now bunched beneath her neck. Flora reached up and yanked as hard as she was able. A loud yelp and Clio once more swivelled round, this time her fists missing their target – Flora was inches shorter – but allowing Jack to take hold of his mother's hand and hurry her towards the castle entrance.

It was as he turned back that he was confronted by a scene desperate enough to stop his heart. Flora and Clio stood facing each other, their figures stiff and unyielding, while the spill of rocks beyond waited patiently. For one girl or the other. Or both. But even as Jack rushed forward in a frenzied attempt to reach Flora, the black-clothed figure swivelled on her feet for the last time and, arms spread wide, dived into the abyss.

Two days later, Jack and Flora sat in a dingy office at Avignon's police headquarters. Their first impression of the building, as they'd walked from the main street, had been one of Second Empire elegance – fancy white stone and ironwork balconies – but inside disappointment awaited, the general shabbiness bringing them down to earth.

'I have good news for you,' the inspector began, waving them into a chair. He was the same detective they had spoken to in the park.

'Alain Frossard has confessed.' He gave a loving stroke to his moustache. 'So, my friends, you will not need to come to the court. You will sign the statements and then you return to England.'

'Confessed to what, exactly?' Jack asked.

He thought the inspector's statement too vague to accept without comment. Frossard could have confessed to trespass, theft, anything. With Clio Falconi dead, there might be nothing to tie the man to the murders.

'But naturally to the murder of Corinne Moreau,' the man said sharply. 'And,' he added, 'to the killing of Miss Ruby King.'

Jack sensed Flora's quick glance. It was what she'd foretold, that the Paris murder would surface once Frossard was arrested, but it had happened far more quickly than either of them had expected. It seemed the police had not needed to dig too deeply.

'Why did he confess so easily?' Flora wasn't interested in vague either. She would share his own suspicions of how such a confession had been obtained.

There was a shrug of the inspector's shoulders, a twist to his mouth and hands that chopped at the air. 'The man, he is in a bad state. He has killed the woman he loved. For him, his life is finished.' The inspector paused, relaxing his hands and fixing a benign smile to his face. A crime of passion evidently ranked high in his estimation. But it hadn't been passion, had it? It had been plotted in the most cold-blooded fashion.

'The scarf,' she asked. 'The scarf we gave you. Did that help?'

The smile grew more benign. '*Mais non, mamselle*. Not at all. The pathologist he confirms it was hands that strangled. Hands in gloves. The scarf – very beautiful – is returned to Madame Carrington.'

'The scarf was left to lay a false trail?' Flora wasn't giving up; Jack smiled to himself. She would keep pressing for details until the inspector lost patience and escorted them to the door.

'*Exactement*. Mamselle Clio gave it to him. This he must use, she said, but he could not bear such a violation.'

'So he killed her with his hands,' Flora said flatly. 'That wasn't a violation?'

'It is easier – to caress the face, the neck, to grasp stronger and stronger.'

Jack saw her give a visible shiver. He agreed with her. It seemed an extraordinary way in which to talk of what had been a brutal crime.

'Frossard says that he had no choice,' the inspector went on. 'Mamselle Falconi told him he must do this. He had killed Ruby King and no one must know.'

'He drove at Ruby King on Clio's orders, presumably?'

The detective nodded. 'At Miss King and your mama, Monsieur Carrington. Mamselle Clio knew that her sister, Allegra, had a friend in Paris. She took Ruby's name and address from her sister's room and offered the woman money to do as she wanted.'

'Money to make friends with my mother and steer her into the path of Frossard's car.' Jack's revulsion grew stronger. 'What was her motive? Evidently, she wanted my mother dead, but why, precisely?'

The inspector shook his head. 'We cannot say. Frossard was interested only in the money and the young lady is dead. Her papa's grief must be respected. He does not wish for more questions.'

Frossard's motive for *his* crimes was clear but for Clio Falconi's, there was to be no official enquiry. The police had been warned off by a powerful man.

'Did Allegra know what her sister planned?' he pursued, wondering how much they would learn from this man.

'She says not. We have spoken to Mamselle Allegra for several hours.' His lips arranged themselves into a small moue. 'It is possible she suspected her sister of bad things but she did not ask and her sister did not tell. Alain Frossard drove to Paris in his car. A large black saloon. We have examined it and there is blood.'

'Where did you find it?' Jack interrupted, wondering what he'd missed.

'The car? A garage in Vaison. A friend of Frossard's had given him a key.'

Flora pulled a face in sympathy, though she'd have been justified in bragging. She had always maintained that looking for the car was a wasted effort.

But everything fitted, he thought. There was the rendezvous with Ruby before the fatal night – the woman he'd spoken to outside Michon's apartment had been adamant it had been a Provençal number plate she'd seen. Ruby would have told Frossard about the event at the Lambert gallery: the evening it would take place, the time she would bring Sybil to the Rue de Rivoli, the place where she planned to cross the road. Nothing must be left to chance. Frossard must have driven around the area that night until he could arrive exactly where he should be at exactly the right time.

Still, it was a mad scheme, fraught with likely mistakes. As, in fact, it turned out. Frossard had got the right intersection, he was there at the right time, waiting for the lights to turn red, no doubt enduring angry honking from his fellow motorists, but then at the last minute he'd got it wrong. He would be unused to the chaos of Paris traffic, was maybe confused by the plethora of lights: street lights, traffic signals, brightly lit shops. And he'd hit the wrong woman.

'What was Clio's response when Frossard returned to Provence, having failed to kill Mrs Carrington? Did he say?' Flora asked directly.

'He told us that he drove all night to get home and next day he tried to speak to Mamselle Clio. He wanted his money. He is getting married. Was getting married, and his garage, it does not do well. He had promised Corinne a beautiful home, so where is the money? He was worried that she will say goodbye to him.'

'And Clio? Did she pay?'

'Every day Frossard waited for her at the entrance to Chateau Constantin. When at last he spoke with her, she told him that he had made a bad mistake. The police had telephoned her sister – they had found Mamselle Allegra's letters at Miss King's apartment – and he had killed the wrong woman. He had killed her sister's friend. She would not pay him the money and if he continued to pester, she would go to the police and tell them what she knew. But he could make things better if he did what she asked. He would be safe from the police then and still earn the money.'

'Why would she say that? Surely, she couldn't go to the police without implicating herself. It was an empty threat,' Flora objected.

'Mamselle is young and quite beautiful. She can say it was all a joke. That Frossard should not have taken her seriously. That the lady's death was not her responsibility.'

'A joke!' Jack exclaimed.

'This is what she can say and maybe it will be accepted. She will be punished a little for the pretence, but Frossard is the one who will lose his life. He dared not take the chance and he still wanted money. When Mamselle Clio rang him at his workplace, it was to tell him that the next day Madame Carrington would be driving to Vaison and it was his job to tamper with the brakes of Count Falconi's car that night. The man knows the car well and it would be easy for him. Also Corinne Moreau is his girlfriend and can give him the key to the chateau garage.'

'Corinne knew what he was doing?'

'No, no, no. He told her some tale that he had left a spanner in the car when it was in his garage. He needed the spanner for his work and must retrieve it. It was only when the count had his accident that she became suspicious. The damaged car was taken to Frossard's garage in Vaison – he is the Falconi's mechanic, after all – and he made safe the brakes that he had made unsafe before.'

I was right! Jack thought. He'd mended them already, when I paid him a visit. No wonder it was only a crumpled panel I saw.

'This time,' the inspector went on, 'Mamselle Clio paid. It was another mistake, although not Frossard's. But Corinne was not happy. She wondered what he had been doing in the chateau garage when she gave him the key. And there had been bad things, too, that happened in the house. It made her more suspicious.' His mother's stolen money, her pills deliberately mixed, Jack thought.

'Corinne was worried that her boyfriend had done something very wrong and told him that she could not marry him if had. He swore to her that this was not so, but soon she heard him on the telephone to Mamselle Clio and knew he had lied. There was another plan to get rid of Madame Carrington and Mamselle Clio wanted Frossard's help. It was then that

Corinne gave her boyfriend... hmm...' the inspector chewed over his words, '*un ultimatum.*'

Flora's eyes were saying clearly, I was right. The ultimatum must have occurred the day she had bumped into a tear-stained Corinne in Place Montfort.

The detective took a long sip from the glass of water on his desk, while neither of them had been offered any refreshment. They were evidently not expected to stay long.

'Frossard made a promise. The bad things were *fini*, but Corinne did not believe him. She said he must go to the police. Tell us he was made to do these bad things. So what is Frossard to do? He is *frénétique.*'

'Frantic?' Jack guessed.

'But, yes. He went to Clio to say they were in trouble, that his girlfriend was making him confess. She told him he must silence Corinne immediately, or they would both go to the guillotine. *Bof!* Now it is only Frossard who will go.' The policeman beamed.

Flora was looking fazed and Jack shared her confusion. Over the last half hour, there had been too much to take in and there were still questions that needed answers.

'After you arrested Frossard,' he said, 'Clio Falconi decided she would take over the role of murderer?'

The inspector nodded happily. 'We have found a note that was sent to Madame Carrington's hotel, asking her to meet Count Falconi at the castle.'

'She must have imitated her father's handwriting so well that my mother believed it had come from the count.'

The detective gave an expressive shrug as if to say people will believe anything if they have a mind to. In all probability that was the truth, Jack thought. His mother had been desperate for a reconciliation and, when the note arrived at her hotel, she grabbed it with both hands, convincing herself it was a true olive branch.

The policeman got to his feet. 'You are free to go,' he repeated with another beaming smile. 'You sign the statements please – they are in English – and then you go.'

But what about the theft of Sybil's money all those weeks ago? Jack wanted to say. Had Clio been the thief? Had she been the one to deliberately mix his mother's pills? And was there any connection between Clio and the maid? Why had Corinne quarrelled with Allegra on the night she died, rather than with Clio? And what possible significance did a chess magazine have? It was enough to make a mind explode.

'You are free to go,' the inspector repeated yet again.

It was clear they would learn nothing more from the Avignon police.

29

For the last few nights, Jack had hardly slept, waking hot and fearful every few hours as he battled to rescue first Flora and then his mother from a deadly fall. Helpless to intervene, he watched as in slow motion the cliff disappeared from beneath their feet and a stony forest of rock sprang up to consume them. Last night had been no different and this morning, stumbling from his bed, it was only when he'd thrown back his curtains that he could believe the nightmare was over.

Feeling every year of his age, he was on his way to the breakfast terrace when the receptionist called his name. 'The telephone for you, monsieur.' She waved the receiver in his direction and, reluctantly, he walked over to her desk. At this rate, Flora would be finished breakfast before he even started.

'It's been the devil's own job to get a ticket,' Alan Ridley said in greeting. 'No idea why September is so popular, but your... Miss Steele... is on the afternoon ferry the day after next. Do I get brownie points?'

Jack wasn't sure how to break the news to him. 'I'll make certain you get them, and thank you, Alan, for all your effort. The only problem...'

'Yes?'

'Things have changed since we spoke. I'm travelling back now with Flora. Look,' he said quickly, hearing an irritated grunt at the end of the phone, 'I'll find a travel agent once we reach Paris and sort things out from there.'

'That's all very well but what do I do with a spare ticket?'

'Treat yourself to a ride on the ferry? You could have a few days in Dieppe. It's a nice town.'

'It might be a nice town.' The inspector's tone was tart. 'But a few days away from this job? No chance. When will you be back anyway?'

'In a couple of days. Why? Do you have a job for us?'

Jack heard his voice sounding hopeful. With Clio Falconi unmasked and very dead, his business in France was finished. A few ends to tidy, his mother to placate if possible, and he and Flora could be on their way home to Sussex. And back to his study. He was uncomfortably conscious of having wasted several weeks already and knew that, once they were home, he should push on with the book. There was always a small part of him, though, that longed for adventure beyond the page.

'I can always do with help, old chap, you know that,' Ridley said, softening a little. 'I presume you've sorted out whatever trouble you ran into over there?'

'I have. Not in the best way, but it's done.'

'So, how about that pint you promised at the Cross Keys when you get back? I can ask the landlord to reserve one of his pies for you.' Ridley allowed himself a rare chuckle.

'Thanks, but if it's OK with you, I'll stick to the crisps. And yes, we'll do that pint for sure.'

Walking out onto the terrace, he found Flora was already on her second *pain au chocolat*.

'I don't know what it is,' she said with a bright smile, 'but this morning I am immensely hungry. Relief probably. That it's all over, bar the shouting.'

'Talking of the shouting.' He took the seat opposite and helped himself to an apricot. 'My mother sent a note round last night – after you'd gone to bed. Massimo has invited us to dinner this evening, to the meal we were promised but never materialised.'

'Really?' Flora looked surprised. 'I would think all he'd want to do was hide under the bed. Certainly not socialise.'

Jack frowned. 'Why hide, and why under the bed?'

'It seems the safest place.' She leaned forward, speaking quietly. This morning they were sharing the terrace with several other couples. 'Think what's happened to him, Jack, this last week. The woman he wants to marry is nearly killed, his ex-wife and favourite daughter are likely to have been conspirators, his youngest daughter is a murderer, or as good as, and just four days ago he was told of her suicide. How can he possibly want to invite us to eat with him?'

'He's trying to look on the bright side?'

'Jack! It's not funny.'

'Sorry, black humour. But there's some truth in what I say. Marriage with Mum is apparently on again and this evening's meal is a kind of celebration.'

'A very uncomfortable celebration.'

'No doubt, but we might get some answers to all those questions our French inspector brushed over. And it will be a good meal. The receptionist caught sight of the restaurant's name – it's the one in Nyons – and she was hugely enthusiastic. It's a popular bistro, she told me. So for all kinds of reasons, I think we should go.'

'We don't have a choice, do we? And maybe you're right about getting answers.'

'That's settled then. But that's this evening. How would you like to spend the rest of the day?'

'I'm not sure... First off, I need to telephone Alice. Let her know we're starting for home tomorrow. And then... I think I'd like to walk to Notre Dame de Nazareth.'

'To say goodbye?' he ventured.

'Something like that.'

'You'll want to go alone, I guess?'

She reached across the table and took his hand. 'Not this time. If you don't mind coming, I'd love you to be with me.'

Once Jack went back to his room to collect his wallet and a light jacket, Flora tucked herself away in the small cubicle that housed the hotel's public telephone and placed her call. She was unsure if Alice was working this weekend but had her fingers crossed that she'd find her friend at home. There was some difficulty initially in getting through but finally the operator managed to connect her.

'Alice? How are you?'

'I'm OK, my love. Better for gettin' this call. It's the arthritis playin' up a bit, you know. It's been that wet here lately, but so good to hear your voice. So are you comin' home?'

'I've good news! We leave tomorrow. We'll be staying the night in Paris. Jack has to return the hire car before we take the train to Dieppe, but we should be in time to catch the afternoon ferry on Monday – as long as we can buy tickets. If we are delayed, I'll try to telephone.'

'It will be good to see you, lass. Abbeymead isn't the same without you. Every time I walk past the All's Well, all closed up, it makes me feel that sad.'

'I can't wait to walk through its door and breathe books again. Has Charlie carried on with deliveries, do you know?'

'Course he has. That boy never stops eatin' but he knows how to work. He's lookin' forward to havin' you back, though. Which reminds me. There's been a man here asking about the bookshop. A right pest, he was. Charlie put him on to me. I said

I'd talk to you, but really it's not somethin' you can say yes or no to over the telephone. I reckon what he's suggestin' will need a lot of organisin' and you might not want to be bothered. Nor Jack, for that matter.'

'What man? What organising? And why Jack?'

'He's from some book society or t'other. Wants to run a kind of writers' conference and wants you to help him. I told him it was Jack he needed to talk to. He's a writer, I said. Flora just sells the books. And he said Jack who and when I told him Jack Carrington, he got very excited. Knows Jack's books, apparently. Anyways, you'll both have to talk to him when you get back.'

'Yes.' Flora sounded uncertain, and was. An excitable man wasn't that appealing – she'd had more than enough excitement for now.

'So how's Jack's ma? If you're comin' back, I imagine everythin' must be OK.'

Death and mayhem was not something Alice needed to hear and Flora passed swiftly over the events of the last few days. 'Things have settled down,' she said, in a cheerful voice. 'Sybil is feeling a great deal safer and even planning to marry again, I think.'

'Really? What's she want to do that for?'

Flora ignored the question, her feelings about marriage more confused than they'd ever been. A month ago, she would have agreed with Alice wholeheartedly, but now...

'We'll know for sure what's happening this evening. We're going to dinner with the count and Sybil and if they intend to make an announcement, that will be the time.'

'And the other business? Your business?' Alice asked delicately.

'Richard Frant was right. My parents are here in Vaison,' she said. 'But that's OK, too.'

She heard her friend give a long sigh of relief and wanted to hug her for her concern. How she'd missed Alice! Missed the whole of Abbeymead. It had been wet in Sussex, Alice said, but somehow that was exactly the weather Flora longed for. To feel again her cheeks damp with rain and the wind skimming the Downs as it buffeted her face. To see a sky of chasing clouds and the gold of autumn all around her. Home.

'Alice, I can't wait to get back,' she said in a burst of feeling. 'I'll see you very soon, I promise!'

30

The bistro in Nyons was buzzing when they arrived that evening, its red-painted doors flung wide to reveal a crowded interior. Black-aproned servers flew from kitchen to restaurant and back again, while bursts of chatter escaped through the open doors, bringing a jollity to the occasion that Flora hadn't expected. A row of small tables lined the open-air terrace, their red gingham cloths offering a cheerful welcome. It was still warm enough to eat outside and Massimo had arranged a table set for four at the far end. Far enough away to save them from eavesdroppers, Flora presumed.

'I must thank you for coming,' Massimo greeted them as they took their seats, 'and apologise for all the bad things that have happened... and for my own... distraction.'

Jack murmured a disclaimer, but the conversation that followed felt decidedly sticky. But then how could it not after the horror of recent events? Mundane observations on the restaurant, the weather, the details of their journey tomorrow, filled the vacuum, and it wasn't until their main course had been served that the count lifted his glass and, smiling around the table, proposed a toast.

'To Sybil,' he said, 'who has promised to be my wife.'

There it was at last. The proposal that had been so long delayed. Jack's mother was smiling, too. A smile that Flora hadn't seen before, its warmth matched by the rose-pink silk Sybil wore, gleaming expensively in the candlelight.

'And I've accepted,' she added, though it was hardly necessary.

Flora hoped Jack would be pleased, or at least reconciled to his mother's marriage. They might have a strained relationship, but he had been apprehensive at the thought of Sybil joining the Falconi family. A fear that had been fulfilled, to put it mildly. But, tonight, his was another smiling face and, whatever his private thoughts, he was hiding them well.

'You will notice,' Massimo said, toying with his filet mignon, 'that I did not invite Allegra this evening.'

I should hope not, Flora thought indignantly. Nor Isabella. She was certain that both women had plotted against Sybil and judged them almost as guilty as Clio.

'Allegra has gone with her mother to Italy,' the count continued heavily. 'Isabella has a house in the Veneto and they will live there together.'

They had been banished. Was that because Massimo suspected their complicity – had, perhaps, definite evidence?

'Is there a reason for their move to Italy?' she ventured.

The count's sadness was in his eyes. 'I have found out much these last few days that has not made me happy. Isabella – I would have expected – but Allegra.' He shook his head. 'She has been a wonderful daughter. I could not have wished for better, but there are things I cannot forgive. I cannot look at her and feel happy so it is best she stays in Italy.'

'What things would they be?'

The second question veered on rudeness, Flora recognised, and she knew that Jack would be wincing, but tonight was likely to be her sole chance of finding the answers she wanted. How could she leave Provence without knowing what role Allegra had played in the tragedy? What stance Isabella had taken? And, surely, it was better that everyone knew the truth. They had all been affected, every person sitting around the table this evening – all changed by the events of these last few weeks.

'Allegra,' the count began with evident difficulty, 'Allegra was not happy when I met Sybil.'

'An understatement,' his beloved snorted, returning for a moment to the Sybil Flora had grown to know.

'She was not happy, as I say, and she was guilty of bad things. She did not realise what her sister was doing – she has sworn to me that it was so – and I must believe her. But...' He paused. 'I feel that in herself she must have known, but never spoke.'

'And that's all?' Surprisingly, it was Jack who asked. 'Silence was Allegra's only crime?'

'No, it was not all. She took her own bad actions to make Sybil leave.'

'She stole my money.' Sybil's mouth set in a hard, thin line. It was plain the transgression angered her still.

'Yes, indeed.' Massimo nodded sadly. 'Allegra has confessed to this and she has repaid the money in full. But there was more, I am afraid – she has told me all – and it is painful. She took Sybil's pills, mixed them with others she found. Pills that have no effect, or maybe worse. A most dangerous thing to do.' The count gave up trying to eat his steak and pushed it to one side. 'Even the scorpion in Jack's room, she has confessed this to me. She wanted him away. For Sybil to be alone. To be weak.' He shook his head. 'Allegra has told me all.'

It was as though by repeating the phrase, he could blot out the sins of his favourite daughter. He hadn't mentioned Pascal Dufour, Flora noticed. The man had almost slipped from sight, except she was determined that he wouldn't. Dufour had been there when the wine rack had tumbled and the glass of shattered bottles cut into her. He had been only yards away – they had smelt his tobacco – when the red-haired boy had sent the block of stone flying in Sybil's direction. If Allegra had told all, had she spoken of him?

'Did your daughter involve Pascal Dufour in her plans?' Flora wondered aloud. 'She quarrelled with him on the night of the feast. We heard them and thought they might have been plotting together.'

'Monsieur Dufour has left us,' the count said impassively. 'He goes as manager to a vineyard in Bordeaux. This is best, I think. But I do not believe he is a guilty man except...'

'Except?' Jack leaned forward.

'His nephew. Clio had dealings with his young nephew. I do not know the true story. Dufour did not want to tell me but he said enough. He was angry that his young relative had been involved.'

The red-haired child. He had been a relation then, just as Flora had guessed. 'The boy was bribed,' she put in, 'to do something very bad. Bribed, I think, with a chess set.'

Massimo looked surprised. 'I do not know,' he repeated. 'Monsieur Dufour did not say, but Allegra, she hoped... But it was not to be. Maybe Dufour made her promises and then nothing. You are right, Mamselle Flora. There was a big quarrel between them on the night of the feast. Allegra told me of it. I did not ask her for details. Her heart was too full and she had much to think about, but I believe that whatever promise Dufour had made was ended.'

That was one quarrel, it seemed, that hadn't been about getting rid of Sybil. It had been personal, Dufour's unquestionable rejection of a woman who'd made her desires all too plain: Allegra's eyes resting constantly on him during that first dinner they'd eaten at the chateau, following him around Vaison until told angrily to stop, her attempt to corner him the evening of the grape celebration – infatuation with a man who had decided his best interests lay elsewhere.

'Did Monsieur Dufour ever mention the accident I suffered in the wine cellar?'

'He told me of it at the time. He was troubled, I could see. Before Allegra left, she told me he knew of the money and the pills. I think now that maybe he worried Allegra had done this, too.'

'But she hadn't?'

Massimo gave a sigh, laden with the sorrow he seemed unable to express. 'I believe, Mamselle Flora, that you were attacked by my younger daughter.' The count was finding it impossible to mention Clio by name. 'She pretended that she had been called to Avignon but there was no second interview. Instead, she stayed at home, waiting for the moment she could cause harm. That incident we cannot lay at Allegra's door.'

'We should lay everything else.' Sybil's voice was harsh. 'Allegra has hurt me and she needs to be punished. Isabella, as well. She hates me, and I am certain, too, that she played a role in this vile plot.'

Massimo looked distraught and, for a moment, Flora felt real sympathy. But there was one thought she could not lose – that it was the count who was behind this mayhem, wittingly or not. It was his favour they had all been fighting to win.

'Isabella knew what Allegra had done,' their host admitted, 'but she did nothing herself.'

'Except harass us constantly.'

'Yes, Sybil, that is true. And true that she encouraged her daughters into wickedness. But she is in Italy now and will bother us no more.' Relief had crept into his voice. 'I will die without seeing either of them again. Allegra will have her share of the money, I cannot prevent this, but no more than the law says. She has lost my good opinion for ever. And Isabella will have nothing. Except to know for the rest of her life that she has caused her young daughter to choose a dreadful death. And to die a criminal.'

'Clio was your daughter, too,' Flora reminded him, earning herself a frown from Jack. His brow was knitted into deep creases. There was something fundamental bothering him, she realised, and it wasn't just her candour.

'Massimo,' he said, 'all the women in your family – Isabella and both her daughters – were hostile to the idea of your marrying again. Allegra harassed my mother, Isabella no doubt encouraged her, but why was it Clio who took such drastic action?'

The relief had gone. Instead, there was anguish in the count's voice. 'I do not know if I can talk about it.'

Sybil reached out and took his hand. 'You should, my dear. You cannot blame yourself for ever.'

'But I must. It is not only Isabella who made mistakes. I, too, am the cause of this terrible trouble. I did not mean... but... I have broken my family, destroyed my children.'

Flora was startled, hearing what had only been a suspicion put into words.

'How could it be your fault?' Jack asked.

Massimo took a long time to answer, seeming to tussle with himself. 'Clio is not my child,' he said at last.

She looked across at Jack and he looked back at her, the same thought flashing bright between them. It was as they'd first suspected. Inheritance had been the trigger for this circus of violence.

'This I discovered only a few years ago,' the count continued.

'It was why Massimo felt he had to divorce,' Sybil put in.

The count nodded. 'After I discovered this awful truth, I could not bear to be with Isabella. The affair she had... I cannot talk of it ... it hurts me too much. To know that after all these years Clio is *illegittima*.'

'And, as an illegitimate child, she would inherit nothing?' Jack pushed home the point.

'Nothing,' the count echoed. 'My heart is not good and I think I will not live to be old. If I marry again, my new wife will inherit much of my estate.'

'But Allegra, you say, is guaranteed a share.'

'*Naturalmente*, but there would be little for anyone else.'

'But...' Flora was flailing, trying to understand why Clio would think getting rid of Sybil would help. 'Even if you didn't remarry, knowing what you did – that Isabella had cheated and Clio was not your daughter – surely, you would not have named them in your will?'

'No. I would not, but if I married Isabella again, then I am bound by law.'

'Marry Isabella again?' She was incredulous.

'That was the plan,' Sybil put in. 'I was to be got rid of and Isabella would provide the tea and sympathy and hope to come away with a brand new wedding ring.'

The count passed a hand across his forehead. Confession was taking its toll. 'This is true,' he agreed. 'Isabella has sworn to me that though she knew what Allegra had done, she had no part in Clio's dreadful plans. She did not know of Frossard and his crimes, and I believe her. But she is not innocent. She was angry and talked much to Clio in a way that inflamed. Told her daughter how poor they would be unless she could persuade me to marry her again. I would forgive her infidelity and, in time, make Clio my child.'

'The affair must have occurred many years ago.' More than twenty years, Flora calculated, thinking of Clio's age. 'Yet, you never knew. How—'

'Was I in ignorance for so long?' He fumbled with his napkin, pleating and unpleating it for several moments. 'How did I discover this? A letter. It arrived one day from this, this *gigolo*. He was very ill and wanted his daughter – his daughter! – to know him before he died. When I asked Isabella why she had a letter from Pisa, she was nervous. She pretended it was from a relative, but I knew that was a lie and I found her out. This was how I discovered the truth.'

Flora was bemused. 'It's an utterly crazy plot. I can't believe they thought it would work.'

'Not only crazy, but wicked,' Massimo said. 'And I am as wicked. Until this letter, I believed Clio was my child and I treated her so. But after, I never spoke of it to her, never asked her how she felt. And I told no one what I had learned. All these bad feelings I kept to myself. Instead, I was unkind. If I had continued to treat Clio as my child, she would be alive now.'

'You couldn't know,' Jack said. 'You couldn't know how she would respond. What terrible things she would do.'

'I should have known. I was a husband to Isabella for many years. *She* has always been a little... mad? And Clio is her true daughter. But now, we must drink again.'

He fixed a smile to his face and raised his glass once more. 'To Flora and to Jack,' he said in a voice that cracked at the edges, 'who saved the woman I love.'

He gestured to a passing waiter. 'More champagne, I think?'

Jack said goodbye to his mother before they left Nyons, walking with her through the cobbled streets to their parked cars. He planned to leave early the next morning – Flora had thought it a sensible idea – forgetting breakfast and hoping they could make Paris by teatime. If the journey went smoothly, he'd return the Citroën to the car hire that evening.

'Massimo has thanked you for what you did. I should, too,'

his mother said gruffly, as they approached the line of parked cars. 'You *and* the girl.'

The way she referred to Flora was enough to push Jack into fighting mode, but he conquered the urge, bit his lip and said merely, 'I'm glad it's worked out.'

'Let's hope.' To Jack's ears, she didn't sound that certain. 'Massimo is deeply upset. He covers it up, but it's going to take time for this ghastly business to stop hurting. If ever. He's had Clio's body flown to Venice, you know, so that her mother and sister can bury her. It will be up to them how they do it. She's a suicide and it won't be easy.'

'They can perjure themselves, I guess. Tell the Church it was an accident. I imagine that's what the death certificate says.'

'Massimo has made sure of it. The police know nothing of what really happened at the castle and, if he has anything to do with it, they never will. They'll continue with their case against Frossard, of course, and they're bound to get a conviction.'

'But Clio will feature in the evidence,' he pointed out.

'She'll be mentioned in the trial, there's no chance of preventing it, but Massimo is hoping it will be brief. As far as possible, he wants to keep her name out of the newspapers.'

'How is that going to work? She was the one who paid Frossard to murder Ruby King and attempt to murder you. Then pushed him into murdering Corinne.'

'The count is instructing a barrister who will argue that Clio was too young and too silly to know she was playing with fire.'

Jack blinked at the idea but, since the inspector had suggested much the same approach, he supposed that Massimo might be successful in shielding his daughter, her true evil never exposed. Instead, she would be seen as a neurotic young woman, playing out her fantasies, with accidental death as an inevitable finale.

'And Allegra?' he asked.

'I'm the only one who can file a charge against her and I won't be doing so. There's some talk of her entering a nunnery. The best place for her, if you ask me.'

Remembering the crucifix around Allegra's neck, the Bible she carried in her handbag and her evident devotion in church, Jack was inclined to think much the same.

'Enough of the Falconi women.' Beneath the lamplight, he saw his mother's expression. Challenging, he thought. 'What about you? What are you going to do?'

'Write the next book, what else? It's what keeps a roof over my head.'

'I don't mean work. I mean the girl.'

'The girl has a name – Flora.'

Sybil gave a loud tut. 'What are you going to do about Flora?'

'Take her home and keep her safe, I hope.'

She looked back along the road. Flora, walking side by side with Massimo, was now a short distance away. 'Marry her,' she said. 'You need a wife and she'll suit you.'

'We'll decide together what's best and when,' he said repressively. He could do without his mother turning agony aunt.

Sybil gave a characteristic snort. 'You'll be fidgeting around until you're eighty. Get on with it.'

His mother was as bad a matchmaker as Alice. Both of them urging him to marry as though it was as easy as simply asking Flora.

'Let me know what happens, if anything does,' she went on. 'I'll be here at the chateau for some while. I can't see Massimo wanting to return to Italy any time soon.'

'And your wedding?'

'It's bound to be a quiet affair and I don't expect you to come.' She gave an unfamiliar grin. 'I might ask your father, though!'

He held up his hand as though to ward off another parental

row, but Sybil took a step forward and, before he realised, had wrapped her arms around him and hugged him tightly. The first hug he could remember since he'd been a small boy.

'Take care on your journey, Jack. And thank you – thank you for coming.'

31

They were on the road out of Vaison by six the next morning and, though Flora's stomach twinged with hunger, she was glad they'd forgone breakfast and made an early start. Her mind now was bent on getting home. She had enjoyed her first taste of 'abroad' – she liked what she'd seen of France, enough to want to explore further – but wished they could have properly enjoyed the trip. Revelled in a peaceful holiday rather than tussling with danger for much of the time. Some peace *had* emerged, it was true, the peace she'd made with her own history, and that was surely a huge win.

They stopped only twice for a break, around ten o'clock for coffee and brioche, and a longer stop at lunchtime in Burgundy to eat a light meal of fish and salad.

'The fish was very good,' Jack said, sliding back into the car, 'but I'll be starving by tonight. Let's hope we get to the big city in time for dinner!'

Flora said nothing, not overly worried what they ate, but three hours later as they were driving through the outer suburbs of Paris, an idea popped into her head.

'Do you know what I'd like to do this evening? Forget the

fancy restaurant and take a walk by the river. We could buy hot dogs from one of the riverside stalls and find somewhere to sit and eat.'

'I am *not* eating a hot dog in France!'

'OK, a croque monsieur then. I'll have the hot dog.'

It turned out to be neither when, after returning the Citroën to its garage, they dropped their cases at the Hôtel Regina and finally made it to the river.

To Flora, it felt as though she'd walked into a fairy tale. Light and dark. Sparkle and shadow. Behind her, a line of buildings, illuminated from top to bottom, splashed brilliance across the dark waters, while every arch of every bridge glowed with brightness, their reflection producing a line of shimmering doubles.

'It was such a good idea to come,' she said, bedazzled by this enchanted world.

'It was,' Jack agreed, 'and these were delicious.' Licking his fingers, he finished the last of the savoury galettes they'd bought at a nearby stall. 'But it was bound to be a good idea. It was yours!'

She turned away from the magic that had held her fast to prod him in the chest. 'Am I that insufferable? And don't say yes!'

'Only occasionally. Most times, I can put up with you! But I agree, it's a good end to a gruelling day. How are you feeling – exhausted?'

'I'm tired but don't let's go back just yet. Let's walk some more.'

Jumping up from the bench, she held out her hand and, arms linked, they strolled further along the river walk.

'It's no wonder we're tired,' he said, as they sauntered past a second brilliantly lit bridge. 'It's been something of a whirlwind, hasn't it? Usually, an investigation takes us weeks, even months, to find our killer, but this time we'd barely caught our breath before the answers tumbled out.' He pulled a face. 'Though we never discovered why Dufour was in his shirtsleeves that evening.'

She laughed. 'We didn't, but in the end, it didn't matter. It has to have been Clio who followed me to the lake and tried to drown me. Massimo never mentioned it – that was a bit odd.'

'I doubt Sybil ever told him. She would have been too busy berating him for her disappointment that night.' Jack came to a standstill and looked down at her. 'So much has happened so quickly that I guess it will take time to work out how we all feel.'

She looked up at him. 'Are you thinking of your mother?'

'A little. She's still the same difficult woman she's always been, but it's strange... I've found myself feeling a sympathy I didn't have before.'

'Yes,' Flora said thoughtfully, 'you're right. This trip has changed things.'

Watching the river traffic as it came and went – the waterway was busy tonight – they walked on. It seemed as though most of Paris had taken to the river. Brightly lit boats plied their trade, their customers eating supper or listening to music. Some even dancing on deck.

'Doesn't it look wonderful? I wish we had time...' She sounded wistful and Jack bent to land a kiss on the top of her head.

'We can come back. Take a trip along the Seine. We *will* come back – only next time, we'll make it a real holiday. Although ... perhaps we should go further afield. Where was second on your list? Rome, wasn't it?'

'It was, but it will be a fair time before I can leave the bookshop again. And maybe we shouldn't think so far ahead.'

'Why not? It's good to plan. We've years to look forward to, and one day...'

'One day?' she asked, feeling stupidly shy.

'It's nothing. Just a thought. Forget it.'

She came to a halt beneath one of the ironwork street lamps that lined the river walk – an old witness, no doubt, to many a similar conversation – and made a decision. 'It's not nothing, is it? Tell me, Jack. Ask me. I've been stubborn, I know, but now I... I feel differently.'

A variety of expressions chased a path across his face. Surprise, hope, joy, doubt. 'Since you found your parents?' he suggested gently.

Flora nodded. 'It's changed me. Changed my thinking. Actually, changed my life. That sounds dramatic, but it's true. There are still things I don't know. Like why Violet never talked to me even after I'd grown up. Like what happened to our home after my parents died. Was it sold and, if so, who benefited? Aunt Violet was silent about that, too. But I have the most important truth now. I know what happened to them, what they shared... and it's made me think and... and I do love you, Jack.'

He ran his finger down her cheek, following the line of her face. Then bent his head and kissed her for a very long time.

'This trip has been just one big surprise,' he said, finally letting her go.

'And?' She looked at him expectantly.

'My mother seemed to think this should be easy – so, will you marry me?'

'She was right.' Flora took his hand and kissed it. 'It is easy and yes, I will.'

Jack's smile brought his face alive. Scooping her up, he lifted her off her feet and danced them both several yards along the pavement, passers-by giving them a wide berth.

'Abbeymead is in for a surprise, too,' he said, as hand in hand, they walked back to their hotel. 'Wait till we tell Alice – she'll be dancing as well.'

Flora laughed. 'If you want to surprise her, you'll have to stop smiling or she'll know immediately.'

'How can I stop? I'm marrying the woman I love. At last!'

32

Jack woke early the next morning, wondering if last night had actually happened. He couldn't quite believe he was getting married. He'd known Flora no more than two years, but for much of that time, making a future with her had been something he'd wanted – consciously or unconsciously. Now it was going to happen. Unless Flora had thought better of it once she was alone, and the lights were no longer twinkling over the Seine.

But when he met her for a hasty breakfast, she greeted him with a happy smile and a kiss.

'Ready for Dieppe?' he asked, tucking one of her waves, this morning more unruly than ever, behind her ear.

'I think so.' She gave a small sigh. 'But the sea... not so much.'

'Thank goodness it's calm today,' she was saying some hours later. They had walked to the stern of the ship and Flora stood beside him, watching the furrow of white surf stretch behind them in the distance. 'I was dreading a repeat of the ferry out.'

'The journey's been worth it, though?'

She circled his waist with her arm and gave him a squeeze. 'It couldn't have been more.'

'What's the betting we'll be met with a reception committee when we get to Abbeymead?'

'Tea and cakes at the Nook?'

'I'm thinking almost certainly.'

And when, some five hours later on the last day of September, his Austin pulled into the kerb outside the All's Well, Alice was waiting, her plump figure poised for a welcome.

'I knew you'd come here first,' she said triumphantly. 'I said to Katie, mark my words, Flora will want to go to that blessed bookshop before she goes home.'

'And you were right. How are you, Alice? It's so lovely to see you.'

Flora had jumped out of the car and was muffling her friend in a warm embrace. She was overjoyed to be home. The trees that lined the high street, she saw, were already ablaze with colour and the cool freshness of an English autumn was on her face. Coming out of his shop door opposite, Mr Houseman, the greengrocer, waved a welcome.

Watching from the driver's seat, Jack nodded to himself. It was clear that he'd never persuade Flora to leave Abbeymead – the village was too tightly entwined in her being. But he was philosophical. There were worst places he could end his days and, clambering from the car, he went to say hello.

'My, you're looking proper spruce.' Alice had advanced on him, standing on tiptoes to kiss his cheek. 'But it's good to have you back, the pair of you. The village hasn't been the same. Charlie, poor lad, has been fair pinin'!'

'That I'd like to see.' Jack's smile was wry. 'Unless he's run out of money.'

'Not yet, he hasn't. But he's waitin' to see you at the Nook.

We all are. Kate and Tony and Sally, too. Come down from the Priory especially, she has.'

'Tea and cakes?' Flora said.

Alice looked surprised that she'd posed the question. 'What else?' Then she noticed their grins. 'Oh! Stop your mockin' – and forget that shop.' Flora had cupped her hands and was peering through the All's Well's window. 'It will still be here tomorrow, but the pot will be cold if we don't get a move on.'

Flora gave a surreptitious stroke to the weathered brick and flint walls, a part of her desperate to walk through the door, to wander the bookshop shelves, run her fingers down spines and simply breathe in the sweet, musky smell. It was a reluctant girl who turned to walk with her companions to the café but, once through the door of Katie's Nook, now closed for the day, she changed her mind.

A loud chorus of hellos greeted them, followed by energetic hugs and cheek-kissing galore. Several tables had been pushed together and an array of sweet treats sat waiting: cakes, tarts, buns and biscuits.

'You're never expecting us to eat all this?' she asked laughingly.

'*I* can help you, Miss Steele.'

A boy's figure, his legs now just a little too long for his body, emerged from behind the counter.

'Hello, Charlie. From what Mrs Jenner tells me, you deserve to eat it all. Keeping my deliveries going – and with no complaints, apparently.'

'Yeah, I did well. And looked after your garden, too, Mr C. Mowed the lawn and weeded the front.'

'Then you're doubly deserving.' He gave the boy a playful punch on the shoulder.

'Come on, sit yourselves down. Katie, love, bring the teapot over, and Tony, you get the cups and saucers.' Their friend was in full Alice mode and, obediently, they took a seat.

'What was France like, Flora?' Kate asked in her gentle way, as she poured lemonade for Charlie and tea for everyone else.

'It was... interesting.' Unsure how much to confide, she took on board Jack's warning look. It was better to keep silent on the details, but she needed to say something. 'Paris was a beautiful city,' she murmured, 'and Provence – beautiful, too, and very hot.'

'We could have done with some of that sun over here,' Tony said. 'The rain's not stopped since you left. It's kept the customers away.'

'Are you definitely working at the Nook now?'

Alice had complained so loudly at losing her number one assistant, it made Flora doubt whether Tony would ever break free of the Priory.

'He's here with me,' Kate confirmed. 'And it's working well, isn't it?' She smiled across the table at her nearly new husband.

'It is,' Tony said contentedly. 'We make a good team, and Alice has a new sous-chef to keep her company.'

Which means we won't have to suffer too many remonstrations, Flora thought, while aloud she asked, 'Who's that then?'

'A chap I heard about from Maud Frobisher,' Alice answered. 'Here, tuck in. I don't want to take this lot home. You know Maud, don't you, Flora?'

She did. Very well. Maud had been a good friend of Aunt Violet's, the best of friends, sharing a passion for books and a delight in auctions. Baking, too – Maud's Victoria sponge could rival Alice's. But Flora was puzzled. Maud ran the mobile library service in this part of Sussex, so what had she to do with staffing a hotel kitchen?

'She's planning on retiring very soon,' Alice said comfortably. 'A couple of years early, but she'll have done enough to get her gold watch! Anyways, this young man is one that Maud knows from the council. Been workin' in the kitchen at County Hall for five years, and really fed up with it. Well, you would be. Who'd want to work for the council?' For local people, the source of all things troublesome.

'Maud Frobisher for one,' Jack pointed out, unable to prevent a smile.

'That's different.' Alice handed round the plate of lemon fondant fancies. 'Maud's out and about meetin' people all day, not stuck in a gloomy buildin' with all them pen-pushers. When she comes to Abbeymead, she's parked on the village green for no more'n half an hour before she's off again.'

Maud Frobisher's route, Flora knew, was a long and winding one, Abbeymead just one stop in a schedule that had her calling at every neighbouring village.

'His name is Hector,' Sally put in unexpectedly. 'Hector Lansdale. When auntie told me about him, I thought he'd arrive for interview in full armour! Wasn't Hector a Greek fighter?'

'He was,' Jack answered. 'A prince and Troy's greatest warrior in the Trojan war.'

'Quite the hero, then. And he is – to Auntie at least!'

'The lad's doin' well,' Alice said grudgingly. 'And I do need help. The hotel's that busy these days, despite the rain. We've been nearly full this month and it's well-nigh impossible to cope on my own.'

Flora watched as the pink of annoyance crept up Tony's cheeks. His departure from the Priory kitchen evidently still rankled with Alice and she wondered what words had been exchanged between them.

'That's splendid news of the hotel, Sally,' she said, filling the silence that had fallen. 'Your hard work is beginning to pay off.'

Sally stuck her thumbs in the air. 'I won't tempt fate, but yes, it's looking good.'

'Talkin' of the hotel bein' busy, before I forget...' Alice poked around in the enormous handbag that was never far away. 'This is the chap who wants to speak to you, Jack. The chap I mentioned on the phone to Flora.'

'What chap?' He looked questioningly at Flora.

'Sorry, it slipped my mind. A man who wants to run some kind of writing conference.'

Jack took the sheet of paper and fished in his pocket for glasses. 'Basil Webb,' he read. 'President of the Dirk and Dagger Society.'

'Have you heard of it?' The name was new to Flora but then she didn't write books and tended to know only those authors who came the bookshop's way.

'Vaguely. Terrible title, but the society's pretty big, I think. It seems that Mr Webb wants to run a crime writers' conference deep in the Sussex countryside and thinks Abbeymead would be a good base.'

'I dunno why.' Alice was dismissive. 'Why not in a town? And why Sussex?'

'If they came, they could stay at the Priory,' Sally said eagerly. 'As long as we know in advance, we can manage a large group.'

'And it would be good for the All's Well,' Kate put in. 'All those book lovers ready to spend!'

'You could hold readings at the bookshop,' Tony offered.

'Hey, not so fast. Don't let's get carried away.' Jack was luke-warm. 'I don't know this chap. I don't know much about the society either. It could be a whim he's dreamt up with nothing solid behind it. I suppose I'd better phone him, though, if only to say I'm not interested.'

Flora helped herself to a slice of Alice's Victoria sponge, her finger scooping up an errant drop of buttercream, and wondered whether eventually Jack would be able to ignore the challenge. He'd found his passion in crime writing and any opportunity to meet and talk books would be difficult for him to resist.

'Maybe just forget it,' Alice said. 'He probably won't come back and you should take it easy after your ma and everythin'.

You, too, Flora. But how are you, lass? You said everything was OK, that you managed—'

'To find my parents? Yes, I did, and learned something of what happened to them all those years ago. But it's too sad to talk about right now. Today is a celebration.'

'Then we'll celebrate Jack sorting out his ma instead. Must be why he's lookin' so jaunty.' Alice stared across at him, studying him closely, while Jack strove to keep his expression blank. She was unlikely to be fooled for long.

'I hope the two of you had somethin' of a holiday, in between all the sortin'.' Alice had her gaze still trained on Jack's face and, as always, it was his eyes that gave him away, their grey changing shade as Flora watched, warming his face from within.

'It was a good holiday,' he offered weakly, looking across at Flora for help.

There was little point in pretending, she thought. The months ahead would be filled with Alice's plans for the wedding – the date, the dress, the flowers and, most of all, the wedding breakfast – and she set herself to endure it with as good a grace as she could.

'Jack and I are getting married,' she said without preamble.

'I knew it!' Alice jumped up and rushed around the table, arms stretched wide, kissing Flora on the cheek, patting Jack's shoulder. 'Didn't I say?' she appealed to her audience. 'Didn't I say that French trip would do it?'

'It's wonderful news,' Kate said dreamily. 'I am so pleased.'

'It was always going to happen.' Sally wore a smile that drooped at the edges. 'You were always so solid together. Not like—'

'You're well rid of that Dominic,' her aunt said stoutly. 'And as soon as you can buy him out of the business, he can pack his bags for good.'

Well, that was Dominic dispensed with, Flora thought,

turning her attention to Charlie who had eschewed the conversation in favour of eating solidly. 'Aren't you going to congratulate us, Charlie?' she asked.

The boy struggled to finish the slice of treacle tart he'd been munching. 'Yeah, it's good news,' he managed thickly. 'Will there be a weddin'?'

'There will,' Jack said, 'with food. Not that you'll need it.'

'Food! I'll have to put my thinkin' cap on,' Alice said briskly, moving seamlessly into wedding preparations as Flora had feared she would. 'A lot of the village will want to come, what with Flora havin' lived here for so long. It will have to be a big weddin' breakfast.'

'Even without Charlie helping to eat it,' Jack said drily.

'A big breakfast means I'll have to have help. And if I can't rely on those I've trained, I'll need to go elsewhere.' She glared at Tony, who looked decidedly uncomfortable.

'Alice!' Flora protested.

She was pained – the wedding was already causing dissension – but, as so often in the past, Jack came riding to the rescue.

'It might be the right time to invite Jessie again,' he suggested. 'I'm sure if we persuaded her hard enough, she'd make the journey from Cornwall.'

Jessie Bolitho had been their housekeeper when last year they'd made a long stay in Treleggan, her home village, looking after them so well they hadn't wanted to leave.

'Yes.' Flora pounced on the idea. 'Jessie is such a good cook and I know she'd love to help out when the time comes.'

Alice sniffed. 'Maybe, though I won't say yes just now. We'll have to wait and see.'

The tea party broke up soon afterwards and Jack walked back with her to the car. The journey to Flora's cottage from the high street took no more than a few minutes and he was soon standing in her hall, her suitcase at his feet, while she checked the sitting room for firewood.

'Do you want this upstairs?' he called out to her.

'There's no need.' Flora emerged, still wearing her jacket. 'It isn't heavy and I can carry it up later. I need to get a fire going – the sitting room is perishing.'

'You can always come back to Overlay,' he said hopefully.

'Except that your house will be even colder.'

He sighed. 'You're right. I'm not looking forward to opening the front door. Wood to chop, coal to fetch, and a mass of post to sort. At least Charlie has looked after the garden. I should be grateful for that.'

'But not mine.' She walked back into the sitting room and peered through the rear window at the straggling borders and grass that was too long. 'The garden must wait, though. The All's Well has to come first. There'll be a huge amount to do.'

'Flora...' he began uncertainly. 'You're still sure? I mean you can keep on with the shop and...' He stumbled over his words.

'And still be married,' she finished for him. 'I know I can and it will work. We'll make it work.'

He looked relieved. 'And the wedding? I know Alice is making for the finishing line already, but soon or not? Have you thought about it?'

'All girls think about their wedding, Jack.'

'Really? Even girls who don't want to get married?'

'Even them. I've always had a yen for a Christmas wedding, ever since I saw photographs in a magazine – all that red velvet and mulled wine. It looked wonderful. But spring means daffodils and fresh greenery, and the world coming alive again.'

'You really have thought about it,' he said wonderingly.

'And today, too – all the way home!' Her gaze fell on the fireplace. 'While you're here, can you give me a hand? I'm going to need coal from the bunker.' She turned back to him, her forehead creased. 'Did you doubt I was serious?'

'I'm... I'm still getting used to the idea, I suppose. There were times when I thought it would never happen.'

'It's a good feeling, though?'

'It couldn't be better,' he agreed, pulling her down onto the sofa beside him, the coal bunker forgotten. Minutes ticked by as dusk became night, until Flora said, 'Do you have to go back to Overlay tonight?'

He wrapped his arms around her a little more tightly. 'I could stay a while,' he said.

A LETTER FROM MERRYN

Dear Reader,

I want to say a huge thank you for choosing to read *Murder in a French Village*. If you enjoyed the book and want to keep up to date with all my latest releases, just sign up at the following link. Your email address will never be shared, and you can unsubscribe at any time.

www.bookouture.com/merryn-allingham

If you enjoyed *Murder in a French Village*, I would love a short review. Getting feedback from readers is amazing and it helps new readers to discover one of my books for the first time. And do get in touch on my Facebook page, through Twitter, Goodreads or my website – I love to chat.

Thank you for reading,

Merryn x

www.merrynallingham.com

facebook.com/MerrynWrites
twitter.com/merrynwrites

Printed in Great Britain
by Amazon